TOUCH OF A THIEF

MIA MARLOWE

D1005134

KENSINGTON PUBLISHING CORP.
www.kensingtonbooks.com

BRAVA BOOKS are published by

Kensington Publishing Corp.
119 West 40th Street
New York, NY 10018

All Kensington titles, imprints and distributed lines are available at special quantity discounts for bulk purchases for sales promotion, premiums, fund-raising, educational or institutional use.

Special book excerpts or customized printings can also be created to fit specific needs. For details, write or phone the office of the Kensington Special Sales Manager: Kensington Publishing Corp., 119 West 40th Street, New York, NY 10018. Attn. Special Sales Department. Phone: 1-800-221-2647.

Brava and the B logo are Reg. U.S. Pat. & TM Off.

ISBN-13: 978-0-7582-6352-0
ISBN-10: 0-7582-6352-X

First Kensington Trade Paperback Printing: May 2011

10 9 8 7 6 5 4 3 2 1

Printed in the United States of America

ACKNOWLEDGMENTS

No book springs to life as the result of only one person's effort. *Touch of a Thief* is no exception. I'd like to send my heartfelt thanks to:

Alicia Condon, my fabulous editor, for believing in the premise of my story and bringing me into the Kensington fold!

Natasha Kern, my tireless agent, for believing in me! She's nothing short of amazing.

Ashlyn Chase, my long-suffering critique partner, for hours of "read alouds" and for her friendship.

Marcy Weinbeck, my beta reader, whose exquisite taste and keen eye I've come to rely upon.

Lisa Mancini-Verges, a reader who submitted the name Greydon Quinn in a contest on my website a couple years ago. The name stuck with me and I'm thrilled that Quinn has finally come to life in this story.

You, the reader holding this book in your hands right now. Without you and your imagination added to my words, nothing magical can happen.

And lastly, I have to thank my Dear Husband. After all these years, he still knows how to show a girl a good time! He is—and always will be—the reason I write romance.

CHAPTER 1

November 1856
Amjerat, a principality of India

On any given day, someone writhed in exquisite pleasure at the home of the most sought after courtesan in Amjerat. Unfortunately for Captain Greydon Quinn, on this day it wasn't him.

"Very good, Quinn-sahib," Padmaa cooed as he lowered his mouth to her neck. She smelled of jasmine and musk and warm, roused woman. "You are fast becoming a master of the teachings of Vatsyayana."

He was fast becoming too much for his trousers, but the exercise was about giving bliss to the woman, so only Padmaa was gloriously naked. When Quinn set out to learn the ancient pleasuring techniques from an obscure Sanskrit text called *Kama Sutra*, he realized there would be times during his sensual odyssey when sacrifice was required.

This was one of those times.

His groin ached in unrelenting need, but he concentrated on Padmaa's hitched breathing and on every shivering muscle beneath her golden brown skin.

"You are the best student I have ever taught," she said, her tone breathless. She took one of his hands and guided it over her belly to the soft, sweet delights between her legs.

By some oriental magic, Padmaa always removed all the small hairs on her body, even the ones covering her sex. Quinn found her smooth pudenda exotically erotic.

"Many of your countrymen come to me for training in the sensual arts, but so few complete the lessons." She made a soft purring sound and tilted her pelvis into his questing fingers. "Why do you think that is so?"

The way his body throbbed for release, Quinn was having difficulty thinking much of anything.

"Attend, Quinn-sahib," she said, when his fingertip slipped away from the spot Padmaa called her "little pearl." "You can do two things at once."

He drew a deep cleansing breath and resumed his intimate caress. Padmaa gave a soft moan of approval.

"I think it's a matter of time that keeps them from completing the training," he said through clenched teeth as he struggled with control. Her skin flushed hotly, sending a message of desire straight to his groin. It was all he could do not to yank down his trousers and bury himself in her soft wetness.

"Do we not all have the same length days, the same . . . heartbeats while we . . . live?"

Quinn was encouraged that Padmaa, an expert in the sensual arts, seemed to struggle with control as well.

"Yes, but we Englishmen divide our days up into nice, practical little hours and minutes." When Quinn first arrived in India, he'd railed at the Asiatic disregard for punctuality. Since then he'd realized there were times when the eternal *now* could not be regimented into a Western schedule.

"No, I think it is because most Englishmen seek only their own satisfaction, not ways to please . . . their . . . women . . . oh!" Her dark eyes rolled back into her head and her body stiffened in preparation for release.

As she came in shimmering waves, Quinn glowed with reflected pleasure. It made a man achingly alive to bring a woman to such a peak.

He was sure she'd demonstrate her gratitude by returning the favor just as soon as she stopped convulsing.

There was a soft rap on the door. Quinn cursed under his breath. Padmaa rose shakily from their bed of cushions and wrapped a length of silk around her body. "Come."

"That was my plan," Quinn muttered. Pleasing a woman was all well and good, but a man had needs too.

It was Sanjay at the door, so Quinn rose to his feet.

"A thousand pardons, my friend." No one would suspect the man in threadbare leggings and tunic was the Crown Prince of Amjerat. Quinn had accompanied him on several incognito adventures when he evaded his guards and slipped out of the palace, but it was the first time he had interrupted Quinn's visit to Padmaa. "There is trouble at the temple."

"What kind of trouble?"

"A Thugee band entered the outer court," Sanjay said. "Already they have killed one of the priests."

Not all devotees of the destroyer goddess Kali practiced ritual murder, but Quinn had heard a group of Thugee were traveling south on the Grand Trunk Road, leaving offerings to their goddess along the way. He usually practiced tolerance when it came to the beliefs of others, but garroted corpses left a particularly unsavory trail of breadcrumbs. Each kill was considered an act of *puja*, a veneration of Kali.

The British had attempted to quash the cult, but obviously some persisted. Now that this new band had reached Amjerat, Quinn could act against them.

He kissed Padmaa's cheek. "My apologies. I must go."

"Then your training is complete." Her musical voice was tinged with regret. "To give bliss without thought of receiving is the goal of the enlightened soul."

"I'm not all that enlightened." Quinn growled in frustration as he shoved his Beaumont-Adams revolver into his belt. "Believe me, I bloody well thought about it."

At a brisk trot, Quinn followed the prince into the sultry night and down a narrow alley toward the imposing temple in the center of Amjerat's capital. They approached the temple's side door in case the Thugs had posted a guard out front.

"What do they want in the temple?" Quinn whispered as he and Sanjay drew near. Most victims of thuggery were caught stumbling home from the local opium den, too wrapped in their lotus-eating haze to put up much of a fight.

"I fear it is *Baaghh kaa kkhuun.*"

"Blood of the Tiger?" Quinn translated for himself as he ran toward the small side door.

Sanjay followed. "Oh, yes. It is the red diamond that makes up the eye in our Shiva. It is said to contain immense power. In the wrong hands, the energy of Baaghh kaa kkhuun turns to evil."

"Then let's make sure it stays in the right hands, shall we?" Quinn drew his revolver, wishing he'd reloaded after target practice that afternoon. He'd been in too much of a hurry to get to Padmaa. He had only four shots instead of the usual twelve.

Quinn kicked open the door and bellowed at the gang to stop. When one was outnumbered, a bit of bravado rarely went amiss.

But it only served to put the gang on alert. Quinn counted ten of them. The Thug perched on two of the four arms of the massive statue at the far end of the temple tossed them a glance and continued prying the eye of the god out with a wicked-looking dagger.

Quinn raised his pistol and dropped four Thugs as they ran toward him and the prince, their long, curved swords glittering. He considered trying for the one clinging to Shiva, but the other four were closer. Besides, Prince Sanjay would take it badly if Quinn accidently put a bullet through his god.

As it was, he and the prince stood back to back, slicing away with their swords, fighting off the rest of the masked gang. Blades arcing, Quinn and Sanjay turned in concert, a stylized dance of death. None who came within their reach escaped without being cut.

It never failed to astound Quinn how battle heightened a man's senses. He noted a hairy mole dividing the eyebrow of one of his attackers, the pungent smell of fenugreek and curry emanating from their flowing robes, and the strident scream when his blade opened a vein and a fountain of red spurted into the air.

He and his friend were both expert swordsmen, but if either of them went down, they were both dead.

The thugee defacing the god suddenly screeched out a high ululation. At the sound, the remaining band turned and ran after the man who had the red diamond clutched in a square of black silk.

Quinn and Sanjay gave chase, but soon lost them in the tangled rabbit warrens of the bazaar. Baaghh kaa kkhuun disappeared like a gob of spit into the Ganges. The red diamond left no trace as it descended into the rotting heart of Amjerat's underworld.

March 1857
London

This is positively, absolutely the last time, Lady Viola Preston promised herself as she squeezed through the ground floor window of the posh London town house.

Viola had contemplated Lady Henson's new emerald necklace over the soup course at Lieutenant Quinn's dinner party, but then the lieutenant let slip that he'd brought back a couple handfuls of uncut stones from India. A newly returned nabob shouldn't flaunt the details of his wealth if he didn't wish to be relieved of it.

Viola's fence would have to chop up Lady Henson's necklace and even then, the gems were large and of a uniquely deep color. They might be recognized. Uncut stones—one of them big as a peach pit, if the lieutenant were to be believed—were nigh untraceable. Viola would get full value for them.

And then she'd stop.

Only once more, Viola vowed silently. Though, like the Shakespearean heroine for whom she was named, she'd miss wearing men's trousers from time to time. They were ever so much more comfortable than a corset and hoops.

From somewhere deep in the elegant town house came a low creak. Viola held her breath. The longcase clock in the main hall ticked. When she heard nothing else, she realized it was only the sigh of an older home squatting down on its foundation for the night.

The room she'd broken into held the stale scents of cigar smoke and brandy from the dinner party of the previous evening. But there were no fresh smells. Perhaps Lieutenant Quinn had taken Lord Montjoy up on his offer to introduce Quinn at Montjoy's club that evening.

Probably visiting a brothel instead. No matter. The house was empty. Why made no difference at all.

She cat footed up the main stairs, on the watch for the help. The lieutenant hadn't fully staffed his home yet, but had brought a native servant back with him from India. During the dinner party, Viola had noticed the turbaned fellow in the shadows, directing the borrowed footmen and giving quiet commands to the temporary serving girls.

The Indian servant would most likely be in residence.

So long as I steer clear of the kitchen or the garret, I'll be fine, Viola told herself. She knew the stones would be in Lieutenant Quinn's chamber.

Her fence had a friend in the brick mason's guild who, for a pretty price, happily revealed the location of the ton's secret stashes. Town houses on that fashionable London street were all equipped with identical wall safes in the master's chamber. The newfangled tumbler lock would open without protest under Viola's deft touch.

She had a gift. Two, actually, but she didn't enjoy the other one half so much.

Slowly, she opened the bedchamber door. *Good.* It had been oiled recently. She heard only the faint scrape of hinges.

The heavy damask curtains were drawn, so Viola stood still, waiting for her eyes to adjust to the deeper darkness. There! A landscape in a gilt frame on the south wall marked the location of the safe.

Viola padded across the room and inched the painting's hanging wires along the picture rail, careful not to let the hooks near the ceiling slide off. She'd have the devil's own time reattaching them if they did. With any luck at all, she'd slide the painting right back and it might be days before Lieutenant Quinn discovered the stones were missing. After moving the frame over about a foot, she found the safe right where Willie's friend had said it would be.

Viola put her ear to the lock and closed her eyes, the better to concentrate. When she heard a click or felt a slight hitch beneath her touch she knew she'd discovered part of the combination. After only a few tries and errors, the final tumbler fell into place and Viola opened the safe.

The dark void was empty. She reached in to trace the edges of the iron box with her fingertips.

"Looking for something?" A masculine voice rumbled from a shadowy corner.

Blast! Viola bolted for the door, but it slammed shut. The Indian servant stepped from his place of concealment behind it.

"Please do not make to flee or I am sorry to say I shall have to shoot you." The Hindu's melodious accent belied his serious threat.

Viola ran toward the window, hoping it was open behind the curtain. And that there was a friendly bush below to break her fall.

Lieutenant Quinn grabbed her before she reached it, crushing her spine to his chest. His large hand splayed over one of her unbound breasts.

"Bloody hell! It's a woman. Turn up the gas lamp, Sanjay."

The yellow light of the wall sconce flooded the room. Viola blinked against the sudden brightness, then stomped down on her captor's instep as hard as she could.

Quinn grunted, but didn't release his hold. He whipped her around to face him, his brows shooting up in surprise when he recognized her. "Lady Viola, you can't be the Mayfair Jewel Thief."

"Of course, I can." She might be a thief, but she was no liar. "I'd appreciate it, sir, if you'd remove your hands from my person."

"I bet you would." The lieutenant's mouth turned down in a grim frown and he kept his grip on her upper arms.

His Indian servant didn't lower the revolver's muzzle one jot. "Did I not tell you, sahib? When she looked at the countess's emeralds, her eyes glowed green." The servant no longer wore his turban, his coal-black hair falling in ropy strands past his shoulders. "She is a devil, this one."

"Perhaps." Quinn lifted one of his dark brows. "But if that's the case, my old vicar was right. The devil does know how to assume pleasing shapes."

That was a backhanded compliment if Viola ever heard one. She hadn't considered Lieutenant Quinn closely during the dinner party. She had little time for men and the trouble they brought a woman. Once burned and all that. She'd been intent on Lady Henson's emeralds. Now she studied him with the same assessing gaze he shot at her.

Quinn's even features were classically handsome. His unlined mouth and white teeth made Viola realize suddenly that he was younger than she'd first estimated. She doubted he'd seen thirty-five winters. His fair English skin had been bronzed by fierce Indian summers and lashed by its weeping monsoons. His stint in India had rewarded him with riches, but the subcontinent had demanded its price.

His storm-gray eyes were all the more striking because of his deeply tanned skin. They seemed to look right through her and see her for the fraud she was—a thief with pretensions of being a lady.

Quinn glanced at his servant. "Looks like I owe you a hundred rupees." He shook his head. "My money was on Viscount Fenway. He's been a cad ever since we were at Eton together. I thought he'd graduated from cheating on exams to lifting jewels." He released her arms and took Viola's hand, making a slight obeisance over it. "My apologies for doubting you, milady. It appears you *are* the light-fingered wretch we hoped to catch this evening."

"There's no reason for rude names." She snatched her hand away. Perhaps if she kept him talking, she might sidle over to the door and escape. It would be his word against hers and no one who hadn't seen her unlock a safe would believe her capable of it. "A liar has very few stones to throw. Didn't you say you'd join Lord Montjoy at his club this night?"

"Yes, I did, but standing up a friend at his club and relieving a man of his jewels are not sins of the same magnitude, are they?"

"Relieving a man of his jewels." She shot a wicked glare at him. "Now there's a thought."

Viola wished she could call the words back as soon as they left her lips. Her association with Willie had exposed her to so many overheard vulgarities while she waited for his shop to clear long enough for them to conduct their business. It was coarsening her sensibilities. No lady would ever think such a thing, much less say it.

Quinn snorted. "You'll pardon me if I don't quake in my boots"—his grin faded—"but I didn't lie. I spread misinformation. A time-honored tactic used with good reason."

"I suppose you think I couldn't possibly have a good reason for my actions." She took a nonchalant step or two toward the door.

Broad of shoulder and narrow of hip, Quinn matched her movement with the sinuous grace of a great cat. If she had to flirt her way out of this predicament, it wouldn't be the most onerous task she'd ever undertaken. But she'd only go so far. If she'd been willing to sell herself in the first place, she wouldn't have had to resort to theft. "I suppose you mean to denounce me and see me ruined."

"I greatly fear I'm too late to be the instrument of your ruin, milady."

Viola brought her hand up sharply to slap him, but he caught her arm in mid-swing and held it motionless. His intense gaze froze the rest of her. There was a thin scar running through one of his eyebrows toward the side part in his sable hair. Lieutenant Quinn might be rakishly handsome, but he was also a man of action. Dangerous. Among the men of the ton, he'd stand out as feral in the midst of domesticated stock.

"My servant has a loaded revolver pointed at your midsection and he's overprotective to a fault." His voice dropped to a low purr of silky menace. "Are you certain you wish to strike me?"

"A lady cannot defend her honor without threat of gunshot?"

"So there is honor among thieves. I'd wondered about that." He motioned for the Hindu to lower his weapon with his other hand, while keeping hold of Viola's wrist. "That'll be all, Sanjay. The lady and I have things to discuss."

"As you wish." The Indian stowed the firearm in his wide sash belt and pressed both his palms together in a gesture of farewell. "*Namaste.* But guard yourself from demons, sahib"— he shot an evil glare at Viola—"however pleasingly they disguise themselves." He slipped out the door as quietly as silk flowing over bare skin.

"I demand you release me." Viola's wrist throbbed in Quinn's tight grip. She didn't want him to become aware of how fast her heart was hammering.

"You're in no position to make demands. Do you plan on taking another swipe at me?"

"Not unless you do something to deserve it."

"Fair enough." Quinn let her go and sat on the foot of his bed. "Now I'm fully prepared to hear why you've chosen to risk shame and prison for a few baubles."

"You would sit while a lady stands?"

"Of course not." He hooked an ankle over one knee. "Should a *lady* break into my bedchamber in the dead of night, be assured I will stand."

Viola narrowed her eyes. If he was set on insulting her, he'd never be moved by her plight. She drew her lips tight together. He did not deserve a front row seat at a recitation of her private pain.

"You're welcome to sit, too, if you like." He patted the brocade counterpane beside him.

"I'll stand." She folded her arms beneath her breasts. "Being a thief and being a lady are not mutually exclusive."

"It'll be hard to convince the magistrate of that."

"If you planned to turn me over to the authorities, we wouldn't still be here." Viola hoped she was right. It would kill her mother if she were arrested.

"Clever girl. I don't plan on hauling you before the magistrate. I shall have to add *astute* to your list of qualities," he said with a grudging nod. "Did you know The Mayfair Jewel

Thief is famous even in Bombay? Stealthy. Only takes from those who can well afford to lose. Never fooled by fake jewels. You see why we set out to catch you."

She knew there was a sizable reward for her capture, but she didn't know word of her exploits had traveled so far. "Then your story about a fistful of uncut jewels isn't true."

"It's *two* fistfuls actually and they're real enough. Mostly." His gaze traveled down her body to her legs, which were encased in skin hugging buff trousers. "I have no need to turn you over for the reward, so you and I will have to come to another arrangement."

"Another arrangement? If you expect me to share your bed in exchange for your silence, you're destined for disappointment."

He chuckled. "That wasn't my plan, but it bears consideration. I'm gratified to hear you're thinking about sharing my bed."

She was quick enough to deliver a ringing slap to his smooth-shaven cheek.

Quinn reacted just as quickly, pulling her onto the feather tick and pinning her beneath him. She sank into the mattress as his long hard body covered hers.

"Release me this instant!" Viola pounded against his chest with her free hand, but he caught it up and joined it with the other one he'd stretched out above her head. He wrapped his legs around hers and held her immobile.

"A woman who sneaks into a man's bedchamber shouldn't expect to emerge without paying a penalty." His mouth descended to swallow her protest in a demanding kiss.

She struggled beneath him, but then his lips softened. He slanted his mouth over hers, as if he sensed exactly how she liked to be kissed. His kiss became a beguiling summons instead of a forced intimacy. Her body responded with a disconcerting flutter in her belly and the beginning of a deep ache.

This is insane. Viola knew better than to let a man use her passionate nature against her. She willed herself to go limp and unresponsive.

He pulled back and looked down at her, curiosity arching his brow.

"Is that your idea of a penalty?" she asked.

"No, kissing you just seemed a good idea at the time."

"You don't think so now?"

"It might be a distraction. You see, we are going to be partners, Lady Viola," he said with certainty.

"Not very gentlemanly of you, Lieutenant, on both counts." She fought to keep her voice even. "Have I no say in the matter?"

"About our partnership, no. Not if you wish to avoid the magistrate." His rough baritone rumbled over her whole body, leaving a shiver in its wake. His eyes darkened as he looked down at her and she felt his hard maleness pressed against the juncture of her thighs. "About whether it's more than business between us, yes, you have a say."

His heart pounded against her breastbone. Her mouth opened and closed, but no sound came out. Heaven help her, she hadn't been this tempted by a man since—she snipped off the thought. Viola knew better than to let her body make the decision. She sucked in a quick breath. "Just business," she whispered.

"I'll accept that for now. But for the record, you're the one who brought up sharing a bed. If I let you up, will you refrain from pummeling me?"

She nodded, not trusting her voice.

Quinn rolled off her and pulled her into a sitting position beside him. He was perfectly still for a moment, bridling himself. Then he rose and walked briskly to the chest of drawers. He pulled out a stocking and a white handkerchief. After spreading the kerchief on the bed, he dumped the contents of the stocking onto it. A glowing rainbow of stones glittered up at Viola.

"You keep your jewels in an old stocking?"

He shrugged. "It seemed more secure than the wall safe with the likes of you prowling about London."

She frowned at the gemstones. It was an impressive pile of riches, but the resonance was off. "Some of these aren't genuine."

He cocked a brow at her and nodded. "Show me."

She drew a deep breath and stretched out her hand. She'd do the pearls first. Their sibilant, watery voices were always easiest to bear. She picked up a gray pearl, a smoky iridescent orb. The low hum began inside her head.

Like a waving bed of kelp, the pearl spoke to her in wobbling, gentle tones. The words were garbled, and in no language she knew, but a quick vision of a wizened old gent with a purple turban and scarlet-dyed beard flashed across her mind. She dropped the pearl before the precious thing could show her any more.

It was unusual for her to receive a vision from a pearl. Perhaps it was because they were never as old as other gems. Perhaps the fragile substance resisted picking up imprints from its owners. Or perhaps pearls realized they too were mortal and didn't want to carry someone else's burden for the course of their stay on earth.

Whatever secret the gray pearl bore, Viola didn't want to know it.

"That pearl is real," she said. "And very old. You'll not find its mate. It will have to be used as a pendant."

"How do you know that?"

"I just know." How could she explain something she didn't understand herself? She only knew she was different.

And people mistrusted those who were different.

She turned back to the rest of the jewels. One by one, she sorted out sweet-voiced carnelians and sultry-toned lapis lazuli, shoving their silent imitations to one side. Then she moved on to the harder gems—the ones with more strident voices. The ones most likely to invade her mind with nightmarish images of their past.

She gleaned out the rasping emeralds, the muttering sapphires, and wailing rubies, sorting the paste gems off in a small pile by themselves. Some of the fakes were quite good and probably would have fooled most jewelers, but if a stone didn't speak to her, she knew it wasn't real.

Finally, she was left with five diamonds. She drew a deep breath to steel herself against them. Of all jewels, diamonds screamed out the atrocities in their pasts most painfully. Perhaps being uncut would help. They couldn't have had contact with too many people.

"Why are you stopping?" Quinn asked. "Can't you tell with diamonds?"

She picked up the largest and breathed a sigh of relief. "Fake."

"You're sure?"

She dropped it on the floor and ground it under her boot heel. The stone splintered into shards.

"Damn. Sanjay had me almost convinced that one was genuine."

"Sanjay was pulling your leg." She winced at the slang that rolled so easily off her tongue.

Viola reached for the next stone. The moment her fingertips brushed it, the diamond screeched at her, a high-pitched squeal on the edge of sound. She bit her lip and pulled back her hand before it could send her an image. "Real."

Quinn moved the gem to the "keepers" pile and it whined softly when he touched it.

How does he not hear that? It was unusual for a stone to speak without her touch merely because she was near. The gem must have a particularly vicious story to tell. That one she would avoid at all costs.

The rest of the diamonds were genuine. Viola managed to handle them quickly enough that only one was able to send her a red-splashed image of the moment the dark-skinned man who first dug it out of the ground was hacked to death for it. She swallowed hard and tried to expunge the horrific scene from her mind.

"So the rumors are true. You cannot be fooled by a fake, no matter how cunningly realistic." Quinn scooped up the genuine stones and replaced them in his stocking.

She stood. Barring that last diamond, she'd escaped rather easily. She doubted any of the visions had lasted long enough to leave her with the grinding headache that usually accompanied the use of her gift. "I'm glad to have been of service. Now, if you'll excuse me—"

"Not so fast. I haven't explained the purpose of our partnership."

"But I've already culled your stones."

"That was only a test. I had to be sure you were the real Mayfair Jewel Thief. Sit," he said curtly.

His tone was so commanding, she obeyed reflexively. Then she stood back up. She wasn't one of his sepoys to be ordered about.

"Very well, *I'll* sit." He claimed the end of the bed again and grinned up at her.

Irritation fizzed up her spine, but she was the one who'd chosen to stand.

"Here are my terms and they are nonnegotiable," Quinn said. "You will render me a burglary service, and at the end of our association, you will receive half the gems you just saw."

"My choice from among them?" Something inside her quivered with hope. It would mean her family's money troubles were over. She'd never have to steal again.

Quinn nodded.

"Very well. I accept your terms. What do you want from me?"

"What do you know about red diamonds?" he asked.

"Red diamonds? They're extremely rare." In all her thievery, she'd never run across one. "And because of that, they're worth the earth. But they aren't for everyone. It's said they often carry curses."

"Are you the superstitious sort?"

"No." It wasn't superstition to believe something true. She'd be able to hear the curse firsthand. "But as far as I know, there are no red diamonds in all of England. Even if there were, I wouldn't steal one."

"Why?"

"Because it would be impossible to fence. And an absolute sin to recut into smaller stones. Red diamonds are never overly large to begin with, no more than five or six carats. What would I do with one?"

"Let me worry about that part." Quinn rose to his feet. "I need to see you home, Lady Viola. You have a busy day ahead of you tomorrow."

She was gratified to hear him use her title, but the rest of his words made her slant him a suspicious look. "What am I going to be doing?"

"You'll be leaving for Paris with me. There is a diamond called Baaghh kaa kkhuun enroute to the Queen's Royal Collection. And I mean to meet the courier in France."

"Baaghh kaa kkhuun?"

"It means Blood of the Tiger," Quinn said. "And you, my Lady Light-fingers, are going to help me steal it."

CHAPTER 2

"We cannot trust a thief. Especially not a woman." Sanjay folded a flowing tunic and stuffed it into a small carpetbag. "A woman muddies every stream she steps in. You know it to be true. When the memsahibs came, did not your countrymen change toward my people?"

Sanjay was right. Social barriers between the white and brown races were swiftly erected once Englishmen brought their wives and sweethearts to the subcontinent.

"I do not like this plan."

"Don't be so pessimistic. It'll work. You'll see." Quinn eyed his friend's luggage, wishing that *his* contained such comfortable garments. When Quinn had lived in India, he often donned indigenous garb. He was a natural mimic and his facility with the language was prodigious. He spoke Hindi well enough to pass as a native in any bazaar where he was not already known as a *Pukka*—devil of a sahib.

"We don't have much choice. Worthington's telegrams are becoming increasingly worrisome." Lieutenant Freddie Worthington shared Quinn's concerns over the growing native unrest. He'd stayed behind in Delhi, but sent Quinn a weekly update on conditions there. Quinn had let him know to send the next report to the Hotel de Crillon in Paris.

"The fact of the matter is we need the Mayfair Jewel Thief and she happens to be female." *Exceedingly female.* Quinn grinned at the memory of her unbound breast in his hand and her soft lips beneath his. He raised a brow at Sanjay. "I've never known you to shun the company of a comely woman, Your Highness."

"No indeed. A woman is useful for a great many things." Sanjay's teeth glinted in a wide smile. Then the smile faded. "But I have a bad feeling about this one. There is a darkness about her." Sanjay's black eyes snapped. "And do not use my title, not even when we are alone. I am no longer a prince of Hind."

"Through no fault of yours." Quinn's lips tightened in a hard line. "It's not just."

"Bah! No one but a child or a fool—or an Englishman—expects the world to be just."

"I don't know why the Home Office wouldn't listen." Frustration made the muscles between Quinn's shoulders bunch into a hard knot.

The Doctrine of Lapse had stripped Sanjay of his rightful place. When the Sultan of Amjerat died, the East India Company deemed that the line died with him because Sanjay was his adopted son. Fostering was common in England, but adoption? Never. Quinn had tried to explain the custom to his superiors till he was blue, but they wouldn't listen.

"It does seem odd. Adopted heirs have been recognized in my country for centuries. What else is a man who begets only daughters to do?" Sanjay shrugged.

"Ah, but you see, for us English, succession is only about bloodlines." Quinn ground the knuckles of one hand into the palm of the other. "As if people were damned racehorses."

The lack of an heir with the previous sultan's blood in his veins was all the excuse the grasping East India Company needed to step in and claim Sanjay's kingdom for itself. Amjerat was a small principality, but strategically located at the apex of several trade routes. Lord Dalhousie possessed the will to back his actions with the full weight of the British military.

Fortunately, Quinn succeeded in convincing Sanjay that Amjerat's half dozen battle-elephants and fighters armed with aging *jezzails* and limited ammunition would have no chance against crack English troops. Sanjay refused to endanger his people by pressing his claim with war.

But the injustice made Quinn ashamed to be British.

He handed the Beaumont-Adams to Sanjay. "Put this in your luggage. You might need it."

"No, sahib. A man of my color in this part of the world would be in more danger if he were caught with such a weapon than if he were naked." Sanjay pushed the revolver away. "You will protect me."

"We protected you right out of your kingdom."

"I trust you."

"I may not be able to change the policy that stole your throne," Quinn said grimly, "but I'll do everything in my power to see Amjerat's treasure restored."

"If the Blood of the Tiger is returned to the temple where it belongs, I will hold your vow fulfilled, my friend." Sanjay clapped a hand on Quinn's shoulder. "The British have brought my country many great things. But they have taken from us as well. The people of Amjerat have a right to feel proud of who they are. The return of Baaghh kaa kkhuun will put heart back into them. It will help my people remember themselves."

Quinn was a soldier. He knew some fights had to be fought. But he respected Sanjay's choice. No one hated war more than one who knew what it really was. "Someday both our people will understand that we have a great deal to learn from each other."

"That is my hope as well. But until that day, the people of

Amjerat will teach their children what every blade of grass knows."

When Sanjay began speaking in riddles, Quinn had difficulty following. The Indian prince saw the world in fluid undulations. Quinn's view was much more black and white. Things were either right or wrong, true or false, just or unjust. The Oriental mind was a puzzlement to Quinn, but one he enjoyed unraveling.

"All right. I give up. What does grass know?"

"Even stone is not forever." Sanjay closed his luggage with a snap.

But England is one bloody big stone.

"The Blood of the Tiger must be returned to the temple," Sanjay said. "Only in the care of Shiva can its evil bent be tempered."

Quinn silently dismissed his friend when Sanjay talked of curses and the evil inherent in the red diamond. Quinn was more concerned about the evil of men.

Mutiny was being whispered in the bazaars. Mad holy men tramped up and down the Grand Trunk Road, spreading the dream of slaughtering hundreds of English women and children. If only the sepoys could be brought to rebellion, they urged, all the *Angrezi* would be driven into the sea and never return.

Quinn had warned his commander that unrest was brewing. Seizing the kingdom of Amjerat played into the fomenters' hands, but he'd been ignored. Worse, he'd been accused of "showing the yellow stripe."

Quinn protested when the viceroy acquired the Baaghh kaa kkhuun from the band of Thugs who'd stolen it. When Quinn continued to rail against the injustice, his commander demoted him and sent him Home with the stern admonition to "remember whose side you're on, Lieutenant."

Now he could only try to right a small portion of the wrong

done to Amjerat. And hope the English civilians living in the cantonments and residencies across Hind wouldn't be made to pay for the sins of the East India Company.

"I still wish you were not putting so much trust into the hands of this thief, this woman," Sanjay said.

"Who says I trust her?" Quinn shrugged into his greatcoat. "In any case, I know how to keep my friends close and my enemies closer."

"And Lady Viola, which is she?"

"Both, I suspect," Quinn said, remembering the strange glint in her hazel eyes when she handled the stones, the way she trembled like some wild young thing, wanting what he offered in his outstretched hand, but fearful at the same time. She was a riddle with feet, a lovely knot he'd enjoy untying. "Either way, it'll be time well spent figuring her out."

"It's unseemly for you to travel to Paris unaccompanied, Viola," the Dowager Countess of Meade said as she grated a carrot into a bowl at the kitchen table. "I don't like it."

"I'll be fine, Mother."

Viola took the bowl from her and worked through the bunch of carrots at double her mother's speed. Eugenia Preston, only occasionally known as Lady Meade now, wasn't accustomed to manual labor. Even after four years of living below her station, she hadn't shown an improved aptitude for working with her hands.

"It's not as if I had to cancel a string of engagements. I shouldn't be gone long enough for anyone to even notice." Viola moved the bowl aside for their servant Martha to deal with later. "I'm not venturing to the wilds of New South Wales. I'm only crossing the channel to France, a thoroughly civilized country."

"*That* is an opinion open to debate," Eugenia said with a sniff. "The only good thing to come out of France—"

"Is French pastry," Viola finished for her for the umpteenth time. As if they could afford any. "Yes, Mother, I know."

"You should at least take Martha with you."

Viola shook her head. "I'd be taking care of Martha more than she'd take care of me." Their decrepit servant was often down with the croup or some other ailment and was rarely able to do a day's work. But Viola kept Martha and her husband Phineas on because they'd been with the family for years and had no place else to go.

Her mother gave a long-suffering sigh. "Then I suppose *I'll* have to accompany you."

That would never do.

"Mother, you get seasick just looking at the Thames. You'd be miserable on the crossing." Viola cast a quick glance at her sister, who was humming in her rocker by the fire. "You're needed here."

"But why must you go so far away?"

Viola bit her bottom lip. Her mother was accustomed to Viola coming home with bundles of banknotes and assorted coin without explanation of how she'd come by them. So long as Viola assured her she hadn't done anything to sully herself with a man, her mother accepted the funds as a gift from God.

When the money ran out, Viola always came home with more. She couldn't explain to her mother. The idea of the dowager countess hearing about Viola's disreputable fence Willie and his sordid little shop made her shiver. Her mother was safer, and happier, not knowing the details.

"I have something I must do and this particular something is in France," she said curtly. "Someone has to provide for this family."

"You know perfectly well we could sell this town house and retire to the country." Her mother launched into the old argument once again. They wrangled over it at least once a week. "We'd have enough and to spare, if we lived simply."

"We do live simply. If we lived any more simply, we'd be going about in potato sacks," Viola snapped back.

She didn't want to live simply. She wanted the life she was born to.

Her father had died without a son, so the bulk of the estate of his earldom, along with the income it generated, went to her weasel of a cousin, Jerome Preston. As her father lay dying, he had penned a letter directing Jerome to provide bountifully for his aunt and cousins, but a letter carried no force of law. The new earl simply pretended the old earl's family didn't exist.

Her father had left Viola his only unentailed property, a London town house, but left her no funds to run it.

Or to live as the daughter of an earl ought.

"I'm sure Father would have wished matters differently for us," her sister Ophelia said from her corner. Her pile of darning was dwindling nicely as her needle clicked in time with the creaky rocker. "He didn't intend to leave us like this."

"Of course not," their mother added. "No one *intends* to die."

But a prudent man might have given the matter more thought, Viola added silently.

"When Teddy comes back, everything will be fine," Ophelia said with confidence. She leaned down to ruffle the hair of the toddler who was playing with a kitten at her feet. "Isn't that right, Portia? When Daddy comes home, it'll be all right."

The little girl grinned up at Ophelia, then turned back to the kitten with a happy squeal. Viola and her mother exchanged a glance. Viola shook her head. There was no need to remind Ophelia once again that her feckless husband was not coming back. She'd only ignore the information and go on with her own version of the world.

When Portia was born, Ophelia hatched the notion that Teddy was off on a tour of the Continent, giving poetry readings for heads of state. Nothing they could say would convince Ophelia otherwise and they finally stopped trying.

She was happy with her fantasy. Who were they to strip it from her?

But someone had to deal with reality.

That lot fell to Viola.

She kissed her mother's sunken cheek and wrapped a cloak around her shoulders. "I'll be home before you know it."

"Good-bye, sister." Ophelia smiled sweetly at her. "Say hello to Teddy when you see him in France."

When Viola had committed her first theft by lifting a jeweled hatpin out of desperation, she'd quickly realized she needed help turning her stolen good into ready coin. She wandered some unsavory streets, wondering whom to trust. In a flash vision the little garnet in the hatpin had shown her Willie's face and the sign swinging above his shop.

When she stumbled across his shop around the next corner, she decided to listen to the stone's advice.

At first, she let Willie believe she was parting with her own ornaments, but when she kept coming in, always in tandem with a reported jewelry theft, he tumbled rather quickly to her gift for larceny.

And heartily approved.

He suggested an arrangement that would benefit them both. He had connections in low places. As the daughter of an earl, albeit a threadbare one, Viola had access to the highest. They could help each other.

Viola knew who owned what valuables. Willie found out through the servants' grapevine and his friend in the masons' guild where they stashed them. Viola never had to enter a home without knowing exactly where she would find the jewels.

When she began stealing more costly pieces, Willie claimed his expenses went up. He had to bring in someone to dismantle the jewelry. Sometimes large stones were recut. It all cost money. Her return for each heist dwindled.

Willie began suggesting specific targets for her housebreaking and promised to increase her share in the profits. So far, she hadn't seen much increase in her take.

He wouldn't be pleased to learn she'd bypassed Lady Henson's emeralds for Lieutenant Quinn's stash and come away with so little. She'd left the lieutenant's home with only the gray pearl in her pocket.

"A show of good faith," Quinn had said.

"One of the diamonds would have shown more good faith," she muttered as she left her hired hansom by the corner after telling the driver to wait. She darted down a narrow alley to Willie's shop.

A veil covered her face, but not because she worried that any fashionable member of society would recognize her there. It wasn't the sort of place frequented by the high-in-the-instep crowd.

The veil was for her. It helped her pretend she couldn't see herself doing those lowering things.

She pushed open the shop door and a little bell tinkled overhead. Willie appeared from the back room, his good-natured, ugly face split in a smile.

"Good day to you, milady," his gravelly voice rasped. He had agreed never to call her by name.

"Hello, Willie." She had never learned his full one. The less she knew about him, the better she slept. The shop was empty so she pulled a handkerchief from her reticule and undid the knot she'd tied around the pearl. "Not much to show for last night, I'm afraid."

She kept on her kid gloves as she nudged the pearl toward him. The last thing she needed was a vision-trance in that seedy little shop. Willie knew she was an accomplished thief, but she resisted letting him learn about her other gift as well. "This pearl is all I have."

"What about that lot of uncut stones the lieutenant was bragging about?"

"Men love to exaggerate." It wasn't exactly a lie. Viola was careful not to add to her list of sins if she could help it. Let Willie make of it what he would. "This pearl is quite unique—very old and very rare."

"And that makes it very hard to move." He named an insultingly low offer for it.

They haggled over the price for a few minutes, but in the end Viola accepted much less than it was worth. Sometimes she was tempted to seek out another fence for her jewels, but the more people who knew about her activities, the more dangerous it became. For better or worse, she was stuck with Willie.

"Don't fret yourself, ducks," he said as he counted out the payment. "You'll see more when you pinch those emeralds."

"I won't be doing that for a while." *Or ever*, she amended silently. She folded the banknotes and stashed the coin in her reticule. She'd deposit it all in her mother's account with the Bank of England on her way to the wharf to meet Lieutenant Quinn. Her mother would need the funds while she was gone. The Blood of the Tiger theft was his plan. He could pay her bills while she was in France. "You won't be seeing me for a bit. I'll be out of . . . town."

"Oh? Anything I should know about?"

"No, this journey is unrelated to our partnership."

"Hmmm." His face broke into a quick, slightly smarmy smile. "God keep ye safe then, yer ladyship."

"Thank you." She hoped it would be the last time she'd ever see him. Once she had the jewels Lieutenant Quinn promised her, she wouldn't have to use Willie's services. She'd make Quinn give her a bill of sale, so she could prove she owned them legitimately. Then she'd take them to a reputable jeweler where she'd receive full value for them.

She'd deposit the money with a venerable man of business

and live as she was meant to. Her mother would never have to grate another carrot. They'd find a doctor to cure Ophelia's troubled mind. No more worries about keeping Portia's pudgy growing feet in a pair of shoes that fit her. No fretting over the unpaid butcher's bill. There'd be endless soirees, nights at the theatre, and as many new gowns as she wished. Viola could even fund her own dowry if she wanted to marry.

No, she decided. *Men are far more trouble than they are worth.*

The important thing was she could put this sordid little shop and all her thefts behind her. Her life would be back to normal.

And she'd never see Willie's tobacco-stained smile again.

"Good day." She pushed out of the shop, eager to breathe the fresher air outside.

"And to you, milady," he called after her.

Willie swiped the pearl off the counter into his beefy hand. It was mighty fine. There was more where that jewel came from or he was a Dutchman. "Duncan!"

His spotty-faced shop boy appeared from the back room. "Wot?"

"Something's not quite coupled up with milady's story. She just left the shop. Nip after her. See where she goes. Find out what you can about where she's off to, who she's with, and what she might be doing once she gets there."

The boy untied the leather apron around his waist.

"Hurry up, boy!"

Duncan jumped, dropped his apron and ran out the door.

"If you lose her, you worthless little bastard, don't bother coming back," Willie shouted after him. "Save me the trouble of takin' it out of your miserable hide."

CHAPTER 3

The *Minstrel's Lady* was tied up at the pier as Lieutenant Quinn had told her it would be. The man himself paced with obvious irritation at the foot of the gangplank.

Viola's lips curved into a satisfied smile. Tall, battle-hardened Quinn was an impressive figure of a man. His trousers and jacket were cut in the first stare of fashion and the lean lines suited his masculine frame. He'd obviously updated his whole civilian wardrobe since returning from India. Traveling with such a presentable fellow would be no hardship.

And if she'd made him fret about whether or not she'd show, so much the better.

It always does a man good to wait. Makes him more appreciative of the honor bestowed upon him once a woman does arrive.

She allowed the cabby to hand her down and fetch her two valises and hatbox from the boot. "Thank you, good sir. Now if you'd be so kind as to wait a moment, the surly-looking gentleman coming this way will pay my fare."

"There you are! Finally. I was within an ace of coming to get you."

"Be thankful I arrived at all. May I remind you I had very little notice for this trip?" Having removed her veil before arriving at the wharf, she tucked a wayward lock of russet hair that always escaped her bonnet back into the lacy confection.

Her hats were the one extravagance she'd not been able to wean herself from entirely, even when her family's need was dire. "There were certain matters that required my attention before I left London."

"Well, you're here now, so hurry or we'll miss the tide." Quinn turned from her sharply and began to stalk away.

"Half a mo', guv," the cabby piped up. "You'll be owin' me for the lady's fare."

Quinn grumbled, but paid the cabby and tipped him handsomely. He started back toward the ship again.

"Lieutenant, aren't you forgetting something?"

"What now?"

"My baggage, of course."

"Of course." He smiled thinly at her. "I thought I told you to pack light."

"I did."

Quinn picked up her hat box, leaving the two heavy bags on the ground. "*This* is packing light."

"But what about my other things?"

He was no longer smiling, merely baring his teeth at her. "Carry them yourself or leave them. It makes no difference to me. Whatever you think you need, I'll buy for you once we reach Paris, but get your sweet little bum on that ship right now. Or I'll rethink my plan and turn you over to the magistrate quicker than you can pick a lock, milady."

He wheeled around for the last time, leaving Viola staring after him.

"Brute," she muttered as she stooped to hoist the luggage herself and scuttle after him.

Sailors pulled up the gangplank behind her and the mooring lines were loosed. The *Minstrel's Lady* wallowed into the main channel of the Thames as her sails filled. She was not a large craft, only about eighteen feet across and little more than twice that in length. Certainly not equipped for luxury travel. Viola saw no other women on deck.

"I need something on my stomach if I'm to be a pleasant sailing companion," Viola said as she followed Quinn. Her mother was plagued with mal de mer whenever she traveled by boat. Viola had never taken an extended voyage, so it was reasonable to assume she might be too. "Bread for choice."

"Don't worry," Quinn said. "I won't let you starve."

"I assume we'll put in at Dover." Her breath came in huffing pants. A corset was such a bother. It would have served him right if she'd decided to make the trip in the male attire she wore when she was working. That would've been packing light. "Won't we board the paddle steamer for the crossing?"

"No, this ship is sailing to Le Havre and then up the Seine all the way to Paris."

"We're crossing the channel in this?" Viola looked around her. The bustling crew swarmed over the small vessel like ants over an upset hill. They tried to make her shipshape, but the gunwale timber was noticeably worm-eaten, the sails patched and much mended. "My estimation of your courage has ticked up several notches, Lieutenant. Sadly, I cannot say the same for your intelligence. Are you mad? This is a river craft, not an oceangoing vessel."

"It's the only ship leaving today for Paris. The captain assures me he's made the trip several times. It saves a dusty carriage ride from Calais. If you have a better way of getting us there, by all means, enlighten me."

Viola clamped her lips shut. She didn't even have fare for a hansom to get herself home.

"No? Then we'll go with my plan. Come, I'll see you to the cabin."

Cabin? There was a ray of sunshine. At least she'd enjoy some privacy on the small vessel. She followed him down the narrow companionway toward the stern. When she snagged the valises on one of the inner hatches, he relieved her of their weight. He lifted one bag, tucked the other under his arm and led the way, holding her hatbox out in front of him.

Quinn glanced back over his shoulder to see if she was following as he stooped under a low beam. The *Minstrel's Lady* was built with much shorter sailors in mind. If Quinn wasn't careful, he'd crack his head before the trip was over.

"The captain has agreed to surrender his cabin, so the accommodations are the best available."

"How kind."

"Kindness has nothing to do with it." Quinn dropped the hatbox in order to open the cabin door.

"Careful with that!"

"How else should I turn the knob, your ladyship? With my teeth?" Quinn stepped aside to let her enter first.

The cabin was spartan, but clean and held the faint tarry smell of carbolic soap. The linens on the narrow bed appeared fresh and there was a small commode with an ewer built into it. A pitcher swung from a hook above. A square table was bolted to the floor in the center of the space.

"I'm paying handily for the use of this cabin," Quinn said. "That means you have *me* to thank for not having to shift for yourself on the open deck."

"If I were making this trip of my own free will, perhaps I would thank you." She flashed him a poisonous smile.

"And if you weren't wanted for larceny in several English shires, perhaps this would be a pleasure cruise," he returned smoothly as he set her luggage on the bunk. "There's not much room in here, but there's a decent porthole and a private head through that door. I suppose we'll make do."

"What do you mean *we*?"

"I'll be sharing the cabin with you. For your protection. We're listed on the ship's manifest as husband and wife."

"Husband and—of all the cheek! This is totally unacceptable."

"It's the only thing that makes sense. A woman traveling alone is—"

"Is what? Mannish? Beyond the pale? Please." She untied

the bow beneath her chin and removed her bonnet. "We are living in the Year of Our Lord 1857, not the Stone Age. A grown woman is perfectly capable of traveling safely by herself."

"Capable, perhaps. But safely, no. Sailors are an unruly lot. If it's noised about that you're under my protection, no one will trouble you."

"And who'll protect me from you?"

One corner of his mouth hitched up. "I've already told you whether our relationship is more than business is your choice. It's a long way to Paris and I'll not deny that shared pleasure makes for pleasant travel." He took a step closer and gazed down at her, his eyes darkening with interest. Her whole body tingled with awareness. "Would you like to amend your previous decision?"

"Ah . . . well." The ship hit a swell and Viola stumbled back till her spine was pressed against the curved hull. Quinn swayed with the movement of the ship, but kept his feet, lifting a hand to the low ceiling to steady himself. He still looked every inch the English gentleman, but beneath the civilized trappings, she sensed a feral quality to his maleness. All that was feminine in her responded.

He reached over and tucked that errant lock of hair behind her ear again. Then he traced her cheekbone with his fingertips, his movement unhurried, his expression both hungry and strangely vulnerable. He ran the pad of his thumb over her bottom lip. The sensitive skin sparked with excitement. She caught a whiff of his scent, a bracing combination of leather and gun oil and something indefinably male. Viola trembled under his touch, not with fear, but with suppressed desire. Her insides churned like a cauldron over a low flame.

She would not let a man control her like that again.

"No." She pushed his hand away. "Don't do that."

He stood stock still for a moment, as if he'd suddenly turned to stone.

"As you wish," he finally said. "But unless you have a der-

ringer tucked in your garter and know how to use it, I suggest
you resign yourself to sharing this cabin with me."

She nodded mutely, refusing to look at him. Her heart was
fluttering so fast, she was sure he must be able to hear it in the
small space. That wild person inside her, the mad part that
had escaped once before and made her do things she regret-
ted, pounded to get out again.

If only they hadn't been such outrageously exciting things.

The wanton she kept under tight control threatened to claw
her way free once again. How could she keep the hidden side
of her from breaking out and doing something stupid?

*Something that would undoubtedly be quite filthy and quite lovely
all at the same time.*

She couldn't risk everything just because her knickers
bunched in a knot every time Lieutenant Quinn glanced sideways at her. She had to be strong. She had to shut down that
part of her. Ladies weren't supposed to like such things.

"I hope your silence doesn't mean you want a quick annul-
ment," he said softly.

If she could stand sharing the small cabin with him without
succumbing, it would prove she was in full possession of herself.

"No, now that I've had time to consider it"—she met his
steady gaze—"I think your plan is a wise one. If we're to pose
as husband and wife, I suppose I should call you something
besides Lieutenant. What is your Christian name?"

"Greydon, but no one except my mother ever calls me that."

"Why not? It's a perfectly respectable name."

"It's one of my father's names." A wall dropped down behind his eyes. "He's many things, but worthy of respect is not
one of them."

"I'd be careful casting stones if I were you. You're about to
embark on a life of larceny in Paris, so if Quinn the elder is
less than respectable, I rather think our partnership proves
you are your father's son, *Greydon*."

"Call me Quinn." His gaze cut to her sharply. "I'm nothing like him. And I'm not the one committing larceny. You are."

"My, my! That's an exceptionally fine blade you slice your conscience with." She leaned toward him, bracing both palms on the table, pleased that she seemed to have the upper hand for the first time since she'd met him. "So long as you only bankroll thievery, your hands don't carry any taint? How convenient."

"I'm not doing this for myself. I—" He closed his mouth abruptly.

"You're stealing that red diamond for someone else," she guessed. She came around the table and walked her fingers up the center of his hard chest. "Are you trying to impress some woman?"

"No." He caught her hand and held it still.

"I'm the one taking all the risks. I think I deserve to know the particulars. You can start with what your father did to make you hate him and finish with why this diamond is so important to you."

"You already know all you need to know." He released her hand and backed toward the door.

"I don't think so." She followed, not willing to let him retreat when she sensed she was winning the skirmish.

"This conversation is over."

"Not until you—"

He grabbed her and pulled her flush against his body. Surprise forced all the air from her lungs. Their gazes locked, and he bent slowly to cover her mouth with his. Her lips parted and his tongue swept in to claim her dark moistness.

She knew she ought to pull away, but his strength would make the contest woefully lopsided. And his warm, wet mouth on hers sapped her will to resist. She tasted brandy on his tongue. His rough chin scratched against her smooth one. His breath feathered hotly across her cheek. She felt herself melt into him without being able to stop it.

She began to kiss him back, chasing his tongue and nipping at his bottom lip. Her fingers curled around his lapel and pulled him closer. He groaned into her mouth.

His hands left her waist and found her breasts, stroking and circling them through the heavy serge fabric. Her nipples hardened and ached beneath their whalebone prison. Longing sang in her veins and pooled between her thighs.

It had been so long.

But she remembered the bitterness that followed bliss.

With reluctance, she slipped her hands into his and pulled them away from her needy breasts. Finishing off their kiss she drew away gently. "You, sir," she whispered, "do not fight like a gentleman."

He grinned down at her, bending to touch his forehead to hers. "I guess that makes us even, because you certainly don't kiss like a lady."

She pushed away from him with a low growl in the back of her throat.

"I didn't mean it like that." He tried to wrap his arms around her again.

She straight-armed him.

"I only meant—"

"I know what you meant," she said through clenched teeth, staring out the porthole as London slipped away from them. "Now leave me alone."

She heard the doorknob turn, and called to him, "Lieutenant."

"Yes?"

"Just so you know." She straightened her spine and turned to look him in the eye. She could be strong when she had to. Traveling to Paris with Greydon Quinn in that little cabin, she'd need all her strength. "I may not have a derringer, but I do know how to use one."

His lips twitched in a ghost of a smile. "I'd have been hugely surprised if you didn't."

CHAPTER 4

Quinn leaned on the gunwale and watched the receding coastline until the Dover cliffs disappeared into the mist. The stiff late March wind and salt spray buffeted him, but the top button of his greatcoat remained undone at his neck.

"I am sorry you must leave your home after so soon returning." Sanjay shivered beside him even though he was more thoroughly muffled than Quinn. Accustomed to India's baking heat, the prince suffered from England's cold dampness in every fiber of his southern body.

Quinn waved away Sanjay's sympathy. Leaving again troubled him far less than he expected. His parents were as tied to the English soil as the two-hundred-year-old oaks surrounding their manor. Quinn was more like a poplar. He thrived wherever he was. Leaving any place, be it England or his adopted India, was a small matter. No place truly seemed like home.

Perhaps he simply wasn't the type to put down deep roots.

"When would you like dinner served, sahib?" Sanjay asked as a sailor passed them with the rolling gait that marks a seaman even on land.

"Whenever it's ready." It bothered Quinn to have the prince pose as his servant, but they'd agreed it was the best way to proceed. Genuine friendship and respect between men of different races was unusual and therefore viewed with suspicion. In order to steal the most valuable treasure ever packed into such a small size, it was best to seem as unremarkable as possible.

"I assume you will dine with *her*." If Sanjay was truly Quinn's servant, he'd have been in grave danger of reprimand for the obvious distaste for Lady Viola in his tone.

Quinn nodded. "I don't like it any better than you do, believe me."

But not for the same reasons.

Sanjay had distrusted Viola on sight. Quinn had no doubt he could keep the lady close enough to not worry if he could trust her. He was more troubled by the fact that his unwilling partner in crime was a woman.

And he was *using* her.

Though Viola was a thief and independent enough he didn't feel obligated to cosset her, his sense of chivalry was offended by their arrangement. It wouldn't bother him a bit to bend another man to his will.

It gnawed at his gut to coerce a woman.

"I sense you share my misgivings," the prince said. "Perhaps we should reconsider this plan."

Sanjay didn't sense the half of it. Not only did Quinn suffer guilt over manipulating Viola into committing yet another burglary, if he hadn't escaped the small cabin when he did, he might have been tempted to seduce her, using the skills Padmaa had taught him.

Since that first time he'd pulled her onto his bed and felt her soft body beneath his, she'd featured prominently in his most wicked imaginings. Already in his mind, he'd undressed the woman and demonstrated a few of Padmaa's lovemaking tricks to devastating effect.

"Pleasure is a formidable chain, Quinn-sahib," the courtesan had told him. "It binds lovers together in mutual need."

Somehow, he never managed to visualize Viola and himself as lovers. The word was too tame, too gentle. When they came together in his mind's eye, it was intense. Fierce.

Like tigers mating.

They'd die of bliss if they didn't kill each other first. He'd never wanted a woman with as much keen-edged hunger as he wanted the one waiting for him in his cabin.

It made no sense to his mind, but his body could care less for logic. A physical entanglement might jeopardize the success of his plans. Once they retrieved the red diamond, what then?

Even though she was wellborn, her larceny meant she wasn't the fine English Rose men of his station expected to wed. There was a raw sensuality in her kisses. She was not a woman to take lightly and forget.

A man would be marked forever by her.

The mere thought of Viola was enough to make him feel achingly male. He'd already visualized her silken limbs, her shuddering sighs. He throbbed to rut her senseless, beating against her like a moth against the glass of a lantern flue.

"... and then we can put the lady off in Le Havre and find another way," Sanjay was saying.

Quinn had missed quite a bit of what his friend thought, but his own about Viola nearly had him spilling his seed in his trousers. It'd been months since he'd had a woman, but he had to get a grip on his reaction to her.

"No," he said with more force than he intended. "We press ahead. This will work. It has to."

He turned away and headed for the cabin, like a man destined for the rack.

When he reached the door, he raised his hand to knock, but caught himself. He was supposed to be her husband. It was his cabin, too. He turned the knob and slipped in.

She'd pulled back the bedclothes, stripped a sheet from the

narrow bunk and hung it from one of the low beams. A lantern flickered on the far side of the sheet, treating Quinn to her shadowy silhouette backlit on the fabric.

Her *naked* shadowy silhouette. Every curve and line of her form danced on the thin sheet.

"Is that you, Quinn?"

"Have you another faux husband on board, madam?"

"No, thank God. One of you is quite enough." She peeped around the sheet, showing one smooth bare shoulder. "I'm taking my bath, such as it is. Kindly remain on that side of the cabin."

"You have my solemn oath that I will not move from this spot." The mingled scents of warm woman and light floral wafted around the sheet. His balls clenched. Wild elephants couldn't drive him away.

"The captain had two chairs brought in for us. I left one on your side in case you returned before I was done."

He was nearly done. He plopped into the chair, not sure his knees would continue to support him.

She disappeared behind the sheet again, apparently oblivious to the fact that he could make out the dip of her waist, the curve of her calf when she propped a foot on the chair, the swell of her breasts as they fell forward when she bent over to soap her leg.

He ached to hold them. When she spread her legs to shoulder width and her hand disappeared between her thighs, he nearly groaned aloud.

"How long will it take us to reach Paris?" she asked.

Quinn cleared his throat to make sure his voice would work. "Three days, if we have fair weather."

Three days of pleasurable agony trapped in the cabin with that siren who'd already turned him down twice. Like Odysseus, he ought to have Sanjay strap him to the mast.

She was toweling off. Quinn stared at the tips of his boots with complete absorption. If she peered around the sheet again, he didn't want her to catch him ogling. It was one thing to want a woman. Another thing to be seen wanting.

"Three days," she repeated. "Well, I suppose it will give us a chance to become better acquainted."

She'd already spurned his efforts on that score. He supposed she meant to *talk* to him for three days. Sanjay's suggestion of putting her off in Le Havre was beginning to have real appeal.

"Tell me, Lieutenant. Why did you go to India in the first place?"

Reverting to his rank was a step backward. "I thought you'd agreed to call me Quinn."

"I agreed to call you *Greydon*, but you didn't seem to like it."

She emerged from behind the sheet, her unbound hair cascading over her shoulders. Auburn highlights sparked in the flickering lamplight and Quinn decided it was one husbandly perk that had been seriously underrated.

She wore a blue velvet robe de chambre. It was a bit threadbare in spots, but the garment covered her decently. If she was at home, she might greet early callers in it, but Quinn couldn't stop thinking about the fact that her breasts were free of their whalebone prison beneath the silver cord frogs that marched down the front of the soft robe.

She reached up to unhook the sheet. It seemed like a stretch for her, so Quinn stood to help her, starting at the opposite end.

When they met in the middle, he handed her the sheet and looked down at her. At close range, the neckline of her robe plunged low enough to reveal the shadowed hollow between her breasts. He jerked his gaze back to her eyes, but not quickly enough for it to escape her notice.

Her lips curved in a slight smile.

The little minx was teasing him. It would serve her right if he swept her up and plunged his hand down her bodice to claim a soft breast. He knew how to tease a woman beyond bearing. She had no idea whom she was dealing with. Of course, if she was aware of the light show she'd just given, he might be in for a sensual surprise as well. In several respects, Viola Preston was no lady.

But he was trying to be a gentleman. Mostly.

Quinn stepped back a pace.

"You haven't answered my question." She moved to close the distance between them again.

For the life of him, he couldn't remember what she'd asked. "There are any number of questions you haven't answered for me either."

"Well, it appears we shall not be in want of topics for conversation the next three days then." She turned and made up the bed, tucking the corners with practiced efficiency.

"For the daughter of an earl, you seem unusually accustomed to domestic chores."

She lifted her chin as she plumped the single pillow. "One does what one must."

"Is that why you steal?"

She shot him a glare. "If it's any of your business, my father died and left my side of the family penniless because I had the misfortune of being born a daughter instead of a son. I steal because I enjoy sleeping indoors and eating regular meals. And want my mother, sister and niece to do so as well. Satisfied?"

Not even close, but his cock would just have to bear the ache till he managed to settle himself.

"Many people live in reduced circumstances without resorting to theft."

"I am not *many people.*" She packed her toiletries back into a small bag and crouched down to stow them in the valise she'd tucked under the bed. "And you're not *many people* either. You're the heir of a viscount. Reportedly far more than solvent even before you left for India. You had no need to make the choice usually relegated to second sons."

"I was born a second son."

"But according to DeBrett's, your brother died in childhood."

"You investigated me."

"It seemed prudent to at least look you up in the registry of peers since you forced me to travel to Paris with you."

He winced inwardly at the word *forced*.

She cocked her head at him. "Why purchase a commission when you could while away your inheritance in gaming hells and brothels like most men who are waiting for a title?"

A captaincy in the military meant putting the greatest possible distance between himself and his father, but he'd already revealed more about that than he should have to her. "It seemed the right course of action at the time."

"No doubt you always choose the right course." Her tone was laced with subtle sarcasm. "Was it for adventure, Lieutenant?"

"It appears you have found me out."

She smiled thinly at him. "Then we are more alike than you might imagine. I freely confess my thefts allow me to do things most women wouldn't dream. Dressed as a man, I've roamed the city at night alone. At first, my heart pounded at every footstep, and I started at every barking dog. But later, I reveled in the choices a man's clothes gave me." She stopped before the porthole and looked out. The first hint of moonlight kissed her cheek. "I know that must sound incredibly tame to you, but for a woman of quality, it's an unheard of freedom."

She turned to fix him with her direct gaze. "What freedom lured you to India?"

Did she know some young bucks chose a stint on the subcontinent because it offered the opportunity for unbridled sexual experimentation? Quinn had limited himself to Pad-maa and her tutelage, but in the Gorgeous East a man of means might purchase any sort of sensual escapade he could imagine.

And some Quinn would never conjure up on his own in a million years.

"Duty to country lured me to India," he said.

Her lip curled. "If that's what you wish to believe."

"Why don't you believe it?"

"Because I think you found waiting around for your father to die boring beyond bearing."

"There's where you're wrong." Satan couldn't collect the old bastard soon enough to suit him.

"Life is beastly unfair, don't you think? My father's death means my family is set aside. Yours means you take your place as a peer of the realm."

Injustice always clawed his spine. Even injustice done to a thief.

"I'm sorry for your misfortune, Viola."

Her robe slipped down one shoulder. The exposed skin glowed with health in the light of the flickering lamp. His soft palate ached to taste that delectable flesh with a string of kisses.

"Do you think the unfairness you experienced gives you license to right the wrong with another wrong?" he asked.

"Apparently you do or we wouldn't be bound for Paris." She adjusted her robe to cover her shoulder completely. "Barring the fact that I've yet to see you on a white horse, this whole desperate escapade smacks of a quest. I suspect you tilt at windmills as often as you can."

"At least my reasons for wanting the red diamond have nothing to do with my own needs."

He realized suddenly that he was still wearing his greatcoat and the cabin was becoming deucedly warm. Or perhaps it was just because he was in it with a beautiful, barely dressed woman. He shrugged out of the coat and hung it on a peg behind him.

"You didn't have to resort to thievery to provide for your family, you know. A woman has other options. Marriage, for example."

"Not if her dowry has disappeared in a blink." She'd been all ginger sauce up to that point, spicy but not the least sour. The sudden bitterness in her tone surprised him.

"You're undoubtedly well educated. You might have become a governess."

"How deliciously lowering. The earl's daughter takes a position tending a baron's brats." She laughed mirthlessly. "The ton would have eaten that for breakfast with a spoon."

"There's another choice they'd consider even more lowering, but some women make it."

Quinn wondered, not for the first time, about her level of sensual experience. She was old for a debutante, probably in her mid-twenties, and hadn't been under a man's protection since her father died. When he'd insisted on sharing the cabin with her, she had protested, but not with a virgin's horror at the scandal of it or with demands that he marry in truth to protect her good name.

And she kissed like a woman who knew what passion was.

"Are you suggesting I sell myself, Lieutenant?"

"As frank a woman as you are, I'm certain you considered it." He moved closer and realized she was trembling a bit but trying to control it. "You'd cut a wide swath through the demi-monde. A gentleman with plump pockets would snap you up in a heartbeat to keep you—"

"As his own private plaything," she finished for him.

"His cosseted, protected, adored plaything. You could name your own terms. What man wouldn't want you? You're well-born . . . beautiful . . . accomplished . . ." Without conscious volition, he found himself reaching to cup her cheek. She didn't pull away. In fact, she inhaled a hitching breath when his thumb feathered over her skin. "Passionate."

"How could you know that?" she whispered, her lips barely moving.

He bent to lower his lips to within inches of hers. "A man just knows."

Then to his very great surprise, she slipped her fingers under his lapels and stood on tiptoe. Eyes wide open, she closed the distance between their mouths.

CHAPTER 5

I'*m going straight to hell.*

Quinn's kisses melted her insides so thoroughly, she almost didn't care.

Her fingers fluttered down his chest, unbuttoning his jacket. Such strong, hard muscles laid beneath that fine lawn shirt. He cinched her tighter to him and she felt a rock-hard bulge in his trousers. Warmth collected between her thighs. She arched into him and rocked her pelvis against him slowly.

He all but growled into her mouth.

That deep ache began to throb in her private place. Hollow. Empty. Needy.

It was wrong for a woman to even have such needs, much less act upon them. Home and family. Those should be her chief concerns.

"Think of the joy a child will bring you and you'll find you can bear those wifely duties," her mother had warned her when she explained the expectations a man has of the woman he marries.

The act was something to be endured with gritted teeth and grim determination.

Not sought out with such languid abandon.

Viola might have been born a lady, gently reared and over-protected, but Nature had played a cruel trick on her.

A wanton lived inside her skin.

Quinn's arms tensed around her. His hands slid down to cup her bum, fondling and lifting. He raised her up, grinding her against his hardness. She hooked an ankle around his leg and moved in rhythm with him.

He lowered her back down and released her lips. His mouth traveled down her neck to the tops of her breasts. She closed her eyes in bliss. Oh, there were his hands, stroking and circling. He parted the robe, unhooking the cord frogs down to her waist. Her nipples strained through the thin silk of her nightgown, aching for him to touch them, to squeeze them. *Oh, please.* To suck.

Quinn thumbed the pearl buttons and her nightgown fell open for him. He plunged his hand into her bodice. She spiraled down into a hot dark place. His mouth followed his hand, finding her taut nipple and suckling it. He nipped her and she gasped at the fiery jolt of need that arced from her breast to her womb.

They moved across the small space, a slow-motion dance of lust leading them toward the bed. It would all happen and Viola was powerless to stop it.

Didn't want to stop it.

Then suddenly, there was a sharp rap on the door. Quinn's head snapped up. "Who is it?" he demanded, his voice passion-ragged.

"Your dinner, sahib. It is ready to be served."

The Hindu's words were a dash of cold water.

"Give us a moment, Sanjay," Quinn ordered.

Viola turned away from Quinn and tucked her exposed breasts back into her nightgown. Her swollen nipples throbbed for more of his rough attention. She pressed her palms flat against both breasts to still the ache.

Quinn wrapped his arms around her from behind and planted

a soft kiss on her shoulder. "Are you all right?" Reaching around to rehook the frogs on the robe for her, his heart pounded against her spine.

She took a shuddering breath. "I shall have to be, shan't I?"

He left her then and opened the door to his servant.

Viola kept her back turned to the men and stared at a knot in the wood of the bulkhead above the bunk. It seemed safer than facing anyone while her heart raced in her chest and echoed between her legs.

She heard the clink of silverware, the snap of fresh napkins being folded just so, the chatter of a cup settling into a saucer. The rich, hearty smell of chowder tickled her nostrils. One of the men eased a cork from a bottle and a faint alcoholic haze wafted toward her.

But none of it cooled the heat in her cheeks.

Could Quinn's servant scent a whiff of her arousal over the yeasty aroma of bread and cheese? Or hear her blood pounding in her veins?

The servant murmured his salaams and she turned her head enough to catch the narrow-eyed glare he sent in her direction. She jerked her gaze away.

Then she heard the click of a latch. She and Quinn were alone once again.

And the madness was passing.

"He doesn't like me a bit, does he?" She turned around to find Quinn holding a chair for her. The table was set with gleaming crystal and china.

"Sanjay doesn't know you."

"Neither do you."

"Not yet. I intend to rectify that soon." His eyes darkened with interest, but he seemed to have recovered from their lusty interlude. Did he still intend on *knowing* her in a manner most biblical?

He swept a correct bow. "Will you dine with me, Lady Viola?"

She swallowed hard and nodded. So formal. Evidently, he needed some distance between them while he decided what to do about what had just happened. Very well. If there was one thing she excelled in, it was distance. She settled into the proffered chair.

"Never say the captain of this vessel knows how to stock a table setting like this."

"No, this is Sanjay's doing." Quinn took his seat opposite her. His face was as flushed as she suspected hers still was. "I'd just as soon travel with a tin plate and mug, but Sanjay keeps reminding me I'll be a viscount one day. He insists on maintaining certain standards."

"That makes one of us," she murmured as he poured blood-red wine for them.

"There is nothing wrong with your standards. Or mine." Quinn fastened his steely gaze on her, not pretending to misunderstand her. "We have done nothing for which we ought to be ashamed. I have not pledged faithfulness to another. Have you?"

"No." Not now, at any rate.

"Then no one is damaged by our actions. We're both adults. We have needs. If we decide to act upon them, it's no one's business but ours." He shrugged. "Unfortunately, we were victims of bad timing."

She sipped the wine, which proved to be an excellent vintage, dusky and plummy with a hint of the oak cask in which it was aged. "Or fortuitous timing. We might have been making a grave error."

"Do you think so?" Quinn filled each of their soup bowls from the filigreed tureen and set hers before her.

"I should amend that." She blew on a spoonful from the steaming bowl. "*I* would be judged to have made a grave error. The world is quite accommodating of a man's needs. It is both ignorant and condemning of a woman's."

"I'm not." Quinn leaned back in his chair, sipped his wine to test its worth, then drained the goblet. A smile lifted his lips. "In fact, I do everything in my power to encourage a woman to acknowledge her needs."

"Of that, I have no doubt." She arched a cynical brow. "How very enlightened of you."

"No, merely practical." He hitched his chair forward and dove into his soup bowl with gusto. "It's folly to imagine that the Creator who gave men their primal urges failed to give women similar inclinations to match."

"A convenient philosophy." But certainly not one she'd ever heard expounded by her vicar. "Has it eased your way into many women's beds?"

"Careful." He scraped his spoon along the bottom of the bowl. "Are you sure you wish to open our past sensual experiences to question? I might ask about the first man you took to your bed."

Did carnal knowledge leave a mark for the world to read? If so, it seemed her Scarlet A was showing. "Why do you assume there's been a man in my bed?"

"Your kiss."

"I may simply be the flirtatious sort who knows her way around a man's lips."

"Perhaps, but you aren't. There's nothing of the coquette about you." Quinn removed the lid from the chafing dish and filled each of their plates with bread, cheese, and a slice of shepherd's pie. "If I were a betting man, I'd stake a considerable sum that you are a sadder, but wiser girl."

Viola blinked hard and focused her attention on her plate. His assessment was disturbingly accurate.

"Let us say for the sake of argument that I am not the virgin society demands I remain until my wedding day."

She clipped her words as she chopped the cheese into bite-sized chunks. She didn't think she'd be able to stomach them, but it gave her hands something to do that would keep her from wanting to scratch his eyes out simply because he was the closest available male.

"Let us imagine that I accepted a proposal of marriage from a fine, upstanding fellow with aspirations to a title and a reputation as sterling as the British pound. Let us further suppose that I was giddy and foolish enough to believe him when he said he would love me all the more if I offered proof of my regard for him prior to our nuptials."

Quinn's lips drew together in a grim line.

"Then suppose my intended cried off on our engagement when my father died suddenly and he learned that my generous dowry would not be forthcoming." She sawed a bite from her pie and speared it with her fork, but couldn't bring herself to raise it to her lips. "I believe it was Sir Francis Bacon who said 'Knowledge is power.' Such knowledge should make me immune to your—how did you put it?—encouraging me to acknowledge my needs."

"On the contrary. Lack of a maidenhead gives a woman the same freedom as a man."

Quinn was apparently the sort to rush in where angels fear to tread. He didn't heed the warning sign she was sure must be affixed to her forehead.

"After the first one, another bed partner more or less"—he sopped up the gravy from his pie with the bread—"doesn't do any further damage."

"Then you think I'm damaged."

"I didn't say that." He looked up sharply and seemed to suddenly realize he teetered on the edge of a verbal precipice. She could almost see him dig in his heels to keep from tumbling off. He dragged a hand through his dark hair. "I think we're all damaged, one way or another. Some types are just easier to guess at than others."

"Really." She laid her fork aside. "How are you damaged, Quinn?"

He refilled his wineglass and drained it in one long gulp. "I find excessive conversation interferes with digestion, don't you?"

"Not particularly." She popped the bite of pie into her mouth. Now that she had him on the defensive, she found she could eat the food before her with relish. "Would you like me to guess?"

When he didn't answer, she plowed ahead.

"Since you seem to intensely dislike your sire, I can only assume something happened with your father. A secret. Something no one else knows." She tried the cheese and found it sharp and crumbly, just as she liked it. "But you know. And it's eating you up."

Quinn pulled his napkin from his neck and dropped it across his plate. He pushed back from the table and stood. "I typically take a walk after the evening meal. Please do not feel the need to wait up. If you will excuse me—"

"No, Quinn, I won't. I won't excuse you. Why do you expect me to share your bed if you won't share the least bit of yourself with me?"

He gave a puzzled shake of his head. "If we shared a bed, you may be certain I would share myself."

"Your body, perhaps." She rose to her feet. "But that's not all there is to you."

"You're muddying the issue," Quinn said. "I suppose I can't blame you, given your history with that cad. He never should have given you those expectations."

"So you imagine I would bed you with *no* expectations?"

"Of course not." He came around to her side of the table and looked down at her. "You should expect pleasure."

He lifted a lock of her hair to his lips and kissed it. "Reams of pleasure."

His fingertips brushed her cheek, traveled down her neck and feathered along the top of her bodice. "Bliss."

He circled her nipples with both hands through the velvet and they rose to meet him, aching for his touch. "A full measure of bliss. Abundant. Pressed down and running over."

He kissed her, open-mouthed, his tongue making love to

hers. One hand left a breast and skimmed over her ribs, past her navel and settled on her sex. Then he slipped his hand through the slit in her robe and cupped her vulva through her thin nightgown.

Oh, God. He'd feel how wet she was.

"You should expect ecstasy, Viola," Quinn said as his fingers stroked her through the silk, leaving a damp spot. "Not once, but many times. You may plead for me to stop, but I haven't a drop of mercy in me. I'll drive you to joy till you're screaming my name. What do you say? Shall I take you there?"

She closed her eyes, aching to let him. He kissed her again and began hitching her nightgown higher. When his hand slipped under her hem and his fingers invaded her, it took every ounce of strength she possessed to grasp his wrist.

"No," she whispered.

He flicked a fingertip over her sensitive spot and she shuddered.

"No." She pushed against his chest. "I can't do this. Not without knowing who you are."

"You knew who your fiancé was, didn't you?" He removed his hand and let her nightgown's hem billow to her feet. "By your own admission that didn't end well."

"No, as it turns out, I didn't know Neville at all. And I will not make the same mistake with you."

"I have no intention of marrying, so I wouldn't offer you a false promise," Quinn said.

"I don't need a promise. I just need honesty."

"What's more honest than this?"

"Nothing if you think we are no more than what we can see. You won't offer me yourself. Only your body." She ran her hands across his shoulders and down his arms. "Magnificent as you are, tempting as you are, that's not enough."

That wall she'd seen behind his eyes once before rose up afresh. He turned and stalked out the door.

CHAPTER 6

Quinn feared he was doomed to a state of perpetual erection. He made six circuits of the ship's rail before his blood started to cool and his body finally settled. He leaned on the gunwale and watched whitecaps flick over the black sea, brief flashes of silver in the moonlight.

"Your dinner was unsatisfactory, sahib?"

"The meal was fine, Sanjay."

"But you and the memsahib are not—"

"No, we're not."

"Good. When a man takes a woman he cannot trust to his bed, it is like taking fire to his bosom." Sanjay leaned on the rail beside him. "The Lady Viola is lovely. A most tempting armful, as you Angrezi say. You have done well to show such restraint, my friend."

"The restraint is not my doing."

"*Hmph.*" Sanjay made a noise of surprise. "The lady is a thief. Such a one has many tricks up her lacy sleeve. I was sure she would use her body to distract you from our purpose, but perhaps she has another plan."

She does, Quinn thought ruefully. A plan to *know* him, God help him.

With Padmaa, it had all seemed so simple. A man and a

woman's bodies were designed to give each other pleasure. Why did women, Western women in any case, have to make a physical relationship so complicated?

"If she manages to pass in your London society as a lady, she is no stranger to deception," Sanjay said. "Baaghh kaa kkhuun exerts much influence over those whose minds are already open to dark forces. Such a one will easily succumb to its power."

Oh, Lord, not the evil diamond diatribe again. Once he started on that saga of gloom and doom, Sanjay would put the chorus of a Greek tragedy to shame.

"Didn't you just hear me say the lady is not the succumbing type?"

Sanjay shook his head. "You misunderstand me. She may well resist your charm, sahib. But you do not have the weight of thousands of years behind your seduction. The diamond tempts people with what they want most. It senses a person's need and feeds it until they are powerless to resist."

"Mm-hmm." Quinn had lived in India long enough to realize that Asiatics didn't share Englishmen's high regard for the truth. They considered truth a dangerous commodity, not one to be broadcast about like a handful of seeds. Why divulge the truth if a lie will serve, a holy man had told him once.

So a number of lies and legends had sprung up about Baaghh kaa kkhuun.

It drove men mad, Sanjay claimed. Hundreds of years ago, the man who gave the stone its original rose-style cut would only handle it long enough to make one strike every seven days and even so, he was drooling and hearing voices of the dead by the time he chipped away the last bit.

"It will drain a man's life force if he does not break free of it," Sanjay said.

"Hokum." The word escaped Quinn's lips before he realized it had formed on his tongue. He sighed. "I mean no disrespect but—"

"You do not believe," Sanjay finished for him. "Whether you believe it or not, the red diamond's history is a bloody one. It has incited murder. War, even. Some say that is how it came by its color in the first place."

"If that were true, why has the East India Company never heard of these killings?"

Quinn would've put a stop to them. He was proud of the way he and the men under his command imposed order and made the streets of India safer. They worked to stop thuggery and put an end to the hateful practice of *suttee*, the custom of burning a man's living widow with his corpse. Using the excuse that a red diamond incited one to commit murder would get short shrift in an English court.

"You think because a white man doesn't know a thing, it hasn't happened?" Sanjay cast him a sidelong glance. "For many lifetimes, Baaghh kaa kkhuun rested safe in the eye of Shiva, its evil quiet."

Then the Thugs stole it for some reason. Several of them would never steal again thanks to him and Sanjay. "Are you trying to tell me the diamond *compelled* them to steal it?"

"No, but did you never wonder why those Thugs gave it up to the British so easily?" Sanjay asked.

"They gave it up for a serious amount of money."

"*Beshak.* Of course," he amended. Sanjay always tried to speak English to Quinn instead of reverting to his native Hindi. "They had to take the Angrezi money to avert suspicion. But the real reason they gave the diamond to your viceroy was so he would send it to your Queen. Once Baaghh kaa kkhuun resides in the royal treasury, it will call to her, as it calls to all people of power. Your Queen will demand to wear it always and it will destroy her. The Thugs have taken to heart the old proverb, you see."

"Which proverb is that? A wise man knows jewelry always fits?"

"No." Sanjay lifted a dark brow at him. "To kill a serpent, one must strike the head."

Despite the fact that Sanjay compared the queen's empire to a snake, Quinn preferred that scheme to get rid of the British in India over the fakirs' cries for the sepoys to mutiny. A new bauble in the royal vault seemed unlikely to result in any actual bloodshed. If the sepoys revolted, hundreds, maybe thousands, would die before order was restored. The return of the red diamond to its rightful place might be all that was needed to show good faith and keep the sepoys from listening to the fakirs.

"Well then, if Baaghh kaa kkhuun is so dangerous to the touch, I'll make sure Lady Viola wears gloves when she pinches it," Quinn said.

Sanjay nodded approvingly. "Now you understand, sahib. But since she is a thief, I do not know if gloves will be sufficient. Did you not hear what happened to the thug who dug the diamond out of Shiva?"

Quinn shook his head.

"Even though he had wrapped it in cloth, he would not release the diamond"—Sanjay's fist clutched tight in demonstration—"so his friends cut off his hand."

"So they could sell it. Blood-thirsty bastards."

"No, they did it to save his life. He could not release it. The diamond was feeding on his heart."

Quinn didn't believe a word of it, but a superstitious shudder passed over him.

"I will see what else may be done to protect Lady Viola from the jewel's malevolence," Sanjay promised. A sailor passed close by them, so Sanjay adopted a more correctly deferential posture. "Shall I clear your dinner away, sahib?"

"Yes." Quinn turned back to the pitching sea. "And while you're at it, see if there's a spare hammock you can string up in the cabin for me. Even if Lady Viola were willing, that bunk is pretty narrow." Nevertheless, Quinn envisioned several positions from the *Kama Sutra* that would allow them to share the small space quite happily. "But since she's not willing, it seems I need other sleeping arrangements."

Quinn waited another half hour before heading for the cabin. He wanted to give Sanjay time enough to clear out. The space was small enough for two people. Three made it difficult to draw breath.

The companionway was dark and he forgot how low the beams were in places until he smacked his forehead on one. He walked the rest of the way in a half crouch, hand on his head, till he reached the cabin door.

No light showed through the crack under the door.

He pushed his way in, pleased to find the porthole provided enough starlight for him to make out the placement of the table, his swinging hammock and the curved form of the woman on the bunk.

Viola had turned her face to the wall, a sure sign she didn't welcome either his attentions or his conversation. He doubted she was asleep, but she didn't stir as he moved past her to his hammock.

She'd braided her hair into one long plait. It draped across her pillow and hung off the side of the bunk. He narrowly resisted giving it a playful tug. She wouldn't appreciate it.

He stripped out of his clothing. He always slept in the nude and didn't see the point in altering his habits to please a woman who wouldn't be pleased no matter what he did. Quinn wrapped his blanket around himself and climbed into the hammock, sighing as it settled into a gentle rocking motion that matched the waves beyond the porthole.

Still, she said nothing. Didn't twitch so much as a shoulder blade.

He wished the sound of her gentle breathing didn't go

straight to his cock. Or maybe it was her scent, warm and clean with an undertone of musk. Perhaps it was that braid swinging in the dark that made his groin ache.

"A woman can please a man with her hair in a number of ways," Padmaa had explained as she loosened her long tresses and dragged them over his prone form. The gleaming black hair was like the caress of a thousand tiny fingers on his skin and left a shiver in its wake.

But Quinn wasn't thinking about Padmaa's jet-colored mane. He was imagining Viola's auburn braid. Undone. Spreading over her shoulders like an autumn mantle. Teasing over his groin. Forming a living tent as she bent to kiss him.

He ached so badly, he suspected he'd never get to sleep.

Then he had an idea. For one of his lessons with Padmaa, she made him concentrate on synchronizing his breath with hers to make their connection as effortless as possible. He closed his eyes and listened to Viola's breathing.

It was a soft sound. He had to strain to catch it over the shushing of the ocean against the ship's hull, but he managed. Once he'd isolated the sound, it was a small matter to match his own breathing to it.

In.

Out.

In.

He settled into her rhythm and closed his eyes.

Her breasts rose and fell slightly as she sat cross-legged before him. Viola's eyes were blindfolded so he let his gaze travel over her without fear of censure. He didn't know why the woman couldn't understand that just looking at her gave him pleasure. At least he didn't have to worry about her trying to cover herself since she thought his eyes were shielded, too. What she didn't know wouldn't hurt him.

Her nipples were the color of a ripe peach and just as luscious. His gaze traveled down her bare body, past her navel to where her yoni was scantily covered with auburn curls. Her slit was pink and glis-

tening. He could smell her, musky and sweet. He ached to rub his face between her thighs, drunk on her scent.

But it wasn't time yet.

"Like this, Quinn?"

"Exactly," *he said, reminding himself to breathe.* That was the whole point. Joined breath led to joined bodies.

His lingam stood stiff as a pole.

"Now we match each other, stroke for stroke." *He reached forward, purposely missing the breast that was his goal, and caressed her collarbone instead.* "If I use my right hand, you use yours as well so we mirror each other."

She reached for him. Her fingertips danced along his sternum and then brushed the hairs whorling around his nipple. He took it as his cue to move down to torment her breast, circling her nipple till gooseflesh rose around it before he took the little bud between his thumb and forefinger and squeezed.

A small gasp escaped her lips.

"Did you like that?" *He rolled her taut nipple between his fingers.*

"Oh, yes."

He dragged his knuckles over that needy flesh. He flicked it with his fingernail. He tugged it gently. She tried to duplicate the motions on him, but her movements were disjointed. It was clear she was too distracted by her own need to focus on the exercise.

That was fine with him. He was happy to fan the flames till she erupted in a fireball. He leaned forward and used his mouth. Kissing her breasts. Licking. Sucking. Nipping.

"I can't . . . can't do that to you at the same time," *she gasped.*

"That's fine," *he murmured as he cupped both breasts and nuzzled between them.* "We'll take turns."

As if he'd play as fair as that.

While he suckled her, he let his hand drift down over her belly. He teased her curls and smoothed his fingertips over the tender skin of her inner thigh.

She drew a ragged breath.

Then he explored her delicate folds. So slick and wet. Her "little pearl" had risen to be stroked and he found the nub of flesh easily.

Her body jerked in surprise.

"Don't you like that?" he asked, all innocence as he circled the sensitive spot. Her mouth went slack.

"Like it?" she gasped. "I may never let you stop."

As if he would.

To his surprise, she put out her hand and searched blindly along his body, her fingertips skimming his belly, then grasping his erect penis. She wrapped her fingers around him and smoothed her palm over his length from root to tip. His balls clenched.

She explored the head, and discovered the patch of rough skin at its base. His breath hissed over his teeth.

"Like that, do you?" she asked slyly.

"I may never let you stop."

A pearl of fluid formed at the tip and he feared he might lose control. Time for a shift in position to distract himself.

He leaned over to kiss her lips again, lifting her at the waist and depositing her on his lap. She wrapped her legs around him and pressed her body from breast to groin against his. Soft and pliant, she was everything he imagined when he thought woman.

His lingam stood upright between her wet folds. He matched her breath and felt her heart pounding between her legs, throbbing around him. If he didn't want a fountain to erupt between them, he needed to enter her now.

He lifted her again, positioning her above him so he could impale her by finger widths, drawing out their torment. The tip of him slid into her yoni. He narrowly restrained himself from driving in his full length in a single quick stroke.

Before he could lower her onto himself, she lifted the blindfold and looked down at him. A cat's smile played about her mouth. "Not until you tell me what happened at the lake," she whispered. "I need to know who you are."

* * *

Quinn jerked awake. It was only a dream. She didn't know anything. She couldn't know. No one did.

Except his father, may he rot in hell.

Viola's gentle breathing was undisturbed but his came in short pants. His cock was set to go off. Only a tug or two would do the trick.

But self-gratification was a cheat, Padmaa had explained. A useful exercise in discovering one's limits of control perhaps, but if one wished to experience the heights of the act of love, one needed to save one's energy and seed for release with a partner.

Quinn wondered if the Indian courtesan wasn't in collusion with his vicar. The man constantly warned of blindness and other ills if young men "abused" themselves.

"Delay brings delight," Padmaa was fond of saying.

Try telling that to my cock, he thought, grinding his teeth with frustration.

Viola had meant it when she'd turned him down. She wouldn't bed him unless he allowed her to ferret out his secrets. Quinn would be willing to tell Viola about his time at Eaton, his stint in the military, even his relationship with Padmaa, but how by all that was holy had she latched onto the one thing he'd never told another soul?

No, his mind was playing tricks on him. That was only in his dream. Viola might have sensed his estrangement from Lord Kilmaine, his father the viscount, but he'd never let anything slip about the lake. Not to anyone.

And he intended to keep it that way.

He rolled onto his side and wondered how much longer it was till dawn.

CHAPTER 7

Willie pushed his way through the knots of passengers on the paddle-wheel steamer and tromped down the gang-plank. He was so eager to get off the ship, he didn't care if he ran someone down. He'd never suspected he had that much puke in him till he crossed the Channel. He narrowly resisted the urge to fling himself to the ground and kiss the cobbles of Calais.

The worst of it was that, even though he'd nipped down the Thames in the fastest riverboat he could find, Lady Viola wasn't aboard the steamer. He'd let her get too far ahead of him. After questioning an unfortunate steward with threats of more than a black eye, he learned no lady of her description traveling with a gentleman of military bearing had been aboard the previous sailing either.

Duncan better not be wrong about this. Willie ground a fist into his other palm.

When his shop boy had come back with the news that Lady Viola was off for Paris in the company of a gentleman, most people would have suspected the lady had found a lover.

Not Willie.

She was too good a thief to be sidetracked by a prick.

He nosed around a bit and came across the rumor of an Indian diamond on its way to the Royal Collection. That made a good deal more sense to Willie's mind. If the lady was bound for Paris, the diamond must be on its way there as well. Lady Viola must have taken a different route than the paddle steamer.

He elbowed his way to the head of the line to purchase a seat on the next coach to Paris. There were only a few hotels in the French capital where the English upper crust would deign to stay. He'd find her right enough.

Lady Viola had to be taught a lesson and Willie was just the bloke to do it. She stole for him and he'd not allow his best set of light fingers to work for someone else. The sooner she realized that was way of the world, and the way it would stay, the better.

As for that Indian diamond, by God, she bloody well wasn't going to cut Willie out of his share.

Sharing the small cabin with Greydon Quinn was even more trouble than Viola expected.

And she'd expected quite a lot.

She took great pains to protect her modesty. Every morning she remained snug in bed until after Sanjay arrived with their breakfast. Then she lifted her robe from its peg and wiggled into it beneath her sheets before she emerged from the bunk to break her fast.

Not Lieutenant Quinn. He greeted her each morning wearing nothing but the blanket he'd slept in and a smile.

"Do you mind?" Viola crossed her arms over her chest.

He took a swig of tea, then set the cup down and stood to hold her chair for her. The blanket rode low on his hips. "Where are my manners?"

"Where indeed?" she murmured as she perched on the chair and allowed him to push her closer to the table. She poured the steaming tea into her cup and added a dollop of milk.

"You're welcome," he said pointedly.

She shot him a glare, then dropped her gaze lest she linger too long over his bare chest. "Why should I thank you for showing me such disrespect?"

His fingers splayed over that incredible chest in a gesture of mock surprise.

He returned to his chair and hooked an ankle over his knee, displaying a bare, long-toed foot. "In what manner have I failed you, milady?"

"We may be posing as husband and wife, but we need only keep up the appearance of intimacy when we are in public." She buried her nose in her teacup to keep from staring at his well-muscled torso. "Did it occur to you that I wouldn't appreciate such a display of flesh in private?"

"Not really." He tapped his boiled egg with the edge of his butter knife and peeled off the shell. "I haven't forced you to look in my direction. But if your sidelong glances are any measure, I'd say you're properly appreciative."

Drat the man! He was right, but it would take an hour with thumbscrews to make her admit it.

"This cabin is small enough to make it impossible not to inadvertently glance your way on occasion." *Only every other heartbeat.* "I would prefer it if you exercised a bit more modesty."

"As you wish." He stood and began untucking the blanket from around his waist.

"What are you doing?"

"Just honoring a lady's request." He held the blanket out in front of him. "I'll attach it to the beam and find my way into a few more clothes." He suited his actions to words and walled himself in on the far side of the table. "Might I suggest you use this time to dress as well? We should be approaching Paris this morning. You'll want to take a turn around the deck and see the sights as we make port. Have you ever been to Paris before?"

"No." There was a threadbare spot in the blanket, thin enough she could see his flesh-toned form through it. She looked at her own lap, trying to steel herself against the temptation. Quinn was totally amenable to discussing matters of the flesh, but he'd resisted all her efforts to draw him into conversation about himself. "I've been wondering something."

"Of course you have. You wouldn't be a woman if you weren't curious. What now?"

She heard the rustle of small clothes being drawn over his body. It reminded her that he tended to dress more quickly than she, so she unfastened her robe and shrugged out of it.

"Your father is Viscount Kilmaine. According to DeBrett's, he also claims a barony. Ashford, isn't it? I was wondering why you go by your military rank instead of your courtesy title, Lord Ashford."

"I may have purchased a commission, but believe me, I earned my rank." His voice held a hard edge that surprised her. "Besides, I wasn't born to the title."

"No, your brother was. I understand that. But still, you're heir to Lord Kilmaine now and you're entitled to use his lesser title." She pulled on her stockings and gartered them at her knee. "A title always smoothes a man's way in the world. I can't imagine why you wouldn't want to use it."

"Ah, I see it now. You want to be introduced as Lady Ashford instead of Mrs. Quinn."

Through the bare spot in the blanket, she caught a glimpse of his navel and the narrow strip of dark hair that led downward from it. Heat crept up her neck.

"Lady Ashford does have a grander ring to it, doesn't it?" His elbow bumped the blanket and her view of his belly disappeared.

"Since I'm not really your wife, it hardly matters." She looked away from the thin place in the blanket, wiggled into her drawers and tied the drawstring at her waist.

Once again he'd deflected a personal question by speculating on why she wanted to know. And put her on the defensive.

"If I were the sort who cared about such things, I'd never have married you in any case." She drew off her nightshift, opened her valise beneath the bunk, and pulled out a fresh chemise. Time to put *him* on the defensive. "A daughter of an earl might be said to have married down since you're merely the son of a viscount."

"Ouch, milady." He was silent a few moments. "Are you the sort who cares about such things?"

At one time, yes, she admitted to herself as she slipped into the chemise. Such things mattered a great deal.

Neville Beauchamp was heir apparent to his uncle, who was a marquis. She'd fully expected to be the ninth Marchioness of Sudbury. But her father died and so did Neville's regard for her. Apparently, his uncle was a light-in-the-pockets marquis and aside from her maidenhead and sumptuous dowry, Viola held no real value for Neville.

Especially once both were gone.

"No, Quinn," she said softly. "Those things aren't important to me."

Her gaze fell on a silver tray where Sanjay had laid out Quinn's wrist studs for the day. Garnets, by the look of them, set in silver.

Garnets weren't the chattiest of gems, but if she were determined to learn more about Quinn, touching a jewel he wore each day would undoubtedly tell her more than he did.

Of course, using her gift was not without cost. If she maintained contact with a gem long enough to establish a link that let the stone send her a prolonged vision, she'd have a pounding headache for the rest of the day. There was also a chance Quinn would catch her mid-trance and discover the secret of her unique ability.

Or he might see her handling his studs and believe she meant to steal them.

If Quinn wouldn't talk to her about himself, how else was she to learn anything about him? She stretched out her hand.

"Did Sanjay leave my wrist studs?"

She started guiltily. "Yes, they're here on a tray."

"Would you mind handing them to me? Or are you dressed enough that I can come round?"

"No, no!" Her breasts were still unbound. She picked up the tray and held them around the edge of the blanket. "Here they are."

"Not terribly grand, are they?" Quinn took the tray from her.

"They seem fine enough."

"They belonged to my uncle. He was a capital chap. Always drunk and disorderly, embarrassed my father every chance he got, but Uncle Bertram knew how to turn himself out well when he put his mind to it. He left me these and a set of pearl ones. And a silver snuffbox I never use but always carry. Odd, I suppose, but it helps me remember him." The pearl studs were supposed to go to his brother, but like so much meant for Reggie, they'd come to him in the end instead.

"You cared a great deal for your uncle. I can hear it in your voice."

"Yes, I suppose I did." Quinn bent to peer through a thin spot in the blanket.

"Why do you just suppose? Don't you know?"

Quinn knew ogling a woman through a threadbare blanket made him a bit of a cad, but he'd like to shake the hand of the man who could resist the tempting bit of lace on the other side of the thin partition. Such a stalwart fellow would have to be a saint.

Or a eunuch.

Viola was fitting her corset around her body. She must have already adjusted the laces at the back to the required tightness. Now she only need fasten the hooks and eyes running alongside the busk.

The corset lifted her breasts and pressed them together. The creamy flesh bulged over the top of her chemise. So soft. So touchable. So—

"Quinn?"

He straightened to his full height and the enticing image blurred. "What?"

"Don't you know whether or not you cared for your uncle?"

Oh, that. Women were always prattling on about feelings and such rot. "Yes, I know. He was a regular corker and I admired him a great deal." Especially Uncle Betram's ability to send Quinn's father into a near apoplectic fit. "But he's gone now. I don't feel the need to dwell on it."

There. That should satisfy her.

"Why not? It's certainly no weakness to admit to tender feelings. The people we choose to love reveal a good deal about us."

"Becoming maudlin over one's feelings, tender or otherwise, serves no useful purpose."

Quinn heard the rustle of taffeta. Against his better judgment, he ducked down to peer at her again. The lace at her neckline was frayed and the petticoats she drew on were patched and mended. Her dresses were several seasons old, but her undergarments were in far worse condition. Only those ridiculous little hats she wore were in the first stare of fashion.

His chest constricted. She kept up a brave front.

"Our first stop in Paris will be at a modiste's," he said decisively. *That should end all talk of feelings.*

"Why? I packed sufficient clothing for all normal purposes."

"Whatever else our purposes are, they are not normal." He pulled on his jacket and straightened his spine. "I think you're right. No more Lieutenant Quinn. Time to put aside my military past. Lord Ashford desires to see his baroness turned out in the latest Parisian fashions. That way our trip to Paris serves three purposes."

"A new wardrobe for me, a red diamond for you. What's the third?"

He lifted the curtain in time to catch her fastening the last button on her bodice. "Why, milady, I'm cut to the quick. How could you forget? We're on our honeymoon."

CHAPTER 8

Quinn delivered on his word. He ordered their cabby to take them to the part of Paris that was home to the most sought after modistes and milliners and to stay at the curb until they'd completed their purchases. In shop after shop, he urged Viola to choose the most expensive, most lacy undergarments and accessories. Two of everything wouldn't do if there was a third or fourth available.

"*Vraiment*, she is the exact size of my dressmaking dummy," one seamstress trilled after taking Viola's measurements behind a chinoiserie screen. "Lady Ashford may choose from any of my sample dresses and *bien sur*, it will fit! Madame, you are most fortunate in your figure."

"I beg to differ," Quinn said gallantly. "I am the fortunate one."

"Ah, *l'amour*!" The modiste tittered and cast him a sly look. "You are not married long, *non*?"

"Long enough for me to thoroughly appreciate my bride's figure."

Viola blushed as if she were his bride in truth. She knew it was all for show, but his words pleased her more than they should.

The dresses were heaven. The linens, the bombazines, the delicate silks—all were delicious on her skin. The styles were all so very *chic*, the newest French term to describe anything on the forefront of fashionable sophistication.

For one glorious afternoon, Viola basked in the glow of cosseted femininity. It was an echo of what her life had been like when her father was alive. If she wanted anything, he saw to it that she had it.

But her father never made sure she had the last item Quinn insisted upon.

A wedding ring.

He steered her into an elegantly appointed jewelry shop.

"Our little ruse won't be very effective if your ring finger remains unadorned," he explained as he started to pick out a set with a large cabochon ruby surrounded by small rose-cut diamonds.

"No, not that one." It was easily the most impressive ring in the case, but the yellow gold setting was designed so the ruby nested deeply. On the underside, the stone would rest on her bare skin. She'd never be free of the gem's voice. "The stone is too big."

"Too big! Oh, monsieur!" The jeweler had bustled over in time to hear her last statement. "Such a woman is a treasure herself, but she protests too much. Her heart is drawn to this ruby, I know it. Surely you will not listen to her."

"Surely I will," Quinn said with a grin. "She's the one who has to wear it. Which one do you prefer, my love?"

My love? He was doing it far too brown. She wished he wouldn't take the game that far. It was almost a sacrilege to feign love, but he certainly seemed to be enjoying himself. She looked over the assortment of rings.

"There." She pointed to a yellow and white gold set fashioned in the style of entwined serpents. The only stones were a pair each of small rubies and sapphires for the snakes' eyes. The jewels were tiny enough not to be a worry. Their voices would be small, barely on the raw edge of sound. With that style, only smooth precious metal would touch her skin.

Neither gold nor silver had ever mumbled a single word to her. She suspected the refining process stripped away all past imprints in a fiery blast. Or perhaps she was unable to receive information from precious metals. She'd never touched a raw nugget, so she couldn't be sure.

"You're certain that's the one you want?" Quinn frowned down at the ring.

"Excellent choice, madam," the jeweler said, which made Viola suspect the ring's artistry made it the ruby's equal in terms of price. "The serpent is a symbol of eternity. Your Queen Victoria, does she not wear a serpent ring for her Prince Albert?"

"I didn't know that," Viola said.

"*Certainement.* A refined choice," the jeweler said as he handed it to Quinn to fit on Viola's finger. "*Tres chic.* Now allow me to show you some necklaces and bracelets to complement your ring."

Quinn slid the ring on Viola's left hand. "I'm beginning to think this new word *chic* means 'hopelessly expensive but an Englishman will pay for it if you get his woman to bat her eyes at him.' "

"I didn't ask for any of this, Quinn."

"No, you didn't"—he pressed a kiss on her hand, no doubt for the benefit of the jeweler who was scurrying back toward them with a couple dozen cases of costly pieces in his arms— "which is why I'm all the more determined to give it to you."

"But no more jewelry, I beg you." She laid a hand on his forearm, which he covered with his. "I prefer to wear a simple ribbon about my neck. Truly."

Quinn refused to be persuaded and she finally agreed to accept a cameo brooch and a pendant watch on a gold chain. The jeweler was quietly livid, but so long as no gemstone touched her skin, Viola was satisfied.

As they left the shop and he handed her into the waiting hansom, Quinn shook his head. "You've confused me royally now. Why on earth do you steal jewelry when it's obvious you've so little use for it?"

"Since it's no hardship to part with, I experience no pangs when I exchange it for funds. I steal because I enjoy seeing my family eat, remember, not because I lack a sufficient number of baubles."

"It appears I misjudged you," he said softly. "I thought you the most acquisitive of women."

She laughed. "Don't admit you're wrong yet. You've only seen the smallest part of my collection of hats."

Quinn had sent Sanjay ahead to bespeak rooms for them at the Hotel de Crillon, Paris's most elegant and oldest inn. It was said Marie Antoinette often reserved suites of rooms there and entertained her guests before the bloody revolution parted her lovely head from her body.

Viola wished she could take Sanjay's room and let him stay with Quinn, but at least the suite on the top floor was large enough to make her forget the tininess of the cabin they'd shared on the *Minstrel's Lady.* If she'd managed to sleep in that little space with him without succumbing to his charm, she could retain possession of herself in the lovely suite of the hotel. The sitting room was furnished in the florid Rococo style. The private bath had running water in the copper tub and a newfangled flushing water closet. And, of course, a sumptuous bedroom.

With only one bed.

"We've been invited to the English Embassy for dinner," Quinn said as he thumbed through the mail Sanjay had collected for them from the concierge. Quinn frowned as he read the telegram that was second in the stack after the invitation from the embassy. He shoved it into his pocket so quickly, Viola decided he didn't want to share its contents.

"How does the ambassador know we're here?"

"Even though we're allies with France now, it's a good idea

to let one's government know one is in country. While you and I were supplementing your wardrobe this afternoon, Sanjay was delivering our calling cards to all the appropriate places in town."

"You think the diamond will be at the Embassy?"

"If it's coming through Paris, I think someone there will know where it is." Quinn crossed to the bellpull. "I believe a real bath is in order for both of us."

The hotel staff was marvelously efficient and Quinn arranged for a lady's maid to assist Viola with her toilette. She'd almost forgotten what a luxury it was to have someone scrub her back or wash her hair or help her lace her corset.

She dismissed the maid when it was time to apply her limited amount of cosmetics. The French were prone to excess in the use of paint. Viola didn't want to look in the mirror and see a stranger staring back at her through her own eyes.

When she finally emerged from the chamber, Quinn was on his feet in a heartbeat. The naked admiration on his face warmed her to her toes.

"You're a stunner, Lady Ashford. I'm almost of a mind to send our regrets and dine in," he said with a wicked grin.

"I do hope you don't think I went to all this trouble for your benefit."

The full skirt of her gown rustled as she stepped lightly across the room. She passed by a long mirror and noticed the green, watered silk flattered her coloring and made auburn highlights sparkle in her hair. "But I don't want you to think me unappreciative. Thank you for these lovely new things."

"I do hope you don't think I went to all this expense for your benefit." He flipped her words back at her. "Believe me, the pleasure is all mine."

She felt her cheeks dimpling. "You don't think the décolletage too daring?"

She knew she was teasing him, but the gown made her feel too delicious not to. The neckline scooped off her shoulders, revealing more flesh than she'd expected. Another couple inches and her nipples would have been laid bare.

"This is Paris," Quinn said. "The French believe there's no such thing as too daring when it comes to the display of a woman's bosom. Damn me, if the Frogs aren't right. Especially when the bosom is as exquisite as yours."

He made a proper obeisance over her hand. The entwined serpents glinted up at him when he pressed his lips in a soft kiss on the back of her hand. "I'm glad to see the ring fits over those gloves. I'd hate for anyone at the embassy to think you unclaimed."

Her smile faded. He was only practicing to pass as her besotted new husband, but he did it with such conviction, she was tempted to believe him. "Careful, Lieutenant or I shall think you missed your calling on the London stage."

The admiring light went out of his eyes.

There was a rap at the door and Sanjay appeared with Quinn's freshly pressed trousers and tailed jacket. He also bore a tray holding a signet ring, an impressive-looking medal on a blue silken stole, and several other pieces of masculine jewelry. Viola might insist on minimal adornment, but it seemed Quinn would sparkle with enough sartorial splendor for the two of them.

The Hindu cast a disapproving glance in her direction and disappeared to oversee the borrowed valet, who'd arrived to draw Quinn's bath.

Quinn undid his tie and removed his garnet wrist studs, depositing them on the tray next to a pair of diamond studs.

Viola didn't mean to ogle. Most people preferred colored stones to white diamonds, but those had been cut in a brilliant style that seemed to release the fire embedded in the stone. Like a magpie, her eyes were naturally drawn to bright shiny things. "I thought your uncle gave you a set of pearls."

"He did. I never said I didn't have any others. My family has many flaws, but fear of ostentation when it's needed isn't one of them." Quinn disappeared into the bedroom and adjoining bath.

Viola paced the room for a bit, not willing to sit lest she wrinkle her skirt. She positioned herself at the window and gazed out at the broad avenue. The streetlamp lighter was making his rounds, his flame on a long pole igniting one lamp after another. Elegant broughams and coaches passed each other, bearing the finer residents of Paris to finer entertainments.

Every few minutes, Viola's gaze flitted back to the tray of jewels.

There were the secrets of Greydon Quinn, encased in crystal, winking at her. Would anyone really be harmed if she touched just one?

Viola peeled off a glove and tiptoed over to the table where the tray rested. She reached out to touch one of the studs, but flicked her gaze toward the bedroom door, ears pricked for the sound of approaching footsteps.

The door had been left ajar. Viola clapped her bare hand over her mouth to keep from betraying herself with the slightest noise. Through the crack in the door, she saw flashes of naked flesh.

Quinn evidently wasn't the sort to linger in cooling bathwater. She was treated to a peek at his chest, the knotty outlines of his muscles standing out around his brown nipples. There was a blur of dark hair at his groin before he turned his back to the door.

He was speaking to Sanjay, giving soft instructions, judging from the tone of his voice. Viola wasn't interested in whatever he might have to say. There was a flash of his muscular thighs, thick and sinewy. When her gaze traveled north, she saw his buttocks.

She bit her lower lip. His butt cheeks were lightly dusted with fine dark hairs. His narrow hips and waist expanded into a broad, muscular back.

Quinn turned and bent over to pick up a dropped stocking. She caught a glimpse of his sex dangling in front of him from its nest of brown curls.

Mercy! Viola sucked her breath in over her teeth.

She'd seen enough. She backed away toward the window, her belly dancing as if a swarm of mayflies were caught there. She'd known Quinn was gifted from the size of the bulge in his trousers, but he exceeded her expectations by a good bit.

Just imagine what he's like when he's roused! Her insides pulsed.

Pleasure, he'd promised her. Bliss. Abundant, pressed down and overflowing. Ecstasy.

The man was certainly equipped by nature to deliver on that promise.

Her corset was suddenly far too tight. She collapsed onto the fainting couch, no longer worried about whether or not she wrinkled her skirt.

Her reasons for turning Quinn down were still valid, but she knew it would be harder than ever to be firm about it now. Why hadn't she just snatched up a jewel and let it send her a vision? Whatever it might have shown her would have been easier to dismiss from her mind than the stolen glimpses of Greydon Quinn in the glorious altogether.

But then again, why should she try to erase that image? If, as Quinn said, no more damage could be done since she was no longer a maiden, why shouldn't she take her pleasure where she willed?

There was no denying her body's need, but she'd been raised to believe she was more than her body. There was a hidden part of her. Unique. Precious. Unseen.

But no less real than her body.

If he was unwilling to acknowledge that part of her by letting her know the hidden part of him, her time with Quinn would end as disastrously as her liaison with Neville.

She didn't think she could bear anything that painful ever again.

CHAPTER 9

Every window of the classically inspired town house of the British Embassy blazed with light. Quinn alighted from their hired carriage to hand Viola down. The early April wind had turned cold once the sun disappeared. He was glad he'd insisted on the mink-trimmed cloak for her.

"You've been exceptionally quiet." *For a woman*, he added silently as they ascended the steps to the grand double doors. At least she'd stopped trying to pry into his past. "Are you troubled by something?"

"Other than by you, you mean?" she said archly.

Quinn made a tsking sound. She'd been different since he emerged from his bath. Pensive. Distracted. "Have a care, my love. People will think we've quarreled. Not at all the done thing for newlyweds."

"Heaven forefend. By all means, we must keep up appearances." She swept through the open doors. "I shall hang upon your arm as if I were a clinging vine."

"Promises, promises."

A liveried footman took Viola's cloak and Quinn's greatcoat and hat, and spirited them out of sight.

Quinn handed his invitation to the butler, who ushered them up to the first floor parlor where the assembled guests mingled in tight knots scattered about the room prior to dinner being served.

"I expected opulence," Viola murmured, "but this room is clearly designed to overawe."

Furnished in the French style, it was ornate without being fussy, the lines of the chairs and occasional tables cleaner than their English counterparts.

"The gilt on the furniture alone might feed a small English town for a year," she said.

"And an Indian one for two," Quinn returned, pleased that their thoughts traveled along the same paths.

"Oh, I say, young Ashford! Is that you?" Lady Wimbly waddled across the room toward them, her long-suffering husband in tow. The couple lived near his father's country estate and had known Quinn since he was in short pants.

"Here we are on holiday in France and whom should we see but our neighbor." Lady Wimbly fluttered her fan with such vigor, Quinn felt his forelock lift in the breeze. "Imagine that. They do say it's a small world, don't they? Of course, they do. So you're back from India now, I collect." She lifted her lorgnette and eyed Viola through the lenses. "And who might this be?"

Quinn introduced her to them as his new bride.

"Preston? Lady Viola Preston? Oh, I say, you knew her father, didn't you, Wimbly?" She poked her husband with her round elbow. Apparently, or perhaps fortunately, Lord Wimbly was hard of hearing. Lady W raised her voice. "Eustace Preston, Earl of Meade, what? You knew him at Oxford, didn't you, Wimbly."

"Why, yes, I remember when he and—"

"So sorry for your loss, dear." The lady patted Viola's arm in sympathy while she trampled on her husband's attempt to join the conversation and hurried on, blithely unaware she'd done it. "And may I say I deplore the straits in which your cousin left you and your mother. It was badly done. Badly done, indeed."

Apparently there was no aspect of life among the ton that went unexamined by Lady Wimbly.

"But now that you're Lady Ashford, no doubt your new husband will do for your family what your cousin wouldn't, eh, what? More shame on him, too. They do say 'All's well that ends well,' don't they? Of course, they do." She rapped Quinn's forearm with her fan. "My dear boy, it was bad of you not to invite us to your wedding."

"Forgive me. It was something of a whirlwind courtship," Quinn improvised, enjoying the excuse to slip a hand around Viola's waist and draw her closer to him. She stiffened, but didn't pull away. "Once I met this lovely lady, I couldn't wait another moment. I confess I convinced her to elope. First, it was off to Gretna Green and now for our honeymoon, we've fled to France."

"Fled?" Lady Wimbly seized upon the word. "So I take it your father is unaware of this . . . ahem . . . happy turn of events."

That was a complication he hadn't foreseen. He should have bitten his tongue before starting down that road.

"Blissfully unaware." Quinn winked at her. "And I rather hope he continues thusly for a good long while. If you're planning to go Home soon, do let me be the one to tell him, won't you?"

Lord Wimbly promised to keep their secret. Lady Wimbly waved to someone across the room whom she'd not yet greeted and begged to be excused.

As the worthy matron duck-footed her way toward her next conversational victims with Lord Wimbly in her wake, Quinn leaned down to whisper to Viola. "I fear Lady Wimbly has no intention of keeping our oh-so-delicious secret."

"It hardly matters since not a word about our matrimonial bliss is true."

Viola hadn't counted on meeting anyone she knew in France. She certainly hadn't expected Quinn to spin such a fanciful tale about their elopement. Word of her exploits would circulate throughout the ton, and once it became known she and Lieutenant Quinn weren't actually married, she might as well become some well-heeled gentleman's mistress and be done with feigning respectability entirely. No decent door would be open to her.

Quinn didn't seem to realize the gravity of her situation. "You look pale." His dark brows beetled with concern. "Are you all right?"

As all right as a ruined woman can possibly be.

There was no point in making a scene, but she couldn't resist whispering through clenched teeth, "You ought not to have used my real maiden name when you introduced me. For all the Wimblys knew, I might have been anyone. You could have told them we met on the boat home from India."

Why hadn't she thought to construct a workable alias and school him on it ahead of time? Too distracted by her new wardrobe and glimpses of Greydon Quinn without one, she supposed.

"How could I give you a false name?" He cast her a puzzled frown. "The ton is really a very small world, even abroad. There may be someone here who already knows you. We'd fool no one."

"We certainly won't now." Her strained smile hurt her face. "You're right about Lady Wimbly. She's not the sort to keep a secret. The whole ton will know we're larking about the Continent together."

"And?"

"What do you think will happen to me when it's noised about that we are not really married?"

"Oh."

"A light dawns." Men never had to worry about their reputations. In fact, his would probably be enhanced by the peccadillo. There was no justice in the world.

"Let me get you a cup of tea," Quinn said as he settled her on a chair near the window. "That's the ticket."

As if tea would help.

As soon as he was gone, she stood and looked out the window. Her mother would hear about it. People who'd avoided the dowager countess since she fell into poverty would make a beeline to their humble town house door to make sure she knew what her daughter was up to on the Continent.

Things couldn't be worse.

"Viola Preston, is that you?"

She was wrong. She recognized that voice. Things were definitely worse.

She pasted a smile on her face and turned around, extending her hand to him. "Neville, how nice to see you. Or are you Lord Sudbury by now?"

"No, and I may never be." Neville kissed the back of her hand and smiled the devastating smile that had once overturned her world. "My uncle the marquis has married again. His nurse, no less, and gotten the woman with child to boot." His smile turned wicked and Viola's belly did a flip out of old habit. "Of course, the events may have occurred in a somewhat different order, but if the brat is a boy, I shall have to remain simple Neville Beauchamp."

He hadn't changed a bit. And he was anything but simple. He'd certainly complicated her life to shreds. Tall, well-favored, his curly blond hair rampant over his golden head, Neville was as strikingly handsome as the day he'd seduced her out of her maidenhead.

He leaned toward her and whispered, "Who'd have thought the randy old goat still had it in him?"

Her lips twitched in spite of herself. Neville was always amusing, always dancing on the wrong side of respectable. It was part of his charm.

"What are you doing in Paris?" she asked.

"I'm the ambassador's secretary. Lord Cowley's right hand, as it were." He leaned a hand on the wall behind her, trapping her with his body and lowered his voice. "You look marvelous, Viola. More lovely than I remembered. And I remember quite a lot."

"Neville, please." Her cheeks were so hot, she knew her face must be scarlet.

"Where are you staying? We must meet. I can get away tomorrow afternoon if—"

"Here you are, love." Quinn appeared behind Neville and stepped around him smoothly, shouldering him out of the way. He handed a cup of tea to Viola.

"Pardon me, old boy." He turned back to Neville who stutter-stepped back a pace. "Didn't see you there."

Quinn put a possessive arm around Viola's waist and bared his teeth at Neville. No one would mistake the expression for a smile. "Who's this, darling?"

Viola swallowed hard and hoped her voice wouldn't quaver. "You were right. I did meet someone I know here. Neville Beauchamp. Neville, may I present—"

"Lord Ashford." He extended his hand to Neville, who cringed at Quinn's grip. "The lady's husband. And how is it you know my wife?"

"As her friend. Her very old friend," Neville said, trying to wring his hand free with limited success.

"And what's an old friend doing in Paris?"

"He's the ambassador's secretary," Viola put in.

"Ah! Well, no doubt Lord Cowley needs someone to open his mail and run errands. You appear marginally qualified for that post." Quinn offered his arm to Viola. "Come, dear. They're opening the door to the dining room."

Neville started to follow them.

"You're coming too?" Quinn turned back to him. "Does Cowley allow the help to dine with guests?"

Neville blinked in surprise. "I'm not the help."

"No doubt that's true. You're probably very little help. Still, very enlightened of the ambassador. I'll tell him so when I see him." Quinn pulled Viola close and escorted her toward the dining room. "I thought you didn't expect to see anyone you knew here."

"I didn't. Least of all, Neville."

"Neville, is it? Not Mr. Beauchamp? Must be a rather close old friend."

"I suppose you could say that. We were once engaged."

Quinn stopped mid-stride. "So that's the cad."

"Yes, but he's down on his luck now. I know what that's like. I don't have it in me to hate him." At least when Neville broke it off with her, he'd tried to be honorable. He let her put about the story that she'd changed her mind and rejected him, so her reputation would remain untainted by their broken engagement. Neville wasn't a bad sort. He was just a greedy sort and Viola no longer represented gain. She leaned toward Quinn. "Why were you so unpleasant to him before you even knew who he was?"

Quinn started walking toward the long dining table again. "I didn't like the way he looked at you."

"Oh? What way was that?"

"Like you were the last strawberry tart on the plate and he hadn't eaten in weeks."

Formal dinner parties were a ridiculous bore. Especially if one was stuck with Lady Wimbly at one's side. The only bright spot for Quinn was that, like the unfortunate Lord Wimbly, he wasn't required to contribute much to the conversation.

Viola on the other hand was seated between the ambassador and his secretary, Neville Beauchamp. Every time Quinn looked in their direction, the man was leaning toward her, trying to engage her in conversation.

The thought of Viola and him . . . Quinn suspected his
blood had turned to molten lava.

"Neville Beauchamp, now there's a name I haven't heard in
a while," Lady Wimbly was saying. "If memory serves, he was
heir apparent to Lord Sudbury with bright prospects until his
uncle married again quite unexpectedly. Ah, well . . . they do
say one mustn't count one's chickens before they're hatched,
don't they? Of course, they do."

Quinn grunted noncommittally and sawed at his beef. It
was a tad stringy and overdone for his taste.

"I believe he and your new wife were quite attached at one
ti—"

"Lady Wimbly, perhaps you can tell me if there are any
here who have recently returned from India," Quinn interrupted, taking a page from her book. If he couldn't quiet her
gossiping tongue, he could at least steer her prattle into something useful. "Since I spent more than a dozen years there,
I'm always interested in comparing experiences with others
who've lived in the East."

"Why, yes, now that you mention it, I believe a gentleman
recently turned up." Lady W scooted her chair closer to
Quinn and lowered her voice conspiratorially. "A Mr. Penobscot, Henry Penobscot. He's seated next to Wimbly on the
left. But I greatly fear you won't get much out of him. Silent as
the grave, that one."

"Oh?"

"He arrived in Paris the same day Wimbly and I did and he
wouldn't speak so much as a word to us while we all waited in
the anteroom to see the ambassador." She chewed a sauce-
laden green bean, her eyes suddenly thoughtful. "He had a
diplomatic pouch attached to his wrist. Attached, I mean, with
a metal cuff. I've never seen the like, have you? Must have
been most important correspondence."

Or a most important diamond. "You didn't hear what might
be in it?"

"Not a breath of a word," she confided. "But not to worry. It's safe as houses now."

"How do you know that?"

"He didn't have it with him when he came out of the ambassador's office. So whatever it is must be in Lord Cowley's safe. One of those newfangled tumbler locks everyone talks about. He brought it over with him when he took the post. Why, they do say it would take the Mayfair Jewel Thief to crack one like that, don't they? Of—"

"Course they do," Quinn finished for her. He looked down the long table at the thief who could open it with a few deft spins. "Of course, they do."

Chapter 10

The ambassador, Lord Cowley, might have had the finest chef in France in his kitchen, but he insisted on "plain, hearty English cooking."

Viola thought the meal would never end. Still, she'd met several useful people, most notably Mr. Penobscot, who was seated directly opposite her. He was freshly arrived from India and staying at the embassy, in Lord Cowley's private suite of rooms as his guest.

That meant he was important enough to merit the ambassador's protection. If she could learn which room in the embassy was Penobscot's, she'd know where to begin looking for the diamond. Surely such an important stone would call to her even before she touched it.

Neville continued to flirt with her. Once, she felt his hand on her knee and had to kick him beneath the table to get him to remove it. He merely smiled at her, as if they were playing a game.

And he knew exactly how it would end.

She was relieved when the men disappeared to the smoking room for their cigars and port. The women sipped sherry and made small talk while waiting for the men to finish discussing whatever it was men talked about—politics or philosophy or whoring—and decided to come collect them. The ladies seemed content to talk only of the weather or pick over the latest gossip from home.

Viola tried to introduce a different topic, since she'd probably figure prominently in the group's next hen fest when the conversation turned to scandal. When she asked what they thought of Dickens's latest installment of *Little Dorrit*, she was met with blank stares.

"I find his satire too tiresome," Lady Wimbly finally said. "Why ever would we want to read something which denigrates the government and those institutions we hold dear?"

Viola bit her tongue to keep from saying, *Because it makes us think. And because we're able to think such things without restriction.*

She wished for the thousandth time she'd been born a man. Not just because she'd have been able to succeed her father in the earldom, but because she longed for the freedom men enjoyed. No one told a man what to think or how to behave, though her vicar sometimes tried.

If she was a man, no one would think it their business who she was traveling about France with. If she was a man, she could take a lover to her bed and none would think the worse of her for it. If she was a man, she might pursue whatever course of study struck her fancy and not be told she was fit only to knit doilies or produce an heir.

One by one, the gentlemen came to collect their ladies. She was still stewing over the general inequity of the world when Quinn finally appeared. He led her to the main vestibule, then went to retrieve their coats since the footman seemed to have disappeared.

Viola paced the hall, pausing to admire a large landscape in an ornate gilt frame. A towering oak overshadowed a narrow country lane that wound along a hedgerow before disappearing around a bend. The painting invited her to step right into the scene, to wonder what was tucked away behind the limits of the canvas.

"I favor that one myself. It's a John Constable." Neville's voice made her turn around. "Whenever I long for Home, this takes me there."

"It's quite lovely," she agreed.

"As are you." He came and stood beside her while they studied the landscape. "This painting reminds me of that time we picnicked by the brook. Do you remember?"

How could she forget? Amid the scent of freshly cut hay, the whisper of water over rocks, and the mating calls of larks she'd given herself to him. Irrevocably.

He must have let that heady time rush back into him as well for he put his arms around her and pinned her to the wall. "Oh, Viola, I made a terrible mistake letting you go."

"Neville, stop it." There was a time when she'd have given anything to hear him say that. She shoved against his chest, but he didn't release her. "It's too late for us."

"Because of Ashford? Don't tell me you have feelings for that pompous ass."

"As a matter of fact, I—"

Quinn appeared suddenly behind Neville's shoulder. He pulled Beauchamp away from Viola and decked him with a solid blow to the jaw. Neville went flying and slid across the marble floor on his belly.

"If you were a gentleman, Beauchamp, I'd demand satisfaction." Quinn's eyes glittered with menace.

"Give me a few months." Neville sat up and rubbed his jaw. "I still have half a chance at being a marquis."

"In that case, I'm willing to give you the benefit of the doubt. Name your choice of weapons."

"Quinn, no!" The bottom dropped out of Viola's stomach. The thought of him dueling Neville for her made her want to retch.

"Don't worry, Viola," Neville said, obviously assuming her concern was for him. He rose to his feet and dusted himself off. "He can't touch me. Dueling is illegal in France."

Relief flooded Viola's being. Neville was a crack shot and a fiend with a blade. With Quinn's military background, she had no doubt he, too, was the dangerous sort. They might well kill each other if they met on a field of honor.

Now that she knew a duel was unlikely since it was forbidden, irritation reared its head. Quinn was overreacting to Neville's attentions to her. As if they didn't have enough gossip circulating about them already.

"Then you're fortunate we're in France, Beauchamp, for whether you chose pistols or blades, I'd have killed you. Instead, I'll give you a promise." Quinn snatched Neville up by his collar. "If you so much as look cross-eyed at my wife again, I'll beat you senseless. Surely the Frogs haven't declared that illegal."

Neville shook his head.

"Am I understood?"

Neville's Adam's apple bobbed. He'd never been one for bare-fisted brawls. It might result in an injury that would damage his handsome face. "Understood."

Quinn tossed him aside and draped Viola's cloak around her shoulders, not taking his evil glare from Neville for an instant. He offered her his arm and when she didn't take it immediately, he snapped, "Come, Viola. We're leaving."

"Indeed, we are." She ignored his arm and stalked toward the door, not caring whether he followed or not.

The driver held the coach door open for her and she mounted the steps without waiting for Quinn to hand her into the hired carriage. He climbed in behind her, pushing her broad skirt aside so he wouldn't sit on it. He rapped on the coach ceiling to signal the driver and they lurched forward.

"There is another seat," she said testily, indicating the empty squab facing her.

"I don't care to ride backward."

"Strange, since you obviously prefer to act in a backward manner."

He drew a deep breath, willing the unaccountable rage inside him to subside. "As far as the world knows, I'm your husband. Did you expect me to simply stand by and ignore the insult while Beauchamp pawed you?"

"He didn't paw me." She scooted toward the other door, trying to distance herself from him in the small space. "I had the matter well in hand."

"No, in another moment he'd have had your arse in hand. Trust me, I know the type."

"That's because you *are* the type," she said with a withering glance. "Have you forgotten how you tried to seduce me the first night we met?"

"When a woman sneaks into a man's bedchamber, she can't rightly blame him for seeing the possibilities in the situation." He pulled off his gloves and shoved them into his pockets. Then he shrugged out of his coat. His confrontation with Beauchamp had heated his blood. He still itched to flatten the man's perfectly formed nose. "If I'd truly tried to seduce you that night, you wouldn't have left my house without spending time in my bed."

She gave a snort. "You've a high opinion of yourself."

"I believe that's a given for us pompous asses." It did no harm to let her know he'd overheard some of her conversation with Beauchamp.

"You were spying on me!"

"I was fetching your cloak and came back in time to keep you from folly."

Her eyes flashed in the dark at him, angry and feral as a hissing barn cat. "I am perfectly capable of keeping myself from folly. I've kept you at bay, haven't I?"

She had him there. She'd been remarkably unmovable. With him, at least.

"You still love him," Quinn said after they'd ridden in silence for several minutes.

She sighed deeply and he could almost see the irritation draining out of her. After a quick glance in his direction, she studied her folded hands. "I wonder if I ever did. I loved the idea of Neville. I loved the thought of being his wife, of having someone to go through life with me, sharing joys and sorrows. But when the first sorrow washed over us, he was gone." She worried her bottom lip. "I didn't know Neville. Not really. How could I love him?"

That explained a good deal. Now he understood why Viola insisted on *knowing* him. But he couldn't tell her about his father. That was a hurt best left alone. If he disturbed the carefully placed plaster on his soul, the wound might never stop bleeding.

But perhaps it would be safe to explain his reasons for wanting to steal the Blood of the Tiger. Since she was helping him with it, he owed her that much. He decided it was worth the risk.

"You asked me once if I wanted the red diamond to impress a woman. I don't."

He told her of the initial theft of the diamond from the temple of Shiva, then the theft of Sanjay's kingdom by the East India Company, and of how it offended his sense of justice and fed the flames of rebellion in Amjerat. He spilled out his hope that returning the diamond would heal a small part of the wrongs done.

"The Sanjay who lays out your clothes and shines your shoes is really a prince?"

"That's right."

"Well, that makes me feel small."

"How so?"

"I felt myself ill-used when my father's death lost my family a comfortable living. The world at least still acknowledges me as an earl's daughter. Sanjay lost who he was."

Quinn's chest constricted. She understood. He'd never expected another westerner to grasp his reasons for wanting to help Sanjay and his people. Certainly not a Western woman.

She completely surprised him by leaning over and kissing his cheek.

"Please don't take this as a complaint, but what was that for?"

"You may not have wanted to steal the red diamond to impress a woman, Quinn," she said as the carriage came to a stop at the curb before the Hotel de Crillon, "but you did, all the same."

He hopped out of the carriage and handed her down. She took his arm without prompting and they strolled up the granite steps to the front door of the massive hotel.

It was comfortable, walking like that, footsteps in time with each other, headed toward the same goal. For a moment, he wondered if that's how it would feel all the time if he and Viola were truly husband and wife.

The thought punched his gut like an unexpected blow.

He shook it off as the fanciful product of a fanciful evening. Pretending to be the lady's husband, defending her honor, even quarreling, then reaching a sort of peace with her, was making him feel far too natural in this matrimonial farce.

"Will you ring for the lady's maid, please?" Viola said once they were back in their suite. "I could have managed with the wardrobe I brought from home, but these new things . . . Don't mistake me. They're lovely, but it's a sad state of affairs when a grown woman can't dress and undress herself."

"It's awfully late." He draped his coat and her cloak over one of the wing chairs flanking the fireplace in the sitting room. "Those girls work such long hours. Let them sleep. You only need a lace or two undone. I'm perfectly capable of helping with that."

"Quinn, I—"

He stopped her with a finger to her lips. "I defended your

honor this night. Don't you think that proves you can trust me?"

She squeezed her eyes closed and he sensed she struggled with herself. When she opened her eyes, he read turmoil in their hazel depths.

"What if I can't trust myself?"

Hope made his cock twitch.

"That is a dilemma." He caught up one of her hands and placed a soft lover's kiss on her palm. Then he folded her hand in his and pressed it against his chest, over his heart. "I promise you, nothing will ever pass between us that you don't want as well. Whatever happens, you may rely upon me, Viola. I'm not the sort who disappears when there's trouble."

"No, I can see you're not."

He led her into the bedroom, then reached up a hand and began taking the pins from her hair. "We'll start with something easy."

Her hair tumbled past her waist as he released it. Her breath hitched when he ran his fingers through one long lock to the curling tips.

"What if it becomes difficult?" she asked in a small voice.

He bent and pressed a kiss on her forehead. "Then we'll find a way to help each other through that as well."

CHAPTER 11

In his fevered imaginings of lovemaking with Viola Preston, he saw their bodies twined together, sweat-slick and aching. He dreamed of rutting her like a beast, slamming into her soft sweetness and hearing her beg him to do it harder. Faster. Deeper. He fancied they'd claw at each other as they strained toward completion, not caring if blood ran.

He never envisioned starting his ultimate seduction by brushing out her hair.

Once he got all the pins out, the shimmering auburn mantle fell in waves. "How many strokes?" he asked, picking up the boar-bristle brush.

"One hundred." She perched cautiously on the vanity chair.

"One hundred it is." Quinn pulled a stool behind her and settled his knees on either side of her hips. He followed each long stroke with his hand, smoothing her hair down every time.

He didn't think he'd ever touched anything so soft. Finer than the finest silk, it smelled of citrus and rainwater and . . . her, a warm, womanly scent that was unmistakably her own. Spicy, sweet and musky at the same time.

He gathered her hair in one hand and ran the brush along the underside starting at her nape. It gave him a chance to graze his fingertips over that delicate skin. She shivered, but he knew she wasn't cold.

The pulse point beneath her ear beat as fast as a hummingbird's wings.

"Ninety-nine, one hundred," he finally said, almost sorry to be done. "Now what?"

"I plait it so it won't tangle in the night." She reached around and quickly worked her hair into a thick braid, tying it off with a ribbon.

His chest constricted with the simple sweetness of the moment. He'd never figured himself for the domesticated type, but if a husband was regularly treated to the sight of his wife in various degrees of delightful deshabille, perhaps there was something to be said for the institution of marriage after all.

"Close your eyes," he ordered.

"Why?"

"Trust me."

She gave him a searching look and amazingly enough, obeyed him. Quinn picked up her braid and teased the loose ends of her hair along her nape and hairline. Then he reached around her to trace it along the top of her bodice over the swell of her breasts.

"What are you doing?" Her eyes popped open and their gazes met in the mirror.

"Giving you pleasure," he said, drawing the end of the plait from the hollow between her breasts up her neck to her chin. Gooseflesh pebbled her skin. "Don't you like it?"

"It feels wonderful and . . . wicked," she admitted. "But that's beside the point."

"No, pleasure is exactly the point." He lowered his mouth to her neck and delivered a string of baby kisses up to her ear. His soft palate ached with the sweetness of her skin. When he took her lobe between his lips, she made a soft sound he recognized.

The sound of a woman caught in needy bliss. His cock throbbed in answer.

He worked the hooks marching down the back of her emerald gown. It parted to reveal her corset and the lacy edge of her all-in-one, two of the wicked, silky underthings he'd bought that afternoon. She thought he'd picked them out for her. When he'd insisted on the black lace confection, it was because *he* couldn't wait to see how she'd look in it.

And out of it.

He pressed kisses on the exposed flesh as her gown fell away, feathering his lips over her shoulder blades and down her spine to the top of the corset.

Looking over her shoulder he met her gaze in the mirror again. She was holding the gown up in front, her lips softly parted.

He reached around and gave the gown a tug. She let the silk slip through her fingers and turned her head toward him.

Quinn took her mouth then. Not in a heated rush. Not with the animal need that clawed at him. He held that in check. He took her softly. Tenderly. So tenderly, he wondered at himself. She opened to him and his tongue swept in to claim her. She suckled him and chased his tongue back into his mouth. He reached around to cup a breast and she groaned.

He plunged his hand into her bodice, pushing back the stiff corset and lifting her breast to rest on the lip of fabric instead of being imprisoned behind it. Her nipple, taut and hard as one of the buttons on his uniform, fairly burned a hole in his palm. He toyed with it, rolling it between his thumb and forefinger while she squirmed. When he gave her nipple a tug, she made urgent noises into his mouth.

He dropped to one knee beside her and covered her breast with kisses. He nuzzled the crease beneath her breast. He licked. He sucked. When he bit down softly on her taut nipple, she cried out.

Not with pain. With fierce joy.

She was so sweet. So perfect.

His hand found its way under the yards of silk, heading for the slit in the all-in-one. The modiste had assured him the racy new garment did away with the need to have a separate chemise and drawers. Less to remove was always a positive development in feminine fashion and the open crotch was pure genius.

God bless the French! He couldn't wait to touch her soft folds and luxuriate in her slick wetness.

But the wire cage that held out her skirts in the required shape stymied his approach.

"Damn fashion," he growled as he stood and raised her to her feet. "What fool ever thought encasing a woman in wire was a good thing?"

She stood on tiptoe, kissing his frown away, her lips a balm on his brow. "Nothing worth having comes easily."

Quinn drew the yards of her gown over her head, leaving her in only her crinoline, corset, and all-in-one. One breast was still exposed, the nipple drawn and tight. He covered it with his hand and squeezed. "You're definitely worth having."

He worked the drawstring that held the crinoline at her waist, but hopelessly fouled the knot. After a frustrating few moments, he pulled out his pen knife and cut the string.

"You're not a very good lady's maid, Quinn. You've just ruined my crinoline."

"I'll buy you a new one." He yanked the wire contraption down to collapse at her feet. He was fast losing patience with drawing out the seduction. Now that the cage was gone, in a pinch, he could bend her over and enter her from behind with her fingers splayed on the Persian carpet.

He could see how it would be. Her lovely curved bum smiling at the ceiling, her pink slit glistening, trembling to receive him. He'd hold her hips steady and plunge into her in long hard strokes, teasing all the sensitive places inside her.

She'd whimper. She'd plead. She'd scream his name.

His cock cheered that line of thinking, but he wanted to make sure the first time with Viola was good for her. Bending a woman over and entering from behind was an approved position in the *Kama Sutra*, but the *Congress of the Cow* could be rough, brutal even, if a man didn't control himself. Padmaa always cautioned that trust must be established before a man initiated that primal sexual position.

Judging from her small frown, he didn't have Viola's trust yet.

"I was very happy with that particular crinoline. How would you feel if I pop all the buttons from your shirt?" She peeled off his jacket and waistcoat and suited actions to words. Then she gasped. "Quinn, you're not wearing any smallclothes."

"Never under formal wear." He grinned. "Neither did Brummel. Claimed it spoiled the line of his trousers."

"So you're a peacock at heart. I'd never have suspected."

"Not a peacock." He took her hand and guided it to the bulge in his trousers. "But definitely a cock."

It was a risk. He knew he was large and might scare her. She might come to her senses and declare the little interlude over. He didn't dare breathe.

Her eyes flared in surprise, but she smiled up at him. "You're magnificent."

He picked her up and twirled her around. She approved of that bit of him—more than approved, she admired him. He felt like a god.

When he set her lightly on her feet, she reached up and pulled his head down so she could kiss him. No missish coquetry from her. Viola was the sort to take what she wanted.

Why was he surprised? He should have expected that from a thief.

His belly jiggled in suppressed laughter.

"What's so funny?"

"Nothing . . . everything . . ." Quinn kissed her again, chasing her tongue, and nipping at her lips. He unhooked the front of her corset and let it fall while she tugged at the buttons over his hips to release the flap front of his trousers.

She plunged her hands into the front of his breeches.

Merciful God.

His balls drew up in a snug mound under her touch and his cock was primed to go off like a Roman candle. He started doing the geometry for cannon firing solutions in his head to keep from spilling his seed into her soft hands.

He slid his palms over her sweetly rounded belly, then moved downward. His fingers found the slit in the crotch of the all-in-one. She was wet and hot and slippery. While he kissed her, he nudged her legs farther apart so he could slip a finger into her yoni and massage her inner walls.

Her knees buckled.

"No, you don't." He picked her up and walked over to pin her to the nearest wall for support. "I won't let you fall."

But he couldn't vouch the same for himself. Viola was a bottomless well. He was in serious danger of falling into her depths of endless delight.

Even knowing that, he couldn't stop himself from kissing his way down the column of her throat. When he reached her breasts, he pushed the all-in-one off both shoulders and peeled the thin linen down her body.

"So beautiful," he murmured, his gaze running over her. He suckled each breast while she ran her fingers through his hair. When he moved down to her navel, her hands rested on his shoulders, holding herself upright.

His kisses continued down her body as more flesh was exposed. He dropped to his knees before her. Her breath was thready, but she stepped out of the undergarment on her own steam.

"Quinn, you . . . you're . . . not going to . . . oh!"

His tongue flicked across her slit. He parted her with his fingers and licked along each of her little valleys, savoring her musky sweetness. He nibbled her labia with his lips. He tongued her "little pearl" which had risen to be stroked.

She chanted his name as she braced herself against the wall. He couldn't decide if she was pleading with him or cursing him.

She arched herself into his mouth.

Her legs began to tremble. He cupped her bum with one hand to steady her. A soft tremor began in the lips of her sex as he thumbed her pearl with his other hand. Her legs went rigid.

She came with a broken cry and a spasm that shook her whole body. He was on his feet, holding her upright with his body against hers, while he sheltered her sex with his palm. She pulsed into his hand.

When her waves subsided, Quinn stooped and hooked his elbows under her knees. She didn't protest when he lifted her, her head lolling like a rag doll.

"Viola," he said as he held her with the tip of his cock poised to enter her. "Viola."

She lifted her head and looked at him, doe-eyed and languid. "Oh, Quinn. I never dreamed . . ."

As she palmed his cheeks and kissed him, he lowered her onto his lingam. Her insides molded around him, tight and welcoming at once.

"You're so snug." If she hadn't told him about Beauchamp, he might not have realized she wasn't a virgin until no telltale blood stained his cock. "Am I hurting you?"

"More." She rocked against him, draping her arms around his shoulders. "Please, Quinn."

He slid into her dark wetness and she expanded to receive him, her inner walls like hot velvet. She pulsed around him twice, aftershocks of her release. He bit the inside of his cheek to keep from coming in answer. He wanted to savor her, to wallow in her scent, to wring every drop of pleasure from the encounter for both of them.

He began to move, slowly at first, drawing almost completely out, then sliding into her again, stopping short of pushing in up to the hilt. Their gazes locked in a connection as intimate as the one between their bodies. While his lingam thrust into her yoni, his soul was in danger of falling into her eyes.

Her breath shuddered when he sheathed himself in her deeply.

"Too much?"

She shook her head, panting shallowly. "More. Give. Me. More. All of you."

A grunt of passion escaped his mouth.

If she knew . . . if she had any idea . . . she'd never want all of him. Some things were best left undisturbed, but he could give her all his body. He let himself drive in completely.

"Oh, yes," she whispered.

A dam inside him burst and he lost the last shred of control. He began to plunge into her, thrusting hard. Her breasts jerked with each deep penetration. She pulled his head down between them.

All conscious thought fled and Quinn became a rutting beast, passion-blind, ruled only by driving need. She was so snug, so sweet, oh, God, so slick.

His balls clenched. Her breath came in short pants and she threw back her head, arcing in a second peak. She cried out his name as her inner walls spasmed.

He really meant to pull out. It was the gentlemanly thing to do. He'd told her she could trust him.

But restraint wasn't in him. The rutting beast wouldn't suffer the insult of interruption. His seed shot into her in steaming pulses as he buried himself deep. She fisted around him, their releases feeding off each other, drawing each other out.

When they were spent, Viola's head dropped onto his shoulder. Their bodies were still connected, but he felt himself relaxing inside her.

"Oh, Quinn. I never imagined . . . I mean . . . I didn't know . . ."

"Didn't know what?"

"That a woman can have pleasure as a man does."

"Actually"—he paused to bend his head and suckle a swollen nipple for a few heartbeats—"a woman can have more pleasure than a man. Or at least more often."

She blushed. "As long as we're counting, it does appear I'm one up on you."

"Something I will never hold against you, love."

Her eyes flared at his words. He bit his tongue.

Love. He'd called her that all night as part of their ruse. He hadn't intended to let it spill over into his seduction. It was simply about need and two lonely adults.

Wasn't it?

His cock, quiescent now, slipped out of her. He felt strangely alone after the joy of their joining. Bereft, almost.

She grinned up at him, mother-naked, except for her stockings. Somehow he hadn't quite gotten to those. The little silk bows at her knees were surprisingly erotic.

She was beautiful. Passionate. Daring.

If a man was inclined to marry, he could do much worse than Viola Preston.

The fact that she was a thief and not to be trusted farther than he could throw her slammed back into him. He shoved that inconvenient little tidbit into a distant corner of his mind.

Though he shouldn't be rousing to her again so soon, his cock didn't get the message. It began to swell. The plump head nudged against her wet nether lips.

"Hmmm," she all but purred and cast him a sly look. "I rather think I shall have to give you the opportunity to catch up."

CHAPTER 12

Viola knew she was being hopelessly wanton, but she couldn't bring herself to care. She kissed him again, tracing his lower lip with the tip of her tongue, then teasing him by withholding it.

Quinn slanted his mouth over hers, and sucked her tongue into submission. Then he lowered her legs so her feet touched the floor.

Just when she thought she might float away.

He scooped her up and carried her to the waiting bed. Someone—Sanjay probably—had pulled back the counterpane to expose creamy white sheets and feather pillows. When Quinn stretched her out on them, they were cool and delicious under her skin.

Quinn's rod had swollen to its engorged state again. As he stood over her, she had the opportunity to examine him more thoroughly. His cock was long and thick, with a raised vein snaking along one side from root to tip. Her womb clenched at the memory of holding something so raw and primal inside her.

She reached out a hand and ran a fingertip along his length. He shivered and a fresh pearl of moisture formed at the tip. A thrill of power raced through her at the realization that she was able to reduce him to such a state of neediness.

"My, he is ready again, isn't he?"

"Ready and wanting."

"He wasn't satisfied before?"

"On the contrary, he was quite satisfied." Quinn cast her a lopsided grin. "But he's a greedy bastard. He can't seem to get enough of you."

She lifted her arms to him in invitation and he sank into them, covering her with his body. Even though he supported himself with his elbows, she reveled in his weight on her. The low ache started afresh and she rocked her pelvis against his groin.

"What about the rest of you, Quinn? Can you get enough of me?"

"The rest of my body is in complete agreement with my cock." He ducked his head to suckle the tender skin of her neck.

The rest of his body.

What about his heart?

She despised herself for the soppy sentiment. Why couldn't she accept the new wrinkle in their relationship as a man would?

Quinn was a thorough pragmatist. Of course, he was gallant and dependable, but he'd never spoken a word that suggested he harbored tender feelings toward her. Just lustful feelings.

Except for calling her *love*.

She wouldn't dwell on that. It didn't signify anything beyond supporting their spurious claim of matrimony. She'd savor the moment. She'd relish the beautiful man who was moving down her body, covering her with kisses. He made her skin dance. She'd take her pleasure as he did.

And maybe give it.

She grasped a handful of his hair and forced him to look up at her face.

"Have I done something that displeases you?" He thumbed a nipple and need zinged from her breast to that emptiness between her legs.

"Not yet." She shuddered with bliss and covered his hand to stop him from tormenting her to distraction. "It would be so easy to just let you play my body as if I were your harp."

He licked the crease beneath her breast and waggled his brows at her. "Are you saying I'm a virtuoso?"

"Yes, I'll admit it, if you like. You're an amazing lover." She lightly smacked the top of his head when he claimed her other nipple with his mouth and sucked. "Keep doing that and I'll sing it for you."

He released her nipple long enough to murmur, "If you like it so much, why do you keep interrupting me?"

"I want to be amazing for you, too."

He lifted his head to meet her gaze. "What makes you think you aren't?"

"I'm not doing anything."

"On the contrary, you're exactly as I'd hoped," Quinn said. "Don't you know how your responses heat my blood? When you make that little drowning kitten noise . . ."

"Drowning kitten?" She tried to sit up, but he was too heavy for her to budge.

"Well, maybe that isn't the best description, but you do sound in dire straits when you're near to coming." He nuzzled along the valley between her breasts. "It thrills me to have put you there."

She palmed his cheeks. "How do I put *you* there?"

His smile was wickedness incarnate. "Are you sure you want to know?

Quinn fisted the damp sheets. It had taken every ounce of control not to end the little exercise by flipping her over and rutting her senseless, but Viola seemed to be enjoying herself, so he gritted his teeth and let her toy with him.

The game required him to lie perfectly still while she touched him wherever and however she liked. She leaned over him, letting her taut nipples graze his chest. She held them tantalizingly close to his mouth, but wouldn't let him catch them between his lips.

"I want to touch you," he said hoarsely.

"Not yet." Though she'd come to him no longer a maiden, she was new to extended loveplay.

But Viola Preston was a very fast learner.

She climbed atop him, her wet yoni positioned over his balls. His erection protruded between her legs, stretching up his belly nearly to his navel. She leaned forward and teased the end of her braid along his ridgeline, dallying at the sensitive patch of rough skin near the head.

He almost wished he hadn't shown her that when she'd asked him to explain the mysteries of a man. She was using her new knowledge to devastating effect. He'd never wanted a woman so badly in his life.

He bit his bottom lip till he tasted blood.

She stroked him hard and his ballocks clenched, tensed for release. He could feel the pressure building. Fluid rose in his shaft like sap in the spring. Thank God he hadn't told her about reaching around to massage the narrow bit of skin between his scrotum and anus, or he'd be spewing over his own belly.

She halted suddenly and he felt as if the world stopped spinning. He clutched the iron headboard to avoid flying off the edge on his own. "You're stopping? Are you finished?"

"Almost." She slid down so she could lean forward and press little kisses along the length of his cock. He wanted to join his body to hers with a longing that was almost a sickness. She whorled her tongue around the head.

If she took him into her mouth, he was lost.

Instead she sat up and slid forward on him again, rocking

her pelvis over his groin. Her head tipped back, her mouth passion-slack, her nipples taut, her yoni leaving a glistening trail on his skin.

Quinn had never seen anything so erotic in his life.

She met his gaze. "When does this stop being a game and start being lovemaking?"

"This ancient dance . . . is always a game, love." The word slipped out again, but he was too far gone in need to worry about it now. "I torment you." He raised his hips beneath her.

"You torment me. And a delicious torment it is."

He broke the rules of engagement to cup her cheek with his palm. She didn't censure him, but leaned into his touch.

"If we stop thinking about each other in bits and parts and start to see each other entire," Quinn said, his voice passion-rough, "then it becomes lovemaking."

She climbed off his groin and settled on her knees beside him. "I'm ready to see you entire."

He sat up and cradled the back of her head, then leaned in to kiss her. A simple kiss. A giving kiss. A kiss with no *take* in it at all.

It might be irrational, but he heard the words tumble out his mouth. "I'm ready to see you, too."

Sunlight shafted through the slit in the damask curtain and made Viola open her eyes. She was lying on her side, with Quinn spooned around her, one of his big hands splayed possessively over her hip. All her joints felt loose and she was tender between her legs, but she sighed with contentment.

Even though she'd done it again.

Granted, it was far more pleasurable this time—what an understatement! The desperate groping in the meadow with Neville couldn't compare with her heart-stopping joining with Quinn. It was almost a totally different act—but the sin was the same.

She'd let her attraction to a man cloud her judgment. And Quinn hadn't even asked her to marry him, as Neville had. He'd just offered her pleasure.

Pressed down and running over.

And delivered on his promise as Neville had not.

Perhaps it was better this way. She'd already decided she'd probably never marry. Once word of her exploits, larking about Paris with a man who was not her husband, reached Society's ears, she was finished. No decent door would be open to her, no matter how wealthy the jewels she'd earn from Quinn made her.

But if last night had taught her anything, it was something about herself. She was an innately sensual person. Her body flared to life in Quinn's arms.

And she couldn't imagine it not happening again.

Often.

But she really ought to have been more careful. Or rather Quinn should have been. Childbed was no light matter, never mind the scandal of bearing a bastard. He shouldn't mind if she insisted that he use a French letter, a sheep's bladder condom, next time.

Quinn stirred behind her and dropped a kiss on her nape. "G'morning," he slurred, his deep voice rumbling through her. His hand slid up from her hip to cup a breast, thrumming her nipple to aching life.

The hard ridge of him pressed against her bum. She rocked back into him. "A very good morning."

She rolled over to greet him with a kiss and a wicked idea of how to make the morning better—even if he didn't have a condom.

If she was going to hell in any case, she might as well make it worth the devil's time.

"How do we get back into the embassy?" Viola asked as she sipped her second cup of tea.

After she and Quinn thoroughly woke each other up with a satisfying romp, they broke their fast en suite when Sanjay delivered a tray of buttery pastry, fresh fruit, eggs, and kippers.

Sanjay had tossed her yet another foul glance, obviously taking note of the fact that she was clad in her robe de chambre and Quinn in his banyan. The Hindu frowned at the bedclothes, the sheets rumpled beyond redemption. His dark glare focused on her again. She'd smiled sweetly at Sanjay in return, which made him scowl all the more before he left them to their meal.

Her vicar was right. Kindness did heap burning coals on an enemy's head.

"Getting back into the embassy will be no problem," Quinn said as he sopped up his eggs with a croissant. He carried no excess flesh, but all his appetites were large. "There's an embassy ball scheduled for tomorrow night and I wangled an invitation for us."

"Good. Climbing in windows is vastly overrated." Viola speared a slice of orange and popped it into her mouth. "I'm sure you realize a ball calls for another ball gown. I couldn't possibly be seen again so soon in the emerald one and all my other new ensembles, while very fine, are not appropriate for a formal occasion."

"We'll nip back to Madame Puisette's this afternoon. Her sample gowns fit you and I've a mind to see you in that burgundy one."

"It was terribly French. Most revealing." So was the Vee neckline of his banyan. A few dark chest hairs peeped at her.

He flashed a wicked smile. "Which is why I want to see you in it."

"But there's a problem with going for the diamond during the ball." She considered helping herself to another scone, but decided against it. All her new things fit glove-tight. Besides, Quinn was the most delicious thing in the room. She was tempted to climb across the table and settle onto his lap.

Wiping away the naughty thoughts, she refocused on the matter of the coming burglary. "It may take a while to locate the ambassador's office and I might be missed. A floor plan of the building or, at the very least, directions would make my job easier."

"Not to worry," Quinn said as he rose. "I know where the office is. I'm going with you."

"But I work alone."

"Not this time. I can't imagine making small talk and avoiding waltzes with Lady Wimbly, while you're at risk. I'm coming, too, and that's final." He leaned down to plant a kiss on her crown. "If we're missed, we can claim we wanted some privacy. Newlyweds, you know."

Warmth pooled in her belly. "You play the devoted bridegroom with devastating conviction."

"And it may prove useful." He turned to go into the adjoining bath, leaving the door ajar. Viola heard the scraping sound of a blade stropped on leather as Quinn prepared to shave. "No one loves lovers like the French, after all. If we find ourselves in danger of being caught, we'll simply make sure we're caught in flagrante delicto. That should remove all suspicion."

"You wicked man!" If he'd been close enough and she'd been armed with a fan, she'd have swatted him with it. But a thrill of the forbidden shot through her. What would it be like to engage in sexual congress knowing you might be caught mid-act at any moment?

"Alas, my love, you don't know the half of it."

My love. There it was again. Her heart fluttered. No, she wasn't his love. He was simply remaining in character for their ruse.

But the rest of his statement was deadly accurate. She still didn't know the half of Lt. Greydon Quinn, Lord Ashford. He held his past and his personal life closer than a gambler clutches his cards.

Perhaps she could learn more about him without the effort of drawing him out.

He'd left his wrist studs, his uncle's snuffbox, the medal, and signet ring on a salver on the lowboy. Viola glanced toward the lavatory door. Quinn was whistling while he shaved, a rather bawdy tune she recognized from her time spent in Willie's disreputable shop.

She'd have time to touch one of the jewels at least. She couldn't be sure how long he'd owned the diamond studs and she despised the screech of diamonds. The medal for valor was ornamented by a small topaz. It would probably show her something military and she wasn't sure she had the stomach for seeing Quinn in mortal danger.

The signet ring would probably yield the most information since he'd been his father's heir for a couple decades and presumably had worn it often. The set was very old-fashioned; the Ashford barony had been created before Cromwell. Heavy gold filigree surrounded a cabochon sapphire carved with the Ashford crest intaglio style. It seemed to wink at her, tempting her with its secrets. If she was quick about it, perhaps she could avoid the sick headache that accompanied prolonged use of her gift.

It was worth the risk.

She ambled over to the tray, cast one last look toward the door, and stretched out her hand for the ring. She picked it up by the gold circle and then pressed the carved crest into her palm.

The sapphire wailed like the damned.

CHAPTER 13

Water shot up her nose. She couldn't breathe. A hand thrashed before her face, stubby fingers with nails bitten down to the quick. Sickly green light filtered through the murky water. The signet ring flashed on the right forefinger. The hand clawed the water. Yarn was wrapped around the backside of the heavy ring to make it fit the childish finger.

Her head broke the surface, but only long enough to gulp a quick breath. Arms and legs pumping furiously, a boy was running along the dock toward her.

No, not toward her. Toward the one in the water.

She struggled to separate herself from the vision, but she continued to see through the eyes of the floundering child. Arms flailing, she sank like a stone.

Slimy dock posts wavered before her. Waterweed grasped at her ankles. Sediment sparkled in a shaft of dying sun.

She looked up. It was hard to tell how much water separated her from the surface. The boy knelt on the dock and leaned out, stretching a hand toward her. The whites showed all the way around his gunmetal gray eyes. His lips were moving. She could hear his voice, frantic and rising in pitch, but she couldn't make out any of the words. The hand with the signet ring strained upward, trying to catch hold.

She looked down, past a bare flat chest with nipples no bigger than *a pair of pimples, past a little boy's penis contracted to almost nothing, and on to the boy's feet. They were churning furiously, knobby knees rising and falling as if he were running uphill.*

She seemed to be moving upward, but not nearly fast enough. Her lungs burned for air.

Then a hand reached down into the water.

Relief melted her bones.

Instead of grasping the stubby-fingered hand, the hand settled on the top of her head, pushing her down. She thrashed and kicked. She clawed at the arm, but the hand wouldn't let go.

She tried to look up, but the hand held her immobile. Its long fingers wrapped around her skull like a vise. Her vision tunneled.

An explosion of bubbles escaped her lips and, muffled by water, she heard one long wavering cry. Her senses couldn't make out the child's last word, but it echoed clearly in her brain, a despairing howl. "Greydon!"

"Viola. Viola." The voice grew more urgent.

She slitted one eyelid. Quinn loomed over her, his gray eyes wide.

Oh, God. The same eyes.

She squeezed hers shut. A claw sank its talons into the base of her brain, sending a shrieking message of pain. She shouldn't have held the ring so long.

But she hadn't been able to turn it loose. She'd never had such a vivid vision, never been inside the body of a jewel's previous owner before. She'd always been able to pull out of an unpleasant Sending, but the jewel had forced her to stay till the bitter conclusion of its tale. It sucked her in. Made her part of the ring's story. It was as if the ring demanded that she see, feel, *know*, . . . something she fervently wished she didn't.

"Viola, what's wrong?" Quinn's voice cut through the pain. Someone was tapping her wrist and trying to make her sit up. "Sanjay, call for a doctor."

Quinn wrapped his arms around her and rocked, pressing her head to his chest.

"No," she murmured, forcing her eyes open. The screaming headache made her clamp them shut again. "No doctor, please."

A physician would only bleed her and make her weaker than she already was. Bile rose in her throat but she swallowed it back. If she allowed herself to be sick, she expected she'd spew murky green water. She tried to pull out of his embrace and rise to her feet.

"No, you don't." Quinn scooped her up and laid her flat on the bed. "Rest now."

She let herself sink into the feather tick and kept her eyes closed. She couldn't meet his gaze yet. Like Adam, who knew with just a look that Eve had eaten fruit from the Tree of Knowledge of Good and Evil, Quinn would see the damnable knowing in her.

What she'd experienced would shoot out her eyes without her conscious volition. He'd see that she *knew*.

"What happened, sahib?"

"I'm not sure. I wasn't in the room."

Quinn's voice sounded worried, but otherwise the same. How could he not sound different? Surely there should be a telltale marker in his tone, the predatory rumble of one who stops at nothing to achieve his ends.

"She must have fainted and knocked over the tray with my effects as she fell," he said. "Look, there's my ring under the lowboy."

"Or she was maybe trying to steal it," Sanjay said sullenly.

Viola peered in Sanjay's direction from beneath her lashes. The Hindu was fiercely loyal to Quinn. Did he know Quinn's dark secret?

"If I was to steal from Quinn, it wouldn't be those trinkets." She forced her voice to remain calm even despite her jittery belly and splitting head. She must give the appearance of normalcy. She mustn't betray herself. "Not when he has a stocking full of jewels in his drawer."

Quinn snorted. "She has a point."

"This sickness of Lady Viola's, it is not of the body. Her aura is different," Sanjay said. "It is a darkness of the heart."

He was right. Her heart had never felt so bleak.

Thoughts darted through her mind like a school of fish, zipping this way and that before she could get a net around one.

Quinn. He wanted to be known as Quinn or called by his military rank, not his title. Not Lord Ashford. Now she knew the real reason why.

Guilt.

Someone pressed a cool, wet cloth to her forehead and a callused hand smoothed over her cheek. She smelled Quinn's scent. How could he be so tender and caring now and so cold then?

Oh, God! The torrent of sensations from last night's lovemaking washed over her. Her chest constricted. Why did she have to have this lump of feeling for him?

And such loathing for herself. What was wrong with her? She discovered she'd made love with a monster and it didn't seem to matter one particle to her wanton insides.

She'd hoped the ring would show her something of the man she'd given herself to. It had, but not as she'd expected. Instead, she was given a glimpse into the previous Lord Ashford. The ring had yanked her into the last moments of life of Quinn's older brother, Reginald.

And showed young Quinn helping him drown.

Quinn paced the room while Sanjay cleared away their breakfast. Viola hadn't stirred. Her chest rose and fell in a steady rhythm, but her cheeks were pale as foolscap.

She'd been fine, flushed and rosy and looking entirely swiveable when he'd left her at their breakfast table. Viola was not the sort given to vapors. She was vibrant. Strong.

But for no apparent reason, she was laid low.

He hitched a hip on the edge of the bed and covered her hand with his. Her fingers were icy. "Is there anything I should do for you?"

"No." Her voice held a repressed sob.

"Are you in pain?"

"Yes." Her lips were nearly white.

"Maybe spirits would help. There's sherry in the decanter." She swallowed hard. "No."

"Laudanum?" He was loath to suggest it. He'd seen too many friends lose themselves to opiates in India, but for this much pain, perhaps it was warranted. "I could nip down to the apothecary and—"

"No, no." She pulled her hand away from his and lifted the edge of the wet handkerchief to peer at him for a moment before letting the cloth drop back into place. Her mouth turned down into a frown. "Please. I just need to be quiet for a bit. This will pass."

"It's happened before?"

She sighed.

"Often?"

"No."

"What brought it on?"

"Please, Quinn." She rolled away from him. "Leave me alone."

Some people preferred to be sick in solitude. Lord knew, he did. When he was recovering from a saber cut in Peshawar, he wouldn't let anyone see him weak and feverish, refusing all visitors and barely allowing the *daai* in to change his sweaty sheets and wound dressing.

He respected Viola's need for privacy. He'd never realized how frustrating that might be to someone who was trying to help the patient.

"Fine, if that's what you wish." He stood and shoved his

hands in his pockets because he didn't know what else to do with them. "I'll see about that burgundy ball gown, then."

She made a small noise he chose to consider appreciative.

"If you need anything, ring for Sanjay."

"No!" she said with surprising force. She sat bolt upright, then seemed to think better of the sudden movement and flopped back down. "I mean, you should take him with you."

"I hardly think it takes two men to pick up a gown."

"But think how it will appear." She grabbed his pillow and covered her head with it. To shut out the light more completely, he guessed. Her voice was muffled, but he could tell her jaws were clenched from the way she clipped her words. "A gentleman shouldn't be seen carrying his own parcel. That's why you have a servant."

"You're right," he said, a weight lifting from his chest. If she was able to scold him, she was on the mend. "We won't be long then."

She mumbled a good-bye and he left, feeling very much dismissed. Sanjay refused to ride in the coach with him, insisting on hanging on the back rail as English footmen did. After rattling along alone for a few miles, Quinn had to talk to someone. He rapped on the ceiling of the coach, signaling a stop several blocks before the modiste's shop so he could get out and walk. Sanjay fell into step with him on his right side, but was careful to maintain a position back a pace in keeping with their supposed relationship as master and servant.

"Sanjay, we've never talked about your domestic relationships, but you're a married man, aren't you?" Quinn asked over his shoulder, trying to sound nonchalant though his gut was jumping.

"Oh, yes, sahib. I have six wives and eight concubines."

Perhaps Sanjay wasn't the right one to give him the counsel he sought, but no one else was available at present. "How did you know it was time to marry?"

"My father told me. Even a prince's marriages are arranged in my country."

"But did you . . . do you love your wife . . . wives?"

"Oh, yes, I love all my wives," Sanjay said with a smile in his tone. "I just love some of them more often than others."

"That's not what I mean." Quinn frowned. "I guess I'm wondering if there's a way to know if a particular woman is the one a man should wed."

"Are you, my friend, considering such foolishness with Lady Viola?"

Was he as transparent as that? He made a mental note to steer clear of the gaming tables until this business was finished.

"Why do you say it's foolishness?"

"In order to wed, a man must first be confident the woman is worthy of his trust. A man gives his wife the protection of his good name, something which is easily lost and not as easily restored."

A good name. Could that be why Viola had turned ill? Last night, she was upset over word getting back home about their posing as husband and wife. Sanjay claimed her illness was a darkness of the heart. Disorder of the spirit could lead to disorder of the body.

Would it be so bad to make their ruse reality? Marrying in truth would solve a number of problems and might very well cure what ailed her. Besides, there was every possibility she might already be increasing with his child. Could the sickness be related to that? Surely it was too soon, but what did he know about the mysteries of women?

"You could not trust a thief to value your name, sahib," Sanjay was saying.

Quinn realized his friend had been talking for the length of a block without him being aware of it. Viola's sudden illness had jolted his heart. She seemed so self-assured, so independent. Now it was obvious she needed his protection.

How better to shelter her than with the protection of his name?

"Please do not tell me you contemplate such a thing, my friend."

"Very well," Quinn said as he allowed Sanjay to come around him to open the modiste's door for him. "I won't tell you."

But he was contemplating the hell out of it.

As soon as Quinn left their suite, Viola dragged herself from the bed. She splashed cold water on her face and fought through the pain to dress herself in one of her old ensembles. She packed one of her valises, leaving behind all the new finery and even her beloved hats. The way her head was pounding, she didn't think she could manage more than one bag.

She rifled through Quinn's drawer, but could find no stocking filled with jewels. He must have taken them with him or deposited them in the hotel's safe. No matter.

She'd have to pawn the cameo brooch and the pendant watch to purchase a ticket on the coach for Calais.

Please God, may there be a vacant seat on the next run!

She'd wait to see if she had enough money left for passage on the paddle steamer to Dover or if it was necessary to part with the serpent ring as well.

"Never tell a man no when he offers to buy you jewelry," she muttered to herself as she pulled the door to their suite closed behind her. A fine necklace, a bracelet even, would have made her escape far easier.

For she must escape. As badly as she wanted Quinn, how could she ever trust a man who would drown his own brother? She tried to puzzle out another interpretation of what she'd seen, but nothing else made sense. The horror of the vision washed over her afresh and she fought back a wave of nausea.

She couldn't put enough distance between her and Quinn.

She was going home. She was done with thievery. She'd sell

the town house and move her family to a small cottage in the country, just as her mother wanted. Somehow, they'd scrape by. If she no longer cared for appearances, she might be pleasantly surprised by what she could do without.

The headache subsided to a manageable throb. She picked up her pace down the Place de la Concorde toward a coaching inn she'd noticed when she and Quinn were shopping. Turning off the well-traveled thoroughfare and down a narrow lane, she was so intent on her goal that she was less observant of her surroundings than she should have been.

"Well, your ladyship, fancy meetin' you 'ere. Ain't it a small world?"

A beefy hand weighed down her shoulder and she turned to look into a face that could frighten a gargoyle.

"Willie, what are you doing here?"

"I was 'bout to ask ye the selfsame question." He eyed her valise. "Going someplace without yer gentleman friend?"

"Not that it's any of your business, but, as a matter of fact, I'm going home."

Willie laughed unpleasantly. "Picked 'im clean already, did ye? Well, that's wot I like so much about ye. Quick and to the point."

He snatched the valise from her and popped it open, rummaging through her chemises and drawers and second-best gown. When he didn't find what he sought, he began to fling the contents to the ground till the bag was empty. "All right, where is it?"

"I have no idea what you're talking about."

They were only steps from a public street, but no one had intervened when he tore through her luggage. She had no hope anyone would come to her aid even if he became violent. Her only recourse was to shelter behind distant disdain and hope that her title would make him think twice before accosting her physically.

"You know. The Indian diamond. I knows that's wot ye're 'ere for."

"I have not done any burglary since I arrived in France," she whispered furiously. Never mind that she'd intended to make use of her skills on the morrow. "My companion and I have decided to part ways and I'm on my way home. That's all there is to it. I told you this trip had nothing to do with you, Willie. You might have saved yourself the trouble and expense of following me."

"Well, I'm 'ere in any case, ain't I?" He swaggered a step closer and she resisted the urge to retreat. A show of weakness would only encourage him. "And I'm out a fair piece of change. Reckon you'll have to make it right for me."

She straightened to her full height, which unfortunately was quite a bit less than his. "I most certainly will not."

"Oh, your ladyship, I wish ye hadn't said that." He shook his head sorrowfully. "Ye see, I have it on good authority there's half a dozen bawdy houses wot would love to have a real English lady in their stable not half a mile from this spot. All I need do is give ye a clout on the head and ye'll wake up chained to a bed."

She scuttled backward, but he snaked out a hand and snagged her wrist.

"But I'm the kindhearted sort, ye see," Willie went on, twisting her wrist as he spoke. "It would pain me to see ye brought so low. So 'ere's wot ye're going to do. Ye nip back to yer gentleman friend, that Lieutenant Quinn, and do whatever ye need do to get back in his good graces. And then ye look for a likely chance to lift his stash of jewels. When ye got 'em, why, ye just take a little walk to stretch yer legs."

He released her wrist and Viola resisted the urge to rub it. If she let him see he'd hurt her, it would only bring him pleasure.

"I'll be watchin' ye, milady. Best ye don't disappoint me.

I'm not always as good-natured a fella as ye see me being right now. So what'll it be? Will ye go back to Quinn and lighten his wallet for me or would ye rather spread yer legs for France's finest?" He raked her with a lascivious gaze and her belly curdled. "Damn me if I wouldn't line up to be first if ye picked the latter."

Viola eyed him coldly, not willing to allow him the satisfaction of her revulsion, and stooped to retrieve her scattered garments. She stuffed them back into the valise, fighting to keep her hands from trembling, and snapped it shut. "Kindly step aside. I'm returning to my suite at the Hotel de Crillon."

She had no choice but to go back to Quinn.

Willie laughed again, a ragged cackle. "Ye wound me heart, yer ladyship, but me purse is like to get fatter this way, so I collect I'll get over it." His face screwed into a fierce scowl and he yanked her so close his putrid breath streamed over her.

She fought the urge to retch.

"But don't ye be thinkin' ye're going to stiff me, Peach. I don't take kindly to it. I don't take kindly to it at all."

CHAPTER 14

"You must be feeling better."

Quinn was relieved to find Viola in the darkened sitting room instead of in bed. The heavy damask curtains had been pulled, blocking out most of the sun's light, but at least she was fully dressed.

Though not in one of the new ensembles he'd bought for her, he noted with consternation. Then he realized she probably hadn't wanted to ring for an abigail to help her dress and decided to muddle through by herself with some of her old things. She was a very private person. In that, they were alike.

Well suited. His resolve strengthened.

But she hadn't acknowledged his arrival yet.

"Viola?"

"Oh, I beg your pardon." She gave her head a small shake and glanced his way. "Yes, my head is somewhat better, thank you."

"Excellent." He turned to Sanjay. "Will you be a good fellow and unwrap that package? The modiste said we should spread it out on a bed so the wrinkles don't set."

"No, Sanjay, I'll do it." Viola rose more quickly than Quinn expected a woman with a sick headache could and moved to intercept Sanjay on his way to the bedroom. "You shouldn't have to wait on me. You're not really a servant, after all."

Sanjay stopped short. It was the first time she'd spoken to him directly unless it was to give him an order.

"Quinn told me your true situation, Your Highness. And may I say, I am dismayed by the injustice done you and your people." She dipped a shallow curtsy, then gentled the parcel away from him. "I believe you and I started on the wrong foot, but that's my fault since we met under larcenous circumstances. I apologize for treating you as if you were my servant in the past. I assure you, it will not happen again."

She smiled charmingly and disappeared into the bedroom, leaving both Quinn and Sanjay staring after her.

"Did she strike her head on something when she fainted?" Sanjay asked.

"I didn't find any evidence of it." Before she'd regained consciousness, he'd checked her thoroughly for injury. Nothing accounted for her fainting.

But Viola was definitely altered by the experience.

"No matter. To my mind, the lady is much improved by her malady."

"You think so?" Quinn wasn't so sure. Something felt off about Viola's abrupt change toward Sanjay. It was as if she were suddenly currying his favor for some reason.

"I wonder if the kitchen has any more of those scones Lady Viola likes," Sanjay mused aloud. "I shall bring some with your tea."

"Sure I shouldn't get it myself?" Quinn drawled. "After all, you're not really my servant."

"No, but we must keep up appearances. At least, for the world's eyes. If the Blood of the Tiger suddenly goes missing and it is known that Amjerat's prince is near, it will not take much to connect me with the jewel's disappearance."

Sanjay let himself out and Quinn went into the bedroom. Viola had spread the burgundy gown across the counterpane and was billowing the skirt to shake out wrinkles.

"Is it to your liking?"

"Yes," she said softly. "It's very fine. Thank you."

She still hadn't looked at him.

It was deucedly hard to propose to a woman who wouldn't meet his eyes.

"I've been thinking," he began.

"Mmm-hmm." She skittered to the far side of the bed and smoothed out the gown's long train.

"I've been thinking I've been unfair to you."

"You've brought me to Paris, bought me a new wardrobe, and tried to shower me with jewels," she said, still not looking up. "Most women would find that exceedingly fair."

"Not if I also compromised their reputation in the process. I confess I hadn't foreseen that outcome when we set out on this venture."

Viola straightened and folded her hands before her fig-leaf fashion. She seemed intensely fascinated with her own thumbs.

"I'd like to make amends for that." This was shaping up to be the most ham-handed proposal in history, but he plowed ahead doggedly.

"I don't see how, since it would be rather like shutting the stable door after the horse has escaped. Gossip flies on swift wings." She began smoothing the burgundy tulle again, her hands nervous as butterflies, alighting and rising again between one heartbeat and the next. "I've no doubt word of our supposed elopement has journeyed toward the Channel already. I'm as good as ruined."

"Not if the elopement wasn't pretend."

She looked at him then, her hazel eyes wide. "What are you suggesting?"

"I'm not suggesting anything," Quinn said, disgusted with himself for doing this so badly and more than a little irritated with her for making it more difficult than it need be. "I'm proposing."

In the silence that followed he clearly heard the mantel clock ticking in the adjoining room.

"I'm proposing we end this sham and marry in truth."

A few more heartbeats trudged by and Quinn realized he was holding his breath.

"Why?" she finally said.

"For the reason I just mentioned. To protect your reputation." Quinn dragged a hand through his hair. "Weren't you attending?"

She looked away from him and furiously rearranged the folds of the gown again. "If you hope for a positive response to your suit, it might behoove you to be less snippy."

He took heart at that. At least she was sounding more like her gingery self.

"I'm not snippy, I'm . . . oh, Viola, I know I'm not doing this well, but—"

"That's not the issue, Quinn. I'm not the sort who needs fair words if that's what you're worried about. But you still haven't answered my question." She stopped fiddling with the gown and fixed him with a stare. "Why would you want to marry me?"

"Do women usually ask that question of the man who proposes to them?"

"I don't know. I suppose they do if they want to know the answer." She fisted her hands at her waist. "I bring you no dowry. I was no virgin when we met. We've known each other less than a fortnight and the main reason for our association in the first place is because I intended to steal from you. So I'm asking, Quinn." Her arms relaxed at her sides as some of the fight seemed to sizzle out of her. "Why do you want to marry me?"

He walked around the bed and put his arms around her. She stiffened in his embrace and turned her head away. He took her chin and forced her to look up at him.

"Because I think . . ."

Her stony gaze spilled a bit of wind from his sails.

"It's quite likely that . . . that I may . . . possibly . . . love you."

He bent to kiss her, but she covered his mouth with her palm to stop him. "Possibly is not good enough."

She pulled away from him and returned to the sitting room. He followed. "I do love you."

She laughed mirthlessly. "Oh, Quinn. Don't start treating me as if I haven't a brain in my head. There may be nothing else between us, but I deserve at least that much respect."

"There's plenty between us and you know it. What about last night—hell, what about this morning?"

"Do I really need to explain to you that sexual congress is not the same as love?"

"Viola, I—"

"No, stop it, Quinn. We barely know each other."

After the toe-curling things she'd done to him and with him, how could she say that? It might not be love, but it was something. He knew the shiver of her sighs, the way her brows drew together in need just before she came, the way her eyes darkened when she wanted him. "I know you better than you think."

"It only seems that way, but you really don't." She stopped pacing and went still as a hare. "And I don't know you."

"You know me better than most."

"You have secrets, Quinn. No doubt you shield them with good reason." She looked sharply at him, but her eyes went strangely out of focus and he got the eerie feeling she was looking right through him. "We barely know each other in mundane matters as well. For example, do you even know if I have any siblings?"

"I know you have no brothers." That was easy since if she had one, her brother would have inherited her father's earldom and would have provided for her as her cousin had not. "And I believe you mentioned a sister."

Her brows shot up in surprise. Score one for a man who listened when a woman spoke.

"Yes, but do you know she's a lunatic? When her husband ran off with an opera dancer, Ophelia went completely off her head. That sort of thing runs in families, I'm told. Why would you want to run the risk of—"

"You are not your sister."

"And you're not your brother," she fired back. "You haven't told me anything about him. Why is that?"

"There's not much to tell," he said uneasily. "Reggie died when we were children."

"How did he die?"

Sweet Christ, why did she ask that? "It was . . . an accident."

"What kind of accident?" she asked, white-lipped.

"The accidental kind." An invisible fist squeezed his heart and for a blink he thought he smelled a whiff of the algae-scummed lake.

"Your brother's death changed your life forever. Tell me about it." *Tell me, Quinn. Oh, God, please tell me I'm wrong. Give me anything that will make sense of the vision. Anything but what I think I saw.*

Her belly writhed like a bucketful of eels. She wanted so badly for him to say something—anything—to wipe away the image that burned in her mind. She realized she'd likely believe him if he lied, simply because she wanted so desperately for the vision not to be true.

She waited, suspended between heaven and hell, barely able to draw breath.

"It happened so long ago. There's . . . nothing to tell really," he finally said. "I fail to see what this has to do with my proposal of marriage."

Her last bit of hope wilted.

"Quinn, if you cannot speak to me of something that must have been a major event in your life," she said softly, because she had hardly any air to put behind her voice, "there is obviously very little you have to say to me. I will not have a marriage full of deadly silence."

"It's not that." He grimaced with frustration. "You've twisted things all around. I'm offering you marriage because I can see that I've created difficulties for you and I want to help you avoid scandal."

"Not a very solid foundation for matrimony. Nor a very flattering one."

"Then let me offer a practical reason for us to marry," Quinn said coldly. "We were careless. You may very well be carrying my child."

"That's possible." Neville had withdrawn the one time they were intimate. She had no idea if she were the sort of woman who quickened easily. "I would not force a child to bear the stain of bastardy. If I find I am increasing, perhaps we'll discuss this matter again."

Her belly churned uneasily. Were there really any circumstances in which she could marry a man who'd murdered his brother?

He narrowed his eyes at her. "What changed you toward me, Viola? Between breakfast and now, I hardly recognize you. It's as if you're a different person."

No, she thought with a leaden heart. She was the same. He was the one who was different. Unnatural. Damaged.

But why couldn't she stop caring for him? Why did he still make her body thrum with his nearness?

Perhaps Quinn wasn't the only damaged one in the room.

"Then you prove my point," she said, wishing she didn't see something like hurt in his gray eyes. "You don't know me as well as you thought."

The latch of the door rattled.

"Oh, there's Sanjay with tea." She bustled over to hold the door for him, relief at his interruption washing over her. If Sanjay didn't know about Quinn's brother, perhaps he'd prove a useful ally when she found a chance to escape. He might even protect her from Willie if she flattered him properly. "Quinn, pull up an extra chair for His Highness. Surely he'll join us for tea. You will? Oh, good. Now I want to hear all about Amjerat."

CHAPTER 15

Quinn had never felt less like dancing, but he was obligated to circulate throughout the embassy ballroom. He collected the partner he'd been assigned to before the upbow for each new piece of music. He shuffled each lady around the floor in the prescribed pattern of steps, then thanked her politely and took his leave before she could initiate conversation.

How could he make small talk with strangers when the only woman he wanted to talk to wouldn't hear him?

He'd tried to engage Viola in another discussion about his proposal after Sanjay had left them yesterday, but she'd deflected him at every turn.

And rejected him utterly when the time came to seek their bed. She complained the violent headache she'd suffered was threatening to return. He offered only to hold her till the weakness passed, but she said she couldn't bear to disturb him in the night with her restlessness.

So he scrunched himself into a pretzel shape and bivouacked on the diminutive sofa in their suite.

He'd slept on rocky ground with the breath of the Himalayas sweeping over him with more cheer.

It was one thing for Viola to reject his suit. It was another for her to be so changed toward him. After a night of earth-shattering passion, he had no idea what he'd done to deserve this . . . shunning.

His gaze followed her about the dance floor. Nimble and light, she was like a faery queen gliding among mere mortals. Spellbinding and unobtainable.

A new adornment sparkled on her wrist. Sanjay had brought her a silver and jet bracelet and connected ring just before they left for the ball. The delicate fancy draped over the back of her upraised right hand, a net of black stars descending from the base of her middle finger and expanding around her hand.

"It belongs to my favorite wife," Sanjay had confided. "She sent it with me because jet and silver have protective properties. Since you will shortly handle Baaghh kaa kkhuun, you are in more need of its shield than I. I beg you to wear it this evening, Lady Viola."

As she slid it on over her long opera gloves, she'd smiled at Sanjay. "Somehow, I don't think it would have fit your finger."

He grinned wickedly back at her. "No indeed. Fatima wanted me to drape it over another part of my body to protect me while I sleep. Alas it will not fit there, either."

They'd shared a laugh and Quinn found himself on the outside of their little circle of two, a street urchin pressing his nose against a bakery windowpane. For the life of him, he couldn't figure out what he'd done to fall so far from her good graces. Why did Viola favor Sanjay with her smiles and hold herself so guarded with him?

"My dear boy, you forgot to collect me for this gavotte." Lady Wimbly's warbling tone interrupted his thoughts. She swatted his shoulder with her closed fan. "Mooning about after one's own wife is not at all the done thing, you know."

"My apologies, Lady Wimbly. In my defense, we have not been married long."

She chuckled indulgently. "Maintain the same level of at-

tentiveness to your bride after you have been married long
and you shall show true quality, young Ashford."

"Excellent advice. We've only missed a few bars." He held
out his arms. "Shall we?"

"No, my bunions are simply beastly this night. Let us sit
this one out and you can keep an old woman company. It'll be
amusing to keep count of how many times my Wimbly steps
on your young wife's toes."

Without giving him an opportunity to decline, she took his
arm and led him from the dance floor.

Viola watched Quinn from the corner of her eye. Why did
he have to be so damnably handsome? Her chest ached at the
sight of him. She missed a step and nearly stumbled.

"Careful, madam." Lord Wimbly held her up with a tight
grip. The old gentleman was a pleasant dancer. Viola much
preferred him to some of the other gentlemen who couldn't
keep from staring at her décolletage as they twirled her about
the floor.

She was also pleased to discover he was an amiable fellow
when his wife wasn't about to monopolize the conversation.
And without Lady Wimbly around, his hearing seemed to improve. It occurred to her that as lord of the neighboring estate,
he would have known Quinn from a young age. Perhaps he
could shed light on Quinn's brother's accident.

"You've known my husband for a long time, I collect," she
said as they dipped in a bow and answering curtsy.

"All his life. Many's the time I chased the young scallywag
out of my orchard. Him and his brother both."

"So you knew Reginald, too?"

"Oh, yes. A good boy, that one. A gentle boy, you understand. One got the sense that he was sickly often, him being
smaller than his younger brother, you know." He narrowed his
eyes and Viola suspected he gazed into the past. "Why, Grey-

don topped him by almost a head that last summer even though he was a couple years the younger."

Viola's heart sank to her toes. Quinn's brother was smaller than he. Weaker. Vulnerable. It made what she'd seen even more hideous somehow.

"Their father, Lord Kilmaine, often said those two were born out of order. Greydon ought to have been the elder by rights. He was always the stronger and the one in the lead. Leastwise, he was when they pilfered my garden." Lord Wimbly laughed good-naturedly. "Poor Reggie was a bitter disappointment to Kilmaine. I suppose if Reginald had been a second son, he might have been more acceptable. He'd have made a good scholar or a vicar, perhaps."

"And then he died."

"Ah, yes, sad business that." Wimbly led her through the gavotte steps without conscious effort. He was evidently used to squeezing his gossip into his dancing time. "And sad for your husband most of all, for he was there, you understand."

"Quinn is not one to dwell on the past."

"Oh, yes. Quite sensible, what?"

He seemed to think she'd given him a signal to stop talking about the topic, so she gave him a gentle nudge. "I'd rather not bring up such a painful subject with my husband. Would you tell me what happened?"

"All my information is secondhand, but it came straight from Lord Kilmaine, so you may rely upon it. Seems Greydon had been teaching Reggie how to swim. He was always very protective of his brother, you know. Lord Kilmaine could be . . . harsh. Never seemed to bother Greydon though. Stoic as a Swede, that one. But Reggie took it very much to heart."

Lord Wimbly turned his lips inward for a moment as if he'd said too much. "Well, a man has to be firm with sons, doesn't he? Spare the rod and spoil the child and all that. Can't mollycoddle one's heir, can one?"

"No, I suppose not."

"Of course not. At any rate, Greydon left his brother at the lakeside and went to fetch their father, so Lord Kilmaine could see how well Reggie was progressing. When they arrived back at the dock, Reggie was in the water by himself and going down for the third time."

"Quinn's father was there?" She hadn't seen an adult in her vision at all. Only Quinn running along the dock as fast as his young legs could carry him.

"Told me himself, poor man. Beastly business."

If Reggie hadn't seen his father, that would explain why Viola hadn't. The vision was unlike the other visions she'd received from gemstones. Usually, she watched a scene from a detached, almost godlike space. This Sending had pulled her into the frantic mind of a dying child. She was bound to have missed a few details.

But wouldn't Reggie have noticed his father's presence? Especially since it seemed he was desperate for Lord Kilmaine's approval.

"Quinn jumped in and pulled his brother out," Lord Wimbly said.

That wasn't true. At least not according to what she'd Seen. Quinn had leaned over from the safety of the dock and reached for his brother.

"But by then, it was too late."

A hand had closed over Reggie's crown and held him down till he spewed the last of his hoarded breath. Viola's belly churned afresh.

The last strains of the gavotte faded. She dipped a low curtsy while Lord Wimbly sketched a florid bow that belonged to the previous century.

"And now give me your hand, my dear— Gracious me! You're pale as a sheet! We shall rescue your husband from the clutches of my wife and find a place for you to sit. I see she has him cornered near the punchbowl." Lord Wimbly led Viola off the dance floor as the string quartet set aside their instruments for a quarter hour break. "She means well, but honestly, my Euphegenia could talk the ears off a donkey."

"There you are, my love." Quinn bussed his lips over her temple as she drew near. He frowned at her with concern. "You look rather blown. Would you like some fresh air?"

It was the signal they'd agreed upon and her pallor at least made his statement plausible. The embassy ballroom was on the topmost floor of the building. A few rooms on the second story had balconies open to the night. It would provide the perfect excuse to venture down the long staircase.

The ambassador's office happened to be on that level as well.

"That would be lovely, thank you." Viola took Quinn's offered arm and excused herself from the Wimblys. Once clear of the ballroom, she dropped his arm and picked up the pace. The fabric of her gown swished with each step. Oh, how she wished she was wearing her male attire. It was ever so much more conducive to speed and stealth.

"Steady on," Quinn said, grasping her elbow as she reached a broad landing on the marble staircase. "We aren't in a race. Are you all right?"

"I'll do"—she tried to shake off the lingering memories of her vision of the lake—"but we need to move with purpose."

"Not necessarily. If we're noticed wandering about, we need to appear casual, not driven."

"But if we are quick, we have less chance of being noticed at all," she whispered furiously. "I don't know how long the lock will take. The more time we waste in the hall, the less time I'll have to work the tumbler."

When they neared the second floor, Quinn brought a finger to his lips and slowed their descent. He glanced around the corner, checking the hallway for guards.

He took her hand and led her down the dim corridor. Only

one in three of the gas wall sconces were burning to discourage unwelcome visitors. When they rounded a corner, Viola caught a whiff of tobacco.

A guard.

Quinn grabbed her and pressed her against the wall.

"What are—"

"Kiss me," he ordered and his mouth descended to cover hers.

Viola expected the knowledge that he had done murder to alter her perception of Quinn, but he tasted the same. When his tongue demanded entrance, her lips parted for him. He groaned into her mouth. Wet suction bound them together in a kiss tinged with desperation.

She wrapped her arms around him, stroking his back. His grip on her waist tightened and his body pressed against hers, his hardness making her soften even more.

This is so wrong.

Her body shouldn't be responding to him. Not after what she'd Seen.

But that didn't stop the low drumbeat from starting between her legs. The ache roared to life, empty and insistent. She arched into him. If he lifted her skirt and tried to take her right there, she hadn't the will to stop him.

"Who goes there?" A voice came from the far end of the corridor.

When Quinn pulled back, Viola peered over his shoulder and saw an embassy guard approaching them.

"Sorry to have bothered you, old chap," Quinn said with a sheepish grin. "My wife and I were looking for a bit of privacy. We haven't been married long, you see."

The guard swept a quick gaze over Viola and winked at Quinn. "I quite understand, sir. Might I suggest the blue room at the far end of this hall? There's a balcony there."

"Much obliged," Quinn took Viola's hand and turned to go. "Oh! You might want to form up a detail to assist Lady Wimbly from the ballroom. She was fair done in when we left her. I don't think she'll be able to make the stairs. Her husband and the ambassador went to school together, you know. They're great friends to this day, aren't they, dear?"

"Utterly devoted friends," Viola agreed.

"I see," the guard said, quick to grasp an opportunity to ingratiate himself with his employer by providing a thoughtful service for his bosom friend. "Thank you, sir. I'll see to it immediately."

Quinn and Viola continued toward the blue room till the click of the guard's heels faded up the stairwell. Then they turned and dashed back down the long hall toward the unguarded ambassador's office.

And its unguarded safe.

CHAPTER 16

"How's it coming?" Quinn whispered from his post at the crack in the ambassador's door.

"The same as when you asked half a minute ago. For pity's sake, Quinn, shut it. I can't think."

Viola stood with her ear to the tumbler, her left glove stripped off, the better to turn the rotating part with precision. Eyes closed, body tense, breasts rising and falling with carefully measured breaths, she was the picture of concentration.

And the picture of swiveable femininity.

Quinn's cock still hadn't settled after that kiss in the hallway. She'd kissed him back! She'd melted against him. He even thought he scented the sweet whiff of her arousal.

But was she only acting? Had she kissed him so soundly merely to throw off the guard?

Viola was a contradiction with feet. Cold or hot, vulnerable or strong-willed, he never knew which side she'd present to him. She was as many faceted as the gem they sought.

How many Violas were there?

Once they had the diamond, he vowed to take the time to find out.

A loud click broke the room's silence.

"There," she said softly. She turned the handle and opened the wall vault.

Quinn left his post as lookout and hurried to her side. There were several tall stacks of various types of bundled currency—pounds, francs, and lira. If they'd been after cash, it would have been a burglar's motherlode. Files in sealed folders were stacked on the bottom shelf, the state secrets of a dozen potentates, no doubt. If blackmail was their game, the vault contained a treasure trove of embarrassing possibilities.

So many paths to wealth, so little time.

But fast ill-gotten wealth wasn't Quinn's aim. His gaze fell on a leather bag. A diplomatic pouch.

He lifted it from the safe and opened it. There was only a small box inside. He started to reach in for it, but Viola stopped him.

"Wait. If Sanjay is right and the diamond is dangerous, I'm the one wearing the protection."

He didn't believe all that Eastern mumbo-jumbo for an instant, but the earnest expression on her face told him she did. If it would make her happy, he'd humor her. He nodded, but watched her with the intensity of a hawk on a vole. If she was going to pocket the stone or make a switch, now was when she'd try to do it.

She drew out the jewel box and opened it for them to see. A red gem sparkled in the gas light. Quinn smiled, but Viola answered him with a frown.

"This isn't the right gem."

"It's red. It's the right size. Are you telling me it's paste?"

"No, it's a precious stone, but I don't think it's a diamond." She picked it up with her gloved hand, the one bedecked with Sanjay's silver and jet, and cocked her head as if listening intently. "The resonance is off."

"What?" Could she somehow *hear* the jewel? In the silence

that followed, he heard nothing but their soft breathing and the blood rushing through his ears.

Viola shook her head and transferred the stone to the palm of her bare hand. Her whole body suddenly stiffened.

"Here you are, Mr. Penobscot," a round man with a fierce set of muttonchop whiskers said to the courier. "Bear this ruby to London using the Paris route. Guard it well. You will have a security detail traveling with you at all times. The more convincing you are about its supposed nature, the safer the real diamond will be."

Viola watched the scene unfold beneath her as if she were a spider on the ceiling. She recognized the stone being handed to Mr. Penobscot. It was the same one she now held in her palm.

"And you, Mr. Chesterton," said Mutton-Chops, "your papers show you to be a returning man of business and not a very prosperous one at that. Your security will be in the appearance of poverty."

Chesterton was a small man, not much taller than Viola herself, with a balding spot on the top of his head no amount of creative combing would cover.

"Your route is through Hanover, Mr. Chesterton. Prince Albert's people will be expecting you. Wait there until an armed contingent arrives to escort you the rest of the way. The closer you come to the queen's collection, the more vulnerable you will be."

Another stone changed hands.

A presence unrelated to the men below her crowded Viola's mind. It was a dark, creeping malevolence, accompanied by a single low tone, so deep it made her chest vibrate. An invisible claw dragged across her spine. Menace emanated from the stone itself, but none of the men seemed aware of it. Panic flooded Viola's mind when she glimpsed the jewel glittering like a bloody eye in Mr. Chesterton's gloved palm.

Could the stone feel her watching it?

Was it watching her?

As if in answer, it turned its evil energy toward her and all the breath exploded from her lungs.

*   *   *

Viola yanked the ruby from her bare palm with her protected hand. Gasping, she blinked up at Quinn. She was still on her feet, waiting for the sick headache to smack the base of her skull.

The blow didn't come.

Sanjay's jet and silver must have offered her some protection, after all. She could almost kiss the Indian prince.

"Viola, what do you mean the resonance is off?"

The way Quinn asked the question assured her he hadn't noticed that anything unusual had happened. The vision must have lasted only a blink. Her secret might still be safe from him.

"I just meant this is not a red diamond," she said with conviction. "It's a ruby. A very precious one at that, but it's not the stone you're looking for."

She secreted the ruby in the small space where the stiff busk slid into the front of her corset, but Quinn's fingers went in after it. Her nipples tingled at his nearness, but he wasn't in pursuit of her charms.

"No, you don't, my Lady Light-Fingers." He came up with the stone, popped it back into its velvet setting and stowed the box in the diplomatic pouch. "We're not stealing anything but what we came for."

"But Quinn, a ruby that size is worth a great deal—not as much as a red diamond, of course, but still . . ."

"We're not simple thieves."

She rolled her eyes at him. "Speak for yourself."

He put the pouch back in the safe and closed it. The click of the latch sounded unnaturally loud. And was followed by the sound of heels on the marble hallway floor.

"Someone's coming!" she hissed.

"We're going to be caught," Quinn said calmly as he turned down the gas lamp. "There's no place to hide here, but I have an idea. Do you trust me?"

"When did you give me a choice?"

He took her hand and pulled her behind the ambassador's
desk. Then he pushed her forward so her upper body was resting on the elegant burled walnut. Quinn pulled up her hem,
and yards of her gown and petticoats layered over her back.

"Quinn!"

"We're going to be caught in any case." He leaned over her
and whispered in her ear, "We may as well be caught doing
something that explains our presence here and will knock any
suspicion of burglary from the guard's mind— Why, Viola!"

She heard a wicked smile in his voice.

"You're not wearing any drawers."

"I don't suppose you'd believe me if I tell you they spoil
the line of the gown. If it's good enough for you and Brummel,
it's good enough for me." In truth, she simply loved the
naughty sense of freedom going without them gave her.

She bit her lip as his hands smoothed over her bare bum
and reached between her legs to tease the small hairs covering
her sex. Moist warmth eased out of her. When he ran a finger
along the length of her cleft, he found her wet and ready.

"Good," he said as she felt him fumble with the front of his
trousers. Then his engorged tip pressed against the soft welcome of her sex. "I don't want to hurt you."

Too late.

He wouldn't hurt her physically, but she was bound to be
hurt in every other way that counted. Everything was such a
muddle—the tatters her reputation would be in once she returned home, the vision of the horrific events at that lake, the
phantom red diamond's evil eye boring through her—it was all
too much. She couldn't think.

She could only feel.

Despite everything, joining her body to Quinn's was the
only touchstone of sanity in her lunatic world.

She tilted her pelvis and he slid his hard cock into her with
the rightness of a homecoming.

Quinn murmured a soft cursing endearment and withdrew

to ram into her again and again. His ballocks slapped against her thighs.

God, yes. Punish me. If you're gentle, I'll think too much and I need not to think.

"Harder," she said through clenched teeth. She gripped the far edge of the ambassador's desk. "For God's sake, harder."

Quinn shuddered into her again, filling her, stoking her sensitive spots, both her sickness and her cure.

Her insides coiled, tensed for release.

She didn't even hear the door creak when the guard opened it. The extra light from his lantern made her raise her head, but her eyes were passion-blind.

Quinn stopped mid-stroke.

A sob escaped her throat. Only a little longer. One stroke more would have sent her over the edge.

The door partially closed and the guard's voice curled around it, tentative and apologetic. "Beggin' your pardon, milord, but you and the lady can't be in there."

"Give us a moment," Quinn said, his voice ragged. He withdrew from her, pulled down her skirts, and buttoned his pants. She was boneless when he raised her from the desktop to stand upright.

"Quinn." His name shuddered out of her, equal parts prayer and curse. He'd used her passionate nature as a distraction for larceny. "I hate you for this."

"Hate me later," he whispered. "Now we need to get out of here."

Viola's whole body thrummed with need and frustration. She leaned on Quinn's chest and somehow her legs carried her along as he led her around the desk and out the door, keeping her on the side of him most sheltered from the guard—a different one from before.

"No one's in the library, your lordship," the guard said helpfully. "Third door on the right."

Quinn mumbled his thanks and a coin flipped between him

and the guard, sparkling for an instant in the lamplight before disappearing into the man's pocket.

As they neared the third door, aching need overwhelmed her and she reached up and pulled his head down to kiss him. She drew all the breath from his lungs in a surprised rush.

He gasped when she released his lips. "I thought you hate me."

"I do." She cupped his genitals. "I hate you very much."

His mouth descended on hers for another bruising kiss.

She'd thought him so unaffected in the ambassador's office, so resolute to pull out of her as if it were nothing, but clearly she'd been wrong. He was shaking with need. They turned together, a stylized dance of lust, barely clearing the library door.

Quinn kicked it shut behind them.

He picked her up and carried her toward the big library table. He set her down and pushed aside the books stacked on either side of her hips in two long sweeps. Spines cracking, they tumbled to the floor, pounding one after the other in a rumble like thunder.

"Careful," she warned, "you'll bring the guard down on us again."

"I suspect he's too busy checking the ambassador's office, making sure nothing's amiss there." He bent and reached under her skirts, running his palms up her legs all the way to the apex of her thighs.

Viola leaned back on her elbows and let her head loll as he caressed her needy flesh. The ache was building again fast. When he brushed his thumbs over her most sensitive spot, she cried out, so near release, but not yet at that place of unraveling madness.

"That's it," he encouraged as he unfastened his trousers again and teased her cleft with the tip of him. "Sing for me, love."

He drove himself into her and she hooked her heels around his waist.

Love, he'd said.

No, she wouldn't think about that. She'd think of this carnal adventure as a man would. It was only a wet, hot joining. A good hard swive.

Quinn feathered his fingertips over her face. She caught two of them in her mouth and sucked. He slid his other hand between their bodies and rubbed her little spot in time with her suckles. When she sucked harder, he stroked harder. If she went faster, he did too.

She was in control and feeling positively wicked. It was as if she were touching herself and could end her torment at any time with the right speed and pressure.

She opened her eyes and met Quinn's gaze. No, it was only the illusion of control. He watched her intently, feeding on her need, turning it any way that suited him.

And it suited him to drive her to completion. Her insides tightened, coiled in on themselves. Her breath came in shallow pants. He arched into her and thumbed her spot in a maddening slow circle.

She flew off in a dozen directions at once, losing control of her limbs as her inner walls contracted around the hard length of him. Someone was speaking in other tongues, the garbled language of lust. The voice sounded like hers. She collapsed back on the table, not sure when or if she'd regain control of her body.

Or if she even wanted to.

Once her pumping subsided, his began.

He came inside her in strong, hot pulses. A throaty growl escaped him as he emptied himself into her. When he was finished, he laid his head down between her breasts, his spent breath streaming hotly over the mounds revealed above her bodice.

So much for using a French letter, she thought absently as her body answered his with a few more gentle spasms, a primal attempt to ease the last bit of his essence into her.

She almost didn't care that she'd risked pregnancy once again. Well-being flooded her body. She ran her hand over Quinn's dark head, ruffling his hair and running her fingertip around the shell of his ear.

"Viola," he gasped, still out of breath from his exertions, "if I ask nicely, will you hate me again sometime?"

"It's a distinct possibility."

"Then I'll live in eager expectation." He raised himself up slightly to look at her, a wicked grin on his face. "Well, Lady Ashford, we've had quite an evening. Perhaps we should be saying our good-byes to the ambassador and heading back to our hotel suite. Should you feel hateful again, no doubt you'd prefer a bed."

She arched a brow at him. He sounded so calm, so collected. "You knew the evening would end like this, didn't you?"

"No, I didn't." He straightened and refastened his trousers. "But you can't blame a fellow for hoping."

CHAPTER 17

"We discussed this possibility before we left Bombay, sahib. You feared there might be a decoy. But if the real Baaghh kaa kkhuun is not in Paris," Sanjay asked, "then where can it be?"

"Anywhere," Quinn answered with a grim frown.

"I don't know about that," Viola said as she unfastened the jet and silver jewelry and returned it to Sanjay with a smile of thanks. It was wonderful to have used her gift for an extended vision without the accompanying blinding headache. She had no idea why the wristlet seemed to work. The silver kept the black stones from touching her skin directly. Perhaps the jet absorbed the psychic emanations of other gems as black cloth absorbs light. She wondered if any silver and jet jewelry would do the trick or if Sanjay's set had particular properties. "There are a limited number of travel routes from India the diamond might take. What are they?"

It was a measure of his faith in her ability to identify gemstones that Quinn hadn't questioned the fact that the jewel in the ambassador's office was not the diamond he sought.

She resisted telling Quinn about her new vision and certainly wouldn't divulge the one she'd received from his signet ring. She didn't feel it was safe to tell him about that part of her gift. Not until she knew what had really happened to his brother.

What she'd Seen varied enough from Lord Wimbly's account to raise questions in her mind. She was cautiously hopeful her version of Reginald Quinn's drowning wasn't as accurate as it seemed.

Maybe it was only her body getting in the way of her reason. She simply couldn't bear for Greydon to be a monster. If there was any other explanation for what she'd Seen, she clutched at it with the desperation of a drowning victim herself.

"I suppose the courier bearing Baaghh kaa kkhuun could stay aboard a sailing ship all the way around the Horn of Africa and straight on to London," Quinn said sullenly.

She caught the tip of her right glove in her teeth and pulled it off. "Is it likely something that precious would be risked on a long ocean voyage?"

"No."

"Overland, then." She removed the serpent ring, peeled off her other glove and rolled the pair together.

"Through a progression of royal residences perhaps," Sanjay suggested. "Does your Queen Victoria have a string of summer palaces someplace away from the dampness of England?"

Viola laughed. "No, we English enjoy our soggy weather and wouldn't dream of leaving our dreary little island on that account." She saw a way to turn Quinn's thoughts in the right direction without revealing how she'd hit upon the correct route.

"But come to think of it, Prince Albert is from the Kingdom of Hanover. The Royal House has many holdings there, so no doubt there's a drafty castle or two on the continent to which the royal couple can escape. Do you suppose the diamond might be routed through there?"

Quinn sank into one of the wing chairs. "I don't know. It

might just as easily have gone round the Horn. Perhaps we should return to London and wait for the diamond to arrive."

"In case it's escaped your notice," she said dryly, "the Royal Collection is not as easy to break into as the ambassador's office."

Not to mention the fact that the Beefeaters who guarded the royal jewels wouldn't be as bemused by finding a couple in flagrante delicto in the vault as the embassy guard had been. Viola had never seen Quinn so discouraged, but she had to discourage him a bit more in order to move him toward seeking the jewel in Hanover. "Once the red diamond is in the queen's possession, it's as good as gone."

"She is right," Sanjay said.

Quinn stared into the dead fireplace for a moment. "I suppose it would make sense to send the diamond into a region controlled by those bound to the English throne."

"Hanover is bound by blood to its past monarchs and by marriage to our queen," she agreed quickly. "Oh! Lord Wimbly said something about hearing that Prince Albert was sending a contingent of his people there this spring for some unknown reason," she extemporized.

"Did he? Well, the old fellow always keeps an ear to the ground, or at least his wife does and he can't help knowing what she hears. If there is a contingent of the Prince's entourage descending on Hanover, the chances the diamond is coming through there are increased." Quinn stood. "I'll arrange a coach for us tomorrow."

"Lord Ashford rides again. No doubt your title will help wangle another invitation for us in Hanover." Viola smiled in satisfaction. She only hoped they arrived in the northern city before the diamond came and went.

And that she had another set of silver and jet jewelry to protect her other hand before she touched the benighted thing in truth, instead of sensing the red diamond in a vision.

* * *

Breakfast was a pleasantly domestic affair. She and Quinn had wakened all tangled up together, their bodies seeking to maintain contact even as they slept. They managed to have a civil and productive conversation about the use of French letters during future bouts of "hatefulness" over their baguettes and tea. Quinn agreed to protect her by procuring a supply of the condoms at once.

By the time Quinn excused himself to shave, she was feeling quite satisfied with the state of the world. Her niggling doubts about the vision at the lake had been shoved aside. When the time was right, she'd talk to Quinn about it. She was all but certain there was something missing from her vision, something that exonerated Quinn.

She'd been in Reggie's head. Perhaps he'd been tangled up in something under the water and only thought he was being held beneath the surface from above.

Quinn couldn't have killed him. No man could have the sense of honor he possessed while hiding a vicious crime like fratricide in his past.

Viola was contemplating a second cup of the fragrant blend of tea when Sanjay arrived to clear their table.

"This arrived for you, milady." He slipped an envelope beneath her napkin. There was no longer any thinly concealed suspicion in his tone. She'd won the Indian prince over. If she needed him, she suspected he'd help her.

"Thank you, Sanjay." She ripped open the wax seal and felt the blood run from her face.

Sanjay couldn't help her. Or Quinn either.

Losing pashuns, the note read in an abominable hand. She deciphered the equally abominable spelling to mean *patience*. *Meet now. And bring a stone if ye no wot's gud for ye. And yer frends.*

It was signed simply *W*.

Her belly curdled. She'd had no idea Willie could write and frankly he'd flown clear out of her mind ever since she'd decided not to leave Quinn. She crumpled the note in her fist, stood and ambled to the curtained window.

"I'll see about our transport to Hanover this morning," Quinn said, his voice slightly altered as he spoke out of one side of his mouth for a smoother shave. "What are your plans for the day?"

Viola peered through the slit in the curtain to the street below. There was Willie, lurking near a fruit seller's newly replenished cart. He cast a look up toward her window and she ducked back behind the curtain.

"A bit of shopping, I think." She tried not to let agitation bleed into her voice. "I liked Sanjay's bracelet so much, I want to look for a similar one to use as a companion piece."

Quinn laughed. "Only because you like the look and feel of it, I hope. You shouldn't be sucked into his fancy about protection and such. Hindus are a superstitious lot."

"Aren't we all?" she said softly. She had no doubt the red diamond was trying to curse her through her vision. If it was powerful enough to sense her presence through the mist of Seeing, she needed all the protection she could get. When she confronted the stone in real life, she'd feel safer dripping in silver and jet.

She rang for one of the hotel serving girls to act as her abigail.

"Why did you do that?" Quinn asked from the lavatory. As long as he was shaving, he left the door ajar so they could continue their conversation. "I'm always happy to help you."

"Yes, but your kind of help is more conducive to undressing than dressing." She kept the conversation light as she eased open one of Quinn's drawers and drew out the stocking filled with jewels. She pinched the smallest emerald and returned the stocking to the drawer exactly as she'd found it. With luck, Quinn wouldn't even miss it until they divided up the lot when they parted company.

Her chest constricted at that. Quinn had offered to marry her once. He'd probably thought better of it since then. If he were going to broach the subject of marriage again, he might have done it at breakfast when they'd settled on using a French letter in the future. There'd be no need to guard against pregnancy if she were his wife.

Quinn had fallen strangely silent in the lavatory. She started to speak to him, but the maid arrived and they disappeared behind the chinoiserie dressing screen together. She noticed Quinn had shut the lavatory door.

Once she was dressed and the chattering maid had left, Viola called out, "I'm leaving, Quinn."

The lavatory door opened and he emerged smelling of sandalwood and spice, but his handsome face was stony and unreadable. "Do you need money?" His voice was flat.

"Just fare for the hansom." She forced a smile. She'd tied the emerald into the corner of her handkerchief and stuffed it into her reticule. Even though it was a small stone, it weighed her down. "I'll warrant your credit is good at that jewelry shop."

"No doubt."

She turned to go, but he stopped her with a hand on her forearm. "No kiss good-bye?"

"Quinn, I'm only going shopping, not to Timbuktu." She stood on tiptoe and kissed his cheek, then hurried out the door before she lost her nerve and told him everything.

It was one thing for Willie to threaten her. She deserved it. But his note threatened Quinn well.

And yer frends.

Malice had shimmered in the malformed letters.

She doubted Willie could harm Quinn physically unless he surprised Quinn on a dark night with a whole gang at his back, but Willie could still make trouble for him. The military career in which Quinn had so distinguished himself probably wouldn't withstand a scandalous connection with a known jewel thief. Willie wouldn't be above turning her in to collect the reward, if he decided she was no longer useful to him.

It would mean her utter ruin.

And by association, Quinn's.

She emerged from the hotel, but didn't wave down a cab. Instead she walked toward the fruit seller. She didn't see Willie anywhere, but she felt the weight of eyes on her. She walked on.

He'd make himself known when it suited him.

She'd stolen from him! Quinn's fingers curled into fists.

Sanjay always warned she would, but he hadn't listened. He wouldn't have believed it, if he hadn't seen her do it, if he hadn't watched her reflection in his small shaving mirror. Cool as ice, she'd opened his drawer and helped herself to his stash of jewels.

He didn't stop to see how much she'd taken. He was too busy shadowing her from the hotel. She walked across the fashionable Parisian street as if she hadn't a care in the world. She was a vision in French lace and frippery.

By God, she should be. He'd paid enough for that bit of French folderol. The price of that ridiculous little hat alone would feed an Indian family for a month. He'd bought her a whole goddamned new wardrobe, hadn't he?

And she'd stolen from him.

She turned suddenly and looked over her shoulder, but he ducked into a bakery doorway. The aroma of fresh bread swirled over him, making him nauseous. The thought of food roiled his belly.

He trusted her. He half believed he *loved* her.

And she'd stolen from him.

Damn it all to hell, he'd have *given* her everything he had if she'd only asked.

He peered around the corner. Viola was on the move again. After a quick glance around, she turned down one of the narrower side streets which seemed to dead end into a decaying court surrounded by sagging tenements. It was lined with refuse and overlooked by rickety balconies of abandoned pieds à terre as the neighborhood shifted abruptly from respectable to seedy. He ducked into one of the buildings and shot up the stairs two at a time. He'd be able to watch her more easily from above.

His chest constricted. A woman alone was much safer on the broad thoroughfares than in the tangled spokes that branched off them. Even in broad daylight, a lady of quality had no business endangering herself by wandering the byways.

It wasn't safe.

But Viola wasn't the type to enjoy safe, he realized. She was unlike any woman he'd ever met. She broke into people's houses and stole their valuables. She wandered London at night, dressed as a man and reveling in the freedom it gave her. She unraveled the mysteries of a tumbler lock as fast as the canniest of light-fingered second-story men. And what lady would have made such enthusiastic love with him in the library after being interrupted in the ambassador's office?

Viola flirted with life on the edge of respectability. She reveled in danger and mayhem.

Why had he ever thought he could cage a bird like that?

He'd dressed her in the trappings of a lady. He'd claimed her as his wife before the expatriate society of Paris, but she was still a thief at heart.

As he crept out onto one of the balconies and looked down on her, he realized she'd certainly stolen his.

CHAPTER 18

"Wot ye got fer me, milady?" Willie demanded from behind an abandoned cart. He stepped around, blocking her way.

Viola dug into the reticule and came up with her hanky. Her fingers trembled as she untied the knot. "An uncut emerald. Untraceable. Gorgeous color. It's very fine."

She handed the jewel to him. "Now, this terminates our association."

Willie grinned and shoved the emerald into his trouser pocket. "Them's mighty fancy words for a simple man like me, but they make me think ye don't want to do business with me no more." His grin faded and his brows beetled in a terrifying frown. "I'd be beside myself if I felt ye didn't want to continue to make use of me services. I do terrible things when I get angry, milady. Terrible things."

"You forget yourself. I am the daughter of an earl." Viola straightened her posture and put on her haughtiest expression. Willie was just the sort of bully to whom one could not afford to show fear. "I will not be threatened by the likes of you."

"I wouldn't be so hoity-toity if I was you. Ye're naught but a common thief, milady. One step up from a light-skirt and not so very long a step at that, what with you cavorting about Paris in the company of a man ye haven't tied no knot with." Willie took a step closer. "And I didn't make no threat. It were a promise. Why, I could wring yer neck like a chicken if I was of a mind to."

Panic raking her spine, she backed away half a step. "We're in a public place."

"Not so public as all that. But the Frogs don't mind a spot o' trouble. They looks at it as entertainment. Don't ye mind how they lopped off all them noble's heads just 'cause they could? Damn me, if they didn't have the right idea."

He shot her a greasy smile. "But ye're worth more to me with yer head on yer shoulders. Lots more. The little green bauble ye brought me is just the down payment. If ye want to be quit of me for good, I can accommodate ye, but I need a last big haul for me troubles. Something to tide me over in me dotage. I want the rest of the lieutenant's jewels."

Viola's jaw gaped. She couldn't steal from Quinn. She didn't regard the emerald she'd lifted as a theft. More like an advance payment on what he'd owe her once they had the red diamond. There was honor of a sort among thieves. While Quinn was encouraging and even joining in her larceny, it wasn't for personal gain. He believed stealing the Blood of the Tiger was a sin mitigated by the greater good of restoring it to Sanjay's people.

He'd never forgive her if she actually stole from him.

"I can't do that."

"Yes, ye can and ye must, if ye don't want something bad to happen to the gentleman. Ye see, a bloke like me can always find fast friends to help him with a bit of skullduggery in a city like this."

In London, people disappeared all the time. It was easy to pretend such things didn't happen in the comfortable West End, even in her threadbare, not-quite-fashionable but still respectable part of it. But on the hardscrabble side of town, bodies washed up in the Thames or were discovered by a dustman in an alley and no one was ever punished for the crimes. It was an unpleasant truth she'd discovered when she first dipped her toe in a life of lawbreaking.

The seedy underbelly of Paris was probably no different.

"But if ye don't get me wot I want, don't worry. Ye can console yerself that the lieutenant won't suffer much," Willie said, his voice smarmy. "In fact, he'll never even see us comin'."

As soon as the words left his mouth, a blur dropped down from one of the balconies above them, landing on Willie. He and his assailant rolled on the dirt-clogged cobbles in a tangle of arms and legs. After a few moments' scuffle, Willie was pinned beneath the big man, who sat astraddle his chest, pummeling the lights out of him.

"Quinn!" Viola was relieved and horrified in equal measure. He must have tailed her to that squalid little lane. Judging by the growled threats proceeding from his mouth, he'd overheard much of the exchange with her fence.

"And if you ever"—Quinn stopped throwing bruising punches and wrapped his fingers around Willie's beefy throat—"bother the lady again—"

Willie made gagging noises and tried to buck Quinn off, but his movements grew more sluggish as his air supply dwindled. His face turned an alarming shade of purple before Quinn released him.

"There won't be a hole deep enough for you to hide in, you miserable piece of filth." Disgust emanating from every pore, Quinn climbed off Willie and stood over him, lip curled. "If you try to make trouble for Lady Viola, if I ever hear your name connected with hers, if I so much as see your ugly face again, make no mistake, I will kill you."

Rage rolled off him in barely contained waves. Viola didn't doubt Quinn's words for an instant. She knew in his capacity as a soldier, he'd probably killed his share of men in battle.

Murder—killing of a very different sort—glinted in his gray eyes.

He bent over and fished the emerald from Willie's pocket. "No man steals what's mine."

Willie gasped for air like a carp on the riverbank and offered no resistance.

Quinn shot a glare at Viola that clearly said *And no woman steals from me either.*

He grasped her elbow and whipped her around, dragging her out of the narrow lane and back onto the broad thoroughfare. She had to trot to keep up with his determined stride.

"Quinn, please, you're hurting my—"

"Madam, for your own safety, I suggest you refrain from speech," he said, tight-lipped. He didn't release her, but he eased his hold a bit.

Viola suspected she'd bruise all the same.

He hustled her down the street to their hotel, through the busy lobby and up to their suite without another word or a single direct glance at her. She might have been no more important than an oversized carpet bag he was forced to lug. Once he slammed the door and locked it behind them, he turned the full force of his angry gray gaze on her. "What the hell was that about?"

"If you can't keep a civil tongue in your head, we have nothing to discuss," she said primly and perched on one of the wing chairs.

"Like hell we don't." He leaned both hands on the arms of the chair, forcing her into the tufted back. "Civil, you say? You steal from me bold as brass. You consort with the lowest sort of riffraff, making God knows what kind of Faustian deal, and yet, you expect me to be civil?"

She lifted her chin. "Did it occur to you that my actions were solely for your protection?"

"Oh, yes. I heard the bugger's threats, but I can't believe

you'd take them seriously. Do you think I can't take care of myself? And you?"

"No one can be eternally vigilant."

"Watch me," he said through clenched teeth. "It still doesn't give you the right to steal from me."

"I didn't steal from you. By rights, half those jewels in that stocking belong to me. Or at least they will once we find the diamond. I merely took a small portion of what is mine in advance."

"Without so much as a by-your-leave." He shook his head and began to pace the small area like a caged leopard. "A bit presumptuous of you, your ladyship, since we've yet to locate the stone. We don't even know we'll find Baaghh kaa kkhuun in Hanover once we get there."

She knew with certainty they would, but she refused to tell him how. If he was this upset over the mundane aspects of her thieving abilities, how would he react to the news that she could hear the voices of gemstones and receive visions from them?

"Who was that fellow?" Quinn demanded.

"My fence," she admitted, slumping a bit under his dark scowl. "Well, a thief can't very well convert stolen goods into cash without one, can she?"

"You mean the man followed you from London?" His mouth tightened in a hard line. "Why did you tell him where you were going?"

"I didn't tell him. I had to visit his shop to sell that pearl the day we sailed. My mother needed the money before I left, but I never breathed a word about Paris or the red diamond. I swear it," she said miserably. "Willie has ways of finding things out."

"So you gave him the emerald to . . . what? Appease him?" Quinn raked a hand through his hair so hard, Viola expected to see clumps of his dark curls come out, stuck between his fingers. "Even if you gave him everything we have, it wouldn't be enough. Fellows of his ilk are never satisfied."

Viola templed fingers in her lap and fixed her gaze on them. Quinn was right. Willie would always threaten, always try to blackmail her.

"How did you know he was here?"

"He sent a note." Quinn didn't need to know she'd run into Willie in Paris once before, when she was attempting to leave him.

"How does he know I possess any gemstones in the first place?"

"I discussed it with Willie before I broke into your town house. He has a friend who knows where all the secret vaults are built into the homes on your street. How else do you think I was able locate the wall safe so quickly?" she said wearily. "Besides, if you didn't want anyone to know about it, you shouldn't have made it known at your dinner party that you had a fistful of jewels."

"I was trying to draw out the Mayfair Jewel Thief at the time."

"Which you did quite successfully. You were just expecting the thief to be a man."

He sank into the wing chair opposite her. "It would have made matters a damn sight easier."

In her mind, Viola heard her father's voice, lamenting that she had not been the son he'd hoped for. It was his complaint all through her childhood and she hated it. God had made her female. It wasn't her fault, then or now.

"How unfortunate. I'm sorry my gender is such an inconvenience to you." Acid crept into her tone.

"I didn't say that."

"The fact that I'm female worked very well for you when we were caught in the ambassador's office. But I suppose you could've dropped a gentleman thief's trousers and buggered him just as easily. Come to think of it, that might have been an even better distraction for the guard."

"Viola!"

He was shocked at her vulgarity. So be it. She was feeling rather vulgar at the moment.

"Swiving one's wife—excuse me, one's pretend wife—isn't nearly as distracting as being caught with a male lover. So once again, my femininity is a detriment."

Choler crept up his neck like a red rash. His eyes glittered dangerously. She was making him angrier, but she didn't care. She could be angry too.

"I didn't say I wished you were a man," he said, clipping his words.

"It was implied."

"Well, imply this." He leaned forward, elbows on his knees. "From now on, you're not going anywhere without me."

"I will not be hedged about as if I were a child."

"If you were a child, I'd take you over my knee and warm your bum good and proper," Quinn said, his gray eyes blazing. "I still haven't abandoned the idea completely, so don't tempt me further."

The only reason she'd taken the emerald to Willie was to protect Quinn. Why couldn't he give her the least bit of credit for good intentions? "You don't trust me."

"Trust has nothing to do with it. I'm trying to protect you, you little ninny." His voice was rough and throaty. "Besides, trust is earned. And you've not done anything to warrant it this day."

He was a fine one to talk about trust. Hadn't she given him the benefit of the doubt after seeing a vision that all but proved him guilty as Cain?

She almost threw her knowledge in his face. But then she'd have to explain about her gift and how she'd seen that horrific vision at the lake. She wasn't prepared to share that part of herself with him.

Not when he wouldn't accept the part she already had shared.

Quinn rose to his feet. "Come. We haven't any more time to waste on this."

Oh, yes, let us not squander time on anything so unimportant as what we are to each other. Viola bit her tongue to keep the bitter words from flying out.

"We have some business to attend to," he said.

"Such as?"

"We still need passage on a coach bound for the German territories." He offered her his hand. She ignored it and rose without his assistance. "And I believe you still want that jet and silver set, or was that just a ruse to get out of the hotel?"

"No, I fully intended to visit the jewelers after I concluded my business with Willie," she said stonily. "You have credit I can exploit, you see."

If he was determined to think the worst of her, by God, she'd show him the worst.

He looked at her sharply. "Yes, I do see. Maybe for the first time."

"Well, let's be off then." She rose, smoothing a strand of hair behind her ear. "At least we won't need to stop by the apothecary."

"Oh?"

"You don't need any French letters," she said with a poisonous smile. "You won't have cause to use them."

CHAPTER 19

When they halted at one of the first coaching inns on the road to Hanover, they were overtaken by Lord Cowley's grand equipage and entourage. Through the servant's grapevine, Sanjay learned the British ambassador to France was on his way to visit the House of Hanover to meet with emissaries from Prince Albert.

"It's a strong indication that we're right about the diamond traveling through Hanover," Quinn said.

It was one of the few things he said at all as he and Viola bounced along in the enclosed carriage day after day. By night, he left Viola alone in the chamber he let for them at each coaching inn and slept in the common room with the travelers who were too poor to afford private accommodations. The one exception was when they caught up to the ambassador in Cologne and happened to overnight in the same inn.

Then Quinn stayed in the room with Viola, but spent the night sleeping on a pallet across the threshold instead of beside her in the bed. Viola had a restless night, fisting her sheets in frustration while Quinn's soft breathing kept her from finding sleep. Her only consolation was that he looked as weary the next morning as she felt.

While they waited for Sanjay to arrive with their breakfast, she watched him in the vanity mirror as she brushed out her hair. Quinn glanced at her several times, but jerked his gaze away each time she caught him at it.

She'd told Quinn she wouldn't have a marriage of deadly silence. She couldn't abide it in a pretend marriage either.

"Is it because of Neville?" she finally asked.

"What?"

"Did you spend the night in this room with me because you know Neville Beauchamp is here at this inn?"

He frowned and studied the plank floor between his boot tips. "I didn't want him bothering you."

"He doesn't bother me. I wouldn't allow him to *bother* me. There's no love lost between us." She turned around and leaned an arm over the straight back of her chair. "Has it occurred to you that he might be useful?"

"How so?"

"Once we reach Hanover, lifting the diamond will be much easier if we stay in the same place the ambassador is staying. That will undoubtedly also be where the diamond's courier will stop to meet Prince Albert's people. If we're in residence, we can scout out the situation before we commit to the theft."

She turned back to the mirror, gathered her hair and twirled it into a quick French twist. Jabbing in a handful of hairpins to hold it place, she plucked a few strands loose to curl at her temples and in front of her ears. It wasn't the most artful coiffure, but it would do.

"Your rank and title may get us an invitation to dinner," she said. "But Neville could arrange for us to stay under the same roof as the diamond."

"At what cost?" he asked sullenly.

She glared at his reflection. "I don't intend to bed him in exchange for an invitation to a house party, if that's what you mean."

What a light-skirt he must think her!

"I didn't—"

"What did you mean then?" she snapped.

"He hurt you once. I don't want you beholden to him. It puts him in a position to hurt you again."

Her heart warmed to him, but she tamped the sensation down. If she let herself lean on him too much, she'd come to need him and she couldn't afford that. No one had tried to protect her since her father died. Not her cousin Jerome, the new earl. Certainly not Neville. But Quinn obviously didn't realize he hurt her by mistrusting her.

"I'm a grown woman, Quinn." She turned back to the mirror to fasten the clasps on her new silver and jet earbobs. Now that she'd discovered there was a stone she could wear without fear, she found she enjoyed jewelry. "I can look after myself."

He bent and placed a soft kiss on the side of her neck. She couldn't bring herself to pull away. His warm breath feathered over her skin and curled behind her ear. "But what if I want to look after you?"

If he could be made to need her, would it be so bad to need him?

When she didn't answer, he kissed her neck again, reaching around to fold his arms across her chest in a snug embrace.

Oh, how she'd missed the warmth of him, the solid hardness of his body. She turned her head and he took her lips, slanting his mouth over hers in a soft, wet kiss.

His kiss said he wanted to make things right between them. His tongue begged forgiveness, teasing along the seam of her lips. She granted him absolution, parting her lips and suckling his tongue softly. She reached up to palm his cheeks.

He unfastened her high collar, one seed pearl button at a time, until the tops of her breasts were bared. Then he plunged a hand beneath her lacy chemise and corset to claim her. Her nipple hardened and ached. She moaned into his mouth as he began unhooking the front clasps of her corset with his other hand.

Viola's body was making her choices once again. It had ended disastrously last time, but she didn't have the heart to resist. Besides, Quinn was not Neville.

"Those are talented fingers you have there, sir," she said when their mouths parted for an instant. "Perhaps I should teach you the mysteries of a tumbler lock."

"I can think of better uses for them at the moment." He demonstrated by drawing out both her breasts and thumbing her nipples in slow circles.

Viola felt herself being sucked into that hot dark place again, where none of the rules of sanity applied, but before she let him lead her there, she had to settle something between them. She covered his hands with hers to still them.

"Will you trust me to see Neville alone long enough to wangle an invitation for us?"

"That depends." He bent to drop a kiss on her breast, whirling his tongue on a small patch of exposed flesh between their splayed fingers. "Will you let me pull out your pins and take down your hair?"

She didn't mistake his real question. "We haven't any French letter."

"There are ways for us to please each other that don't require one," he said huskily. "Let me show you, Viola. Trust me for this."

She'd trust him with anything. She pulled out the first pin and a long lock tumbled down over her left breast. "I didn't really do a good job on this style in any case."

He smiled and pulled out the rest of the hairpins. He smoothed her hair over her shoulders. "It looked fine, but I love it down best."

"Hardly appropriate for public display."

He shook it out, feasting his eyes on the long auburn locks.

"I wouldn't want your hair on public display. Call me greedy, but I like being the only one to see you like this." He raised her to her feet and went to work on her buttons and laces again. "This way when you're all done up in public, I can look at you and imagine you as you really are."

"So you think you know how I really am?"

"Probably not. Not yet," he amended. "How much can anyone really know of another person? Only what they let us see."

Or what I see when I touch your signet ring, she thought guiltily. She'd never deliberately used her gift to spy on another person that way before. When she handled a gem, a vision came unbidden, not sought out. Perhaps that was why the images at the lake were so terrifyingly immediate, why she'd seen it all through Reggie's dying eyes. Now that she thought about it, what she'd done had been a terrible violation of Quinn.

And it had only brought her doubt and mistrust.

"It takes a great deal of time to know another person," she said. With or without aid from a gemstone's stored memory.

"But I'm willing to take the time to know you, Viola."

When Sanjay rapped on the door a few moments later, he was greeted with Quinn's surly growl and told not to bother with a breakfast tray.

"The lady and I will break our fast later." Quinn's voice was ragged and Sanjay heard the telltale creak of a bed frame.

"As you will, sahib." The prince smiled. It had saddened him to see the rift between the pair, especially since he'd revised his opinion of the lady upward. His friend had deprived himself of Lady Viola's company long enough and he suspected Quinn was breaking that fast now.

About time, my friend, he thought as he headed back down to the kitchen with the tray. *About bloody good time.*

Quinn had imagined Viola's mouth on his cock several times. She'd delivered a few licks and teasing kisses to that part of him during their previous loveplay, but she'd never taken him in.

Until now.

His imaginings couldn't begin to compare with reality.

Quinn's world dissolved in the warm wetness of her mouth. The soft grate of her teeth against the head of his cock, the swirl of her tongue over the rough patch of skin that was so ultrasensitive. The suction. The saliva. He was drowning in her and not caring a whit.

Of course, he'd given as good as he was getting.

He'd insisted on pleasuring her first. Well, that was a little dishonest because it was his pleasure to do it. Seeing her brought to incoherent need made him feel achingly alive.

And giving her bliss gave him a reason to keep breathing.

When she turned her mouth on him, without him asking her to, he thought his heart would leap out of his chest.

He closed his eyes, the better to revel in the delicious sensations, all the while scrolling images of Viola across his mind's eye—her whole body glistening with a light sheen of perspiration, as her mouth went passion-slack; the way her breasts thrust upward when she arched her back; the incredible secret view of her delicate parts when she spread her legs, knees lolling to the sides, giving herself over to him completely.

How like a flower she was, all soft petaled and quivering. How sweet when he licked at her wet little puss. He'd rolled his tongue and delved deep.

When he'd pressed his teeth against her "pearl" she'd come, her inner walls clenching around his tongue in fierce pulses.

His scrotum tightened at the memory.

He opened his eyes and watched her lavish him with her tongue. She worked with diligence, like a beautiful cat running her tongue over his length. She made an appreciative noise, as if he tasted better than a baguette.

"I can't . . . hold back . . . much longer," he warned her.

She swirled her tongue over the head. She sucked his aching spot, still turning her wide eyes toward him to see how what she did affected him. "Don't hold back."

She grasped his rod and slipped her mouth over him, taking him as deeply as she could. Then she cupped his bag with one hand, fondling his balls. His muscles tensed. Her fingers eased down to massage the spot just behind his scrotum.

His eyes rolled back and the top of his head nearly flew off. He came in her mouth, throbbing against her soft palate. When the last pulse faded, she sat up, an incongruously angelic smile on her face. What she'd done to him was wickedness itself, but he wallowed in it. To be accepted so completely, to be wanted in total—his heart galloped in his chest at the unwarranted grace of her mode of loving.

"You were right, Quinn," she whispered as she draped herself over him.

He had no idea what she meant and didn't think his voice would work in any case. So he pressed a kiss to her lips and tasted himself, musk and salt all swirled with her natural sweetness.

Where was the dividing line between them? He couldn't find one. They were more firmly joined than he had a right to hope for.

She nuzzled his neck and sighed. "We really don't need a French letter, do we?"

CHAPTER 20

Hanover was a charming city of tall half-timbered houses and cobbled streets. Ale houses had brewed their own special recipes for three hundred years in the shadow of massive *Marktkirche*, the church that had safeguarded the town's souls since the 1400s. The thriving market was filled with produce from neighboring farms as well as more exotic wares.

The city was a long-standing member of the Hanseatic League, the medieval trading guild. Goods from a thousand ships were unloaded at Bremen and carted or towed on river barges to Hanover's bustling heart.

Somehow in that frenetic city, Quinn and Viola had to finagle a chance meeting with Neville Beauchamp, plague take him.

"I still say catching the man at the market would answer our needs better." Quinn led Viola through a section of rosebushes, their tight buds beginning to uncurl enough to hint at the blossom's color, but not enough to release their perfume.

He wasn't immune to natural beauty, but neither did he seek it out particularly. The Royal Gardens of *Herrenhausen* were all well and good, but not the sort of place a man might make a point to visit unless he was squiring a woman on his arm. However, having Viola at his side made up for any inconvenience. "You're sure Beauchamp will turn up here?"

"I'm certain." They took a turn around the beds of tulips and daffodils, whose drooping heads were at the end of their blooming cycle. "Neville fancies himself something of an amateur botanist. Sanjay tailed him this morning in the market. Neville was arranging for additional provisions for the ambassador's entourage to be delivered to the *schloss* at Celle where they are staying. He wouldn't be at leisure to speak to me while he was working."

"Beauchamp isn't that industrious," Quinn said with assurance, wishing Viola weren't on first name terms with the man. He knew Neville Beauchamp's type, always sniffing around women's skirts like a dog looking for the nearest bitch in heat. "He'd make time to speak with you."

She smiled up at him, obviously taking his gruff statement as a compliment of sorts. He ached to plant a kiss at the upturned corner of her mouth, but she'd already warned him to behave himself when he tried to pull her behind a lilac bush earlier.

"The fact that Neville is provisioning the castle means they must intend to stay in Celle for a while. Which tells me the diamond and the prince's delegation isn't there yet. Even though I'm sure he's frightfully busy, Neville won't be able to resist the Royal Gardens long."

Quinn hoped not. The sooner Viola had her "chance" meeting with the man and teased out the invitation to stay at the schloss where the ambassador was staying, the better. Quinn's gut clenched at the thought of her spending any time at all with Beauchamp, but he couldn't fault the logic of her plan. Staying at the same drafty old castle the diamond would pass through made perfect sense.

"Oh, there he is," Viola said.

Neville alighted from a hired gig, a sporty little conveyance that would have caught plenty of eyes in Hyde Park. His gaze swept over the gardens with as much joy as a glutton surveying a feast.

"Time for my 'husband' to make himself scarce." Viola nudged him with her elbow.

Quinn reluctantly left her on the path, disappearing behind a lush wall of ornamental grasses. Though he was perfectly hidden in the dense foliage, he could see through the greenery quite well.

So this is how the tiger feels watching his prey from the tall grass, Quinn thought, glaring at Beauchamp so hard he wondered that the man didn't feel the vehement heat. If Neville put so much as one toe out of line with Viola, Quinn would pounce.

Not that he had a real right to protect her. Though they'd made world-altering love several times, the fact that she'd turned down his proposal of marriage still stung. He hadn't realized when he'd made the offer that her answer meant so much to him.

He'd never gathered his courage to broach the subject again. Not when he wasn't sure what her answer would be. A second *no* would be the last. He sheltered behind their sham marriage as his excuse for trying to keep her from renewing her acquaintance with her old beau.

Viola meandered in Neville's direction, careful to keep her attention on the plantings. When she was near enough to be sure Beauchamp would notice her, she stopped and fanned herself languidly.

"Doing it a bit too brown, aren't you, girl?" Quinn murmured. "It's not that hot a day."

But the graceful motion of the fan was all it took to draw Beauchamp's eye to her.

Neville called out and hurried to her side. Quinn was too far away to hear the conversation, but he could read the lust on the man's face well enough.

He didn't merely stand near Viola. He hovered over her. She was adept at maintaining a discreet distance, but she had to lead him a delicate dance as they moved along the graveled pathway.

Quinn shifted from one place of concealment to another, careful to keep them in sight. His gut roiled. He'd scrambled from one rocky outcropping to the next avoiding Afghani tribesmen in the Khyber Pass with less agitation.

Beauchamp placed a possessive hand on the small of Viola's back to steer her toward a particular sort of peony that wasn't even in bloom yet. He captured her hand and pressed her gloved fingers to his lips.

Quinn gritted his teeth so hard he thought he might crack a molar. He reminded himself why it was so important to retrieve the Blood of the Tiger for Sanjay's people. He tried to summon his old outrage at the Doctrine of Lapse. The cries of the mad holy men rang in his ears and he knew he ought to fear for the innocent British women and children in the cantonments of India, unless the diamond was returned and the unrest could be quelled before it erupted into a full-blown rebellion.

But all he could see was Viola, playing a dangerous game with a man who'd hurt her once. If she still harbored tender feelings for Beauchamp, she was bound for sorrow. He had already proven himself a cad, but if she was set on him, Quinn didn't know how he could protect her heart.

Or his, he realized with a start. The thought of her with another man made his eyes burn.

Viola dropped her handkerchief and Beauchamp bent to retrieve it. It was the signal. She'd wangled the invitation and it was safe for Quinn to join them.

He returned to the path and sauntered in their direction with studied nonchalance. "Ah, there you are, my dear." He gave Neville a curt nod. "Beauchamp."

Neville returned his surly courtesy.

"Isn't it wonderful, darling?" Viola cooed. "Mr. Beauchamp has invited us to stay at the castle at Celle. The ambassador's party is there so we won't lack for good English conversation over dinner."

Quinn knew he was expected to speak, so he ground out the words. "Damned decent of you, Beauchamp. Bratwurst and pig's knuckles, I can manage. Conversing in German is beyond me." Then something made him turn to Viola. "Are you sure you wish to remove from our hotel? Castles are so drafty and I wouldn't want you to catch a chill."

She tossed him a bewildered glance. "Of course, dear. Who wouldn't want to visit such a charming old place? A castle may be drafty, but I'm sure it simply reeks of romance."

Neville's smarmy smile confirmed that was precisely his hope. Quinn resisted the urge to knock the grin from his face but it required serious effort.

Viola promised Neville they'd start for the castle that very afternoon and bid him good-bye. Quinn caught a flicker of lusty potential in Beauchamp's eyes when he made his too-long-to–be-proper obeisance over her gloved hand.

She strolled away on Quinn's arm, laughing and chattering about the budding garden for the benefit of any who might be curious about them.

But Quinn couldn't help wondering what Viola had promised Neville in exchange for the invitation to the castle. His pride wouldn't allow him to ask.

Whatever it was, he'd make sure she was never alone with Beauchamp long enough to make good on it.

The castle at Celle was located several hours' drive from Hanover, over rutted roads that were barely more than cart paths. Quinn allowed that his perception might be a bit colored by his generally surly mood, but the fact that Viola was so blithe about recent developments did nothing to ease his disquiet. She was almost giddy about staying under the same roof as that bounder Beauchamp.

"Neville has promised to give us a tour of the place as soon as we're settled," she said as they jostled over a particularly bumpy stretch of roadway.

Bugger Neville. "We're going there for the diamond, not for sightseeing," Quinn grumbled.

"If we know our way around the castle, it'll make pinching the stone that much easier once it arrives. Neville's providing us with exactly what we need." She rolled her eyes at him. "What's gotten into you, Quinn? You're being a regular muttonhead."

"Maybe I'm tired of hearing 'Neville this' and 'Neville that.' He's not doing this out of the goodness of his heart. It's clear to anyone with eyes what his game really is."

She cocked her head at him. "If I didn't know better, I'd say you're jealous."

"Of him? Don't be ridiculous. I just don't know how you can stand the sight of him. Given your history with the man."

She laced her fingers and stared out the window at the rolling meadows, bright with the pale green of spring. "So that's it. *You* can't bear my history with him."

"No, it's just—"

"Correct me if I am wrong"—her tone was icy and her knuckles whitened as she drew her fingers tighter together— "but I have the distinct impression I am not the first woman you've taken to your bed."

"No, of course not, but that's not what I—"

"So a man may have as many amours as he pleases, but God help the woman who cannot present him with a maidenhead the first time he's with her," she said, tight-lipped.

"That's not important to me. What happened before we met is none of my business." That wasn't strictly the truth. He was jealous of every man who'd ever looked sideways at her, but she didn't need to hear that. "I only care that you not be hurt now. Viola, I will never reproach you for the past."

She looked at him then, her hazel eyes welling. "But what if *I* reproach me?" she said miserably.

"Don't." He gathered her up and pulled her onto his lap. His chest constricted when she came willingly. "Will it make you feel better if I tell you I wish you'd been my first too?"

"You do?"

Surprisingly, that *was* the truth.

He'd tumbled a few willing serving girls in his youth. There'd been a manic summer when he first discovered the miracles his cock could perform. His groin had given him no peace. At the sight of a curved waist or a slim ankle, only mindless rutting or a few minutes behind a shed with his own hand would ease his complaint.

Once he finished school, he shipped out to India, where he'd learned control and the finer points of loving from Pad-maa. Those couplings were studied and strangely sterile. Almost as if he were standing at stud, trained to perform. During his sessions with the Indian courtesan, he seemed to hover outside his own body and watch while she put him through his paces.

With Viola, it was different. She reached inside him and touched the part of him he thought no one else could bear. Perhaps it was because she didn't really know yet.

He kissed her temple. "I do wish you'd been my only one. And I wish I'd been yours. But since there's nothing we can do about that, I suggest we forget it."

"We could pretend, I suppose," she said, blinking hard to keep the tears in her over-bright eyes. "We could pretend that there had never been anyone else for either of us."

"We could," he agreed.

She snuggled deeper into his embrace and he was suddenly

glad for the jostling bumps of the ride. His cock rose to meet her soft bum, straining against his smallclothes and trousers with as much erotic hope as the most callow youth.

"So if we were both younger and more impetuous and eager to learn," she said softly, "what would we do on a long ride in an enclosed coach?"

"First, I'd say it'd be important for us to remain more or less fully clothed. After all, one never knows when a coach might come to a halt," Quinn said as he untied the bow under her chin and removed her straw bonnet. "But as a younger, more impetuous and eager-to-learn fellow, I'd be dying to see your breasts."

She smiled naughtily at him. "You mean you're not dying to see them now?"

"You know better than that. I'd be delirious if you put them on display at all times." If no one else but he were about to see them, of course.

He claimed her mouth and began working the mother-of-pearl buttons marching down the front of her bodice. The high, tight collar parted, revealing the pale, soft skin of her neck. He kissed his way down to the slight indentation at the base of her throat.

Her breath hitched as his fingers continued to work the buttons till her corset and lacy chemise were bared. He tugged at the bow holding the chemise closed. Once loosened, the thin garment fell away, revealing the soft mounds of her breasts straining above the whalebone corset.

"Beautiful," he murmured, running his fingertips over her silky skin and teasing the shadowed hollow between her breasts.

She bit her lip, but didn't make any effort to shield herself from his gaze.

He steadied her on his lap, lavishing kisses on her breasts and gently tugging at the top of the corset with his free hand. He exposed a taut pink nipple, and settled her breast on the stiff lip of the corset. Then he did the same for the other one till they were framed by the blue serge of her traveling ensemble.

"There you are." He leaned back to survey his handiwork. He pinched one of the pink buds. She gasped. The little nub puckered above its darker rose areola as if begging for more impudent play. His cock throbbed and he imagined rubbing it in the soft hollow between her breasts. "You have, without doubt, the loveliest bosom in England."

"We're not in England," she said, her tone breathy.

"I'd have said the world, but I feared you'd think I was exaggerating so you'd allow me to take more liberties." He bent to take a nipple between his teeth and bit down lightly.

An involuntary moan escaped her.

"Take all the liberties you like, Quinn."

CHAPTER 21

Her whole body hummed with anticipation. Her nipples ached and when Quinn plucked them, she jerked at the zing of longing that streaked through her. She no longer cared that she was behaving in a shockingly fast manner.

Wanton, really.

All that mattered was Quinn's mouth on her skin, his breath raising the small hairs on her nape, his skillful hands playing her body like the finest virtuoso.

Her corset's boning jabbed under her breasts in a tender spot. The slight pain was buried under the torrent of sensations that washed over her simply because her breasts were exposed and Quinn was fairly worshipping them.

How perfectly wicked to imagine running about with them out like this all the time.

Quinn had put the idea in her head, but she found going about her normal life bare-breasted was a tantalizing prospect to consider while he suckled and licked at them.

"What would it be like to ride a horse with my breasts bared?" she murmured.

"You'd be dazzling. A charging Amazon"—Quinn released her nipple long enough to say—"with sunlight kissing your bouncing bosom and wind whipping past your nipples."

He whorled his tongue over the tight bud and blew his warm breath across her charged flesh to demonstrate. She shivered with delight.

"What if I were to stroll along Hyde Park with my charms thus displayed?"

"You'd cause a sensation in short order." He laughed. "There'd be a surge in traffic of all sorts. Who knows? You might start a new fashion, but you'd have to arrange your parasol to keep your bosom shaded lest it freckle unbecomingly."

"You dislike freckles?"

"I misspoke." He kissed her neck and nuzzled her earlobe while he rolled a nipple between his thumb and forefinger. Warm moisture gathered between her legs. "If *your* breasts were freckled, I'm certain they'd be entirely fetching. Soon all the best Society would wear their bosoms with spots even if they had to be drawn on each morning with a stick of charcoal."

She giggled at that. "How perfectly scandalized my modiste will be if I ask her to alter my wardrobe to bare my breasts at all times."

"Seek out a French seamstress," he advised soberly. "The French are, in all matters of the flesh, far more worldly and less easily shocked."

He bent his head to lavish attention on her breasts once more. Viola fought the downward pull in her groin. If Quinn had taught her anything, it was that delay meant delight and she was enjoying their nonsensical lovetalk.

"But perhaps it need not be my whole breast on display," she suggested as she arched into his mouth. He suckled till she made a helpless little moan.

"Speaking for the male of the species, I cannot support anything less than baring your entire bosom." He cupped her breast in his palm and thrummed her nipple, taunting and teasing it into an aching peak. "I'm growing exceedingly fond of the fashion concept of an open bodice."

The hard ridge of him pressing against her bum was solid proof of his fondness.

"What if the neckline of my gown were simply cut a bit lower?" She drew a thumb across her bosom beneath both nipples. "Just low enough to make sure my nipples were visible above a froth of lace?"

Quinn met her gaze and his storm-gray eyes glinted with dark fire. "What a little minx you're becoming."

"And do you like minxes?"

"More than breathing." He dipped his head and suckled her again. A low drumbeat throbbed between her legs.

"Or perhaps my nipples might only be visible at certain angles so I might pretend I'm unaware of the sensation I'm causing."

"How considerate, milady," Quinn said, as he reached under her skirts and rifled through the layers of her petticoats. "It's kind of you to forewarn me of your innate wickedness."

His hand found her knee and slid up her thigh. Her legs parted slightly of their own accord. She pressed her lips to the crown of his head since he'd bent to cover her breasts with kisses once more.

"My wickedness is not innate. You must take credit for some of it," she said breathlessly when his fingers found the slit in the crotch of her all-in-one. "You make me . . ."

Quinn lifted his head and watched her intently as he began playing a lover's game on her hot mound. She was so slick and wet, his fingers slid between her legs with languid ease.

"I make you what?" he prompted.

"Feel outrageous things," she admitted as her head fell back with a sigh. He trailed a row of kisses along her neck and delight shivered over her whole body while his fingertips teased along her intimate folds. "Think outrageous things."

"Like what?" He circled her little sensitive spot, which had risen to his touch, with maddening slowness.

She forced her mouth to form words, but his stroking was

making conscious thought more difficult by the moment. "I picture myself in a formal assembly. I dip a low curtsy to the ambassador with the rosy tips of my breasts winking at him, bold as brass."

Quinn's fingers moved with more speed and increased pressure right where she needed him. Her insides tightened, coiling for release.

"His monocle will no doubt slip from his rheumy eye in surprise, but I won't even blush."

"Jezebel," he murmured as if it were an endearment. Quinn slipped a finger inside her to stroke her slick inner walls while his thumb continued to rub her spot.

"My nipples will do the blushing for me," she said, rocking her pelvis into his questing hand. She cried out when Quinn bit down on one of her tight pink buds. Viola dissolved in heat and friction and blinding need. She spiraled downward, nearly there, nearly incoherent with need, but he seemed to enjoy her naughty thoughts, so she went on. "I throb under the appalled, . . . roused, . . . unblinking gaze . . . of everyone . . . in the room."

"Everyone," he repeated. Quinn's hand stopped and he sat up straight. His face was stone. "Everyone like Beauchamp, you mean."

She suppressed a sob. She'd been so close. "No, I didn't . . . Quinn, there's nothing . . . I was just . . . ."

Her body screamed at him, begging him to finish her, but she knew he couldn't hear it. She teetered on the ledge of a precipice, unable to stay as she was, unable to tumble over. A tear of frustration slid down her cheek and she tasted salt when it found the corner of her mouth. He pressed a kiss on that juncture of smooth skin and moist intimacy.

Then he cupped her sex with his whole hand and the firm pressure was all she needed to push her over the edge. She pulsed into his palm as her insides unraveled. He cradled her head against his chest with his free hand, crooning urgent endearments in some language she couldn't understand, while her body shuddered with the force of her release.

When she settled, he continued to hold her, rocking her in time with the movement of the coach. Their breathing fell into rhythm with each other.

"I'm an ass," he finally said, breaking the silence.

She lifted her head so she could look at him squarely. "Not that I'm contradicting you, but why do *you* think so?"

"You were having a harmless little fantasy and I ruined it for you."

She lifted one shoulder in a small shrug and her lips twitched in a smile. "It wasn't completely ruined."

"I don't share well, love. I can't bear the thought of anyone else seeing you like this, anyone else holding you while you—"

She palmed his cheeks. "No one else has ever made me feel the things you do, Quinn."

"Truly?"

"Truly."

The coach slowed. Viola slid off Quinn's lap and peeked out a slit in the curtains at the sleepy little village of Celle. Their coach lumbered through the narrow lanes, barely able to squeeze through in spots. Viola could have snatched a posy from the window boxes as they passed if she'd wished.

A blindingly white lime-washed castle loomed over the cluster of thatch-roofed homes.

"We're nearly there," she said covering his bulging groin with her palm. "I'm sorry to leave you so dissatisfied."

"Not dissatisfied. I prefer to think of my current state as hopeful."

He was lying, of course, but he did it with such charm she couldn't help smiling at him.

"Hope is a good quality in a man."

"Then I shall try to remain hopeful," he said with a wicked grin. "But if we are nearly there, we need to put you back together. However delicious it may be for me to enjoy your bare breasts, I don't want to extend that pleasure to others."

He wanted her only for himself. It wasn't a declaration of undying love, but her heart warmed to his words.

He eased her breasts back beneath her corset and tied up her chemise. She was just fastening the last button at her neck and retying the bow of her bonnet when the coach rumbled to a stop.

Quinn opened the door and handed her down from the coach. The moat had been filled in so there was no drawbridge to cross. They had already entered the central courtyard and were stopped in the center of the bailey, a broad parade ground surrounded by the outer castle walls. A fair complement of Hessian soldiers patrolled the top of the curtain wall and manned the turrets at each of the four corners. A loud thud told Viola the portcullis had been lowered behind them.

"There you are!" Neville emerged from one of the many doors opening onto the bailey and hurried toward them with a pair of liveried footmen flanking him. He snapped his fingers and the servants unloaded Viola and Quinn's baggage from the carriage boot. "Welcome to Celle."

Viola smiled and nodded her thanks. After Quinn's display of jealousy, she didn't want to add fuel to that fire with a more effusive display of gratitude.

"You didn't bring your Indian servant?" Neville asked Viola.

"Sanjay is in Hanover, waiting for a telegram from one of my regimental friends," Quinn said, yanking away from her the opportunity to answer Neville.

She stifled her irritation at his high-handedness.

"The telegram is late and we nearly delayed our trip to Celle on account of it," she told Neville. "But we're glad to be here now."

Every third day or so, Quinn received a *tar* from a Lt. Worthington with news about developments in India. The lieutenant had missed the last designated day for a missive and

Viola suspected Quinn worried over it, though he said little about it beyond making excuses for his distant friend.

"My servant will rejoin us once he collects the telegram coming from Delhi," Quinn explained.

Neville curled his lip slightly. "Still reliving your glory days in the Gorgeous East? Well, it may interest you to know we're expecting a fellow who's come directly from India any day now. Perhaps Mr. Chesterton can sate your need for news of the exotic."

Viola and Quinn exchanged a quick glance. Based on her vision from the ruby in the ambassador's office, she'd been certain the diamond would come through Hanover. Now Quinn was, too.

"In the meantime, I'm sure we can scare up a valet for you, milord," Neville said. "And an abigail for you, Lady Ashford. This way, if you please, and I'll show you to your rooms."

"Rooms?" Quinn said. "The lady and I are on our honeymoon, Beauchamp. One room will suffice."

"Your recent nuptials notwithstanding, it's not at all the done thing for a husband and wife to share the same quarters in Celle," Neville said with a frown.

Quinn placed a proprietary hand on Viola's waist and pulled her close. "Do I look as if I give a tinker's damn whether it's the done thing?"

Viola flashed Neville a look of entreaty. The last thing they needed was another brawl to break out.

"As you wish," Neville said stonily. "This way, if you please."

The interior corridors of the castle stored cold better than an ice house. Chill leached from the bare stone walls and floors. It slipped beneath Viola's hem and crept indecently up her shins. Her teeth threatened to start chattering by the time they mounted the third set of stairs that led up to the guest rooms.

"This is your chamber, milady," Neville said as he opened one of the heavy plank doors leading off the frigid corridor.

The room was sun-splashed since the shutters had been thrown open onto the bailey below. The bed was built into the wall in Teutonic fashion with curtains to enclose it against nighttime chills. The footmen carried their luggage into the space and left them for the abigail and valet to unload later. There were half a dozen hat boxes, along with her valises and a good sized trunk. Those held only her wardrobe. Viola was mildly surprised by how much she'd accumulated in the way of worldly goods since joining forces with Quinn.

"The chamber is a bit small. It was designed with one guest in mind, and at a time when people seemed to be a good deal shorter. Many of the private chambers are snug like this." Neville shot a look at Quinn. "The room I'd chosen for you had higher ceilings, Ashford, if you'd care to change your mind about sharing."

"Not bloody likely." Quinn bared his teeth in a feral smile.

"This room is lovely. Thank you," Viola said, untying her bonnet. "We'll be quite cozy here."

Fortunately, a blue tiled stove squatted in one corner of their accommodations. Someone had banked a small fire in it and the room was a comfortable temperature compared to the hallway. An overstuffed chair bathed in the shaft of sunlight streaming through the window. Beside it on a small table, fresh cut tulips nodded in a Delft vase.

Viola's heart gave a small lurch. Neville had remembered how she loved tulips.

"Now perhaps you'd like a tour of the castle?" Neville directed his suggestion to her, pointedly ignoring Quinn.

"Not really," Quinn intervened. "We've traveled a good way this afternoon. I think perhaps a nap before supper is warranted. When is supper, by the way?"

Neville's narrow-eyed gaze was just shy of a glare. "Nine o'clock. Attire is formal."

"Very good. Arrange for a bath to be brought up for us around seven then, there's a good fellow." Quinn yawned hugely and stretched his arms, filling the space and brushing the low ceiling with his extended fingers. "Off you go now, Beauchamp."

Neville turned to Viola. "Is there anything else you require?"

"A dressing screen would be nice," she said.

"But not necessary," Quinn added as he started to unbutton his own collar. He flashed a wicked grin at Viola. "Honeymoon, you know."

Neville swept a low bow to Viola and gave the shallowest of nods in Quinn's general direction. Then he turned and stalked out with the retreating footmen.

"Did you have to do that?" she demanded once Neville was gone.

"Do what?"

"Rub his nose in it with all that honeymoon talk. The man has feelings."

"And none of them do him credit, I assure you." Quinn stripped off his jacket. "The jackal used you once and he'll do it again in a heartbeat if you give him the least encouragement."

"There are those who might say *you're* using me as well."

"I'm using you? Hmpf!" He sat down and toed off his boots, stretching out his long legs. "As I recall, only one of us was forced to remain merely 'hopeful' on the drive here."

"I'm not talking about that," she snapped. Devil if she'd give him anything to hope for now. "Aren't you coercing me into committing a burglary?"

The irritation drained from his face. "I won't make you do anything you don't want. You always have a choice, Viola."

His silky bass washed over her, but she resisted the way his deep voice made her knees wobble.

"You didn't give me one when we started this."

"No, I didn't." He rose and crossed over to test the bed for firmness. "But to be fair, when I set out to capture the Mayfair Jewel Thief, I expected you to be a man."

"The way you keep bringing that up makes me think you're disappointed."

His hot gaze sizzled across the room toward her. "You know better than that."

She refused to be sucked in by the desire in his eyes. "For tuppence, I'd—"

A sudden wave of nausea coursed through her and she nearly doubled over. As it was, she had to grasp the back of the chair to keep from going down.

Then she heard it, a low vibration on the farthest edge of sound. It reverberated in her chest. She swallowed the lump in her throat with difficulty.

"Viola, what's wrong?" Quinn was by her side in a heartbeat. "Are you ill?"

She wiped her clammy hands on her skirt. Though she'd been cold not five minutes before, a bead of perspiration slid hotly down her spine.

The bass note droned on in a slow pulse. It echoed in her head, boring deeper into her mind with each ponderous blat of sound.

"Do you hear that?" she asked in a whisper.

There was a clatter of hooves and the clack of wheels on cobbles in the bailey below.

"Sounds like another carriage has arrived," Quinn said.

"No. That's not what I mean," Viola said as she collapsed into the chair. Her vision tunneled, but she fought the pull of darkness with a gulping breath. "It's the diamond."

"The Blood of the Tiger?"

"Yes," she gasped. "It's here."

CHAPTER 22

Quinn scooped her up and carried her to the bed. Viola could only moan. Her cheeks flamed with scarlet patches. He put a hand to her forehead, then jerked his fingers away.

"You're burning with fever."

Panic rising in his gut, he sprinted to the washstand and poured water onto a cloth to drape across her forehead. It didn't help.

"No, I don't need . . ." she mumbled, pulling the cloth off and letting it drop to the floor. Tears streamed from the corners of her eyes, but she didn't seem to be aware of them.

"I'll fetch a doctor."

He started to go, but she snatched at his arm with a surprisingly strong grip. "No. No doc—"

One of her eyes was nearly black with a fully dilated pupil. The other was glazed over, the pupil no bigger than a pinprick. Her irises were pale, drained. Instead of their usual rich hazel, they were a sickly grayish green. He feared she saw nothing through either of them.

"Jet. Silver," she whimpered. "Get them."

"Hush, love. I'll take care of you. They surely have a doctor here." Quinn thought she must be delirious.

Lord, how had it happened? One moment she was spitting

mad and doing her best to pick a fight with him. The next she was so suddenly ill, he feared she'd slip away from him between one gasping breath and the next.

"Jet. Silver," she said between clenched teeth. A small muscle in her forearm jerked involuntarily beneath her skin. "Please."

It dawned on him that she wanted her damn jewelry. Quinn didn't see what good it could do, but he was afraid to leave her side to shout down the echoing corridor for a doctor. He rifled through her valise for the black-stoned set.

"Here, love." He pressed them into her hands. He'd seen plenty of men die during his years as a soldier, fighting to the last breath against the inevitable pull of the great dark. For no reason he could tell, Viola was unexpectedly on the edge of that great gulf. She drifted from him by inches and he was helpless. There was nothing he could do but give her the baubles she asked for. "They're right here."

Viola made no move to put the jewelry on. She simply clutched the jet between her breasts like a talisman against evil.

As Quinn watched, the deep furrow between her brows relaxed. Her whole body loosened, the muscles unclenching, and she drew a slow deep breath. She closed her eyes and her head lolled to one side.

"Viola, no." Alarm shot through him as he cupped her cheek. The raging fever was gone. Her skin was eerily cool to the touch. "Stay with me."

Her chest rose and fell a couple times in measured breaths. Then she opened her eyes. To his relieved surprise, they were normal. Her pupils matched and her hazel irises were once again flecked with gold.

She looked up at him and smiled thinly.

"Good Lord, what happened to you, Viola?"

Her lips pressed together for a moment as if she held back

words she didn't wish to speak. Then she whispered, "It's nothing. It's passing now."

"It's not nothing, damn it! What brought this . . . this fit on?"

"Please don't shout." She closed her eyes again and put a hand to her temple.

Quinn was instantly contrite. He retrieved the discarded cloth, wet it afresh, and placed in on her forehead. She didn't strip it off. He moved across the room and yanked on the bellpull to signal for a servant to bring tea. By the time he returned to Viola's side, she was trying to fasten the clasp on one of her bracelets, without much success. The rest of the jewelry still rested between her breasts.

"Help me do this." Her voice was hoarse as if she'd screamed for an hour. "Please."

She'd never seemed to care too much for jewelry, but she was certainly intent on it now. Quinn helped her don both bracelet and ring sets. Then he propped her upright and fastened the jet and silver necklace at her nape. Her fingers worked at the row of buttons on her bodice.

"Touch. Must . . . be touching," she murmured disjointedly. Her breathing seemed more steady once the silver and jet was draped across her exposed skin.

"The earbobs too." Her voice sounded almost normal, but he insisted she lie down after he affixed a bob to each of her lobes.

The maid arrived with tea. Quinn helped Viola sit up again and held the steaming cup to her lips while she sipped.

"Lady Ashford is unwell," he told the maid. "Pray arrange for a supper tray to be brought up to us when it's time."

"No," Viola said with surprising force and took the cup from his hand. "I'll be better by then. Truly. I'm feeling much stronger already."

Quinn cocked a brow at her, but she seemed adamant. He rescinded his order to the maid, who bobbed a curtsy.

"Are you going to tell me what's going on?" he asked Viola as soon as the door closed behind the maid's dark skirts.

She sighed. "I don't know. All of a sudden I was . . . overcome by nausea." She buried her nose in her teacup again. "That was a long, bumpy carriage ride, you know."

Quinn had never seen a carriage ride, bumpy or otherwise, result in a flash fever or pupils that would do credit to an opium fiend. But he didn't think it would do Viola any good if he argued the point. He was satisfied when she drained the teacup and lay back down to rest. In a few moments, she drifted into a gentle sleep, her eyelids twitching, her breathing rhythmic and deep.

It's the diamond, she'd said just before succumbing to the terrifying malady. Sanjay had always claimed the Blood of the Tiger was powerful and malevolent, that its evil could reach out and strike people down. Quinn hadn't believed it for a moment.

He was beginning to reconsider that position.

What about her insistence on the jewelry all of a sudden? Sanjay had planted the idea of the supposed protective properties of silver and jet in her head. His friend swore by them, but Quinn dismissed his claims as Eastern superstition, the sort of hokum the British Empire felt honor bound to stamp out whenever possible.

Hokum or not, Viola's alarming symptoms retreated when she slipped on the black stone set. She knew more than she was telling about that episode, he was certain. He'd press her for a further accounting once she was healthy enough for a row.

Quinn pulled the chair next to the bed and watched her as she slept. She'd scared him so badly with the thought of losing her, he didn't dare look away.

Viola rested her fingertips on Quinn's arm as he led her down to supper. He wore his dress uniform, resplendent with rows of ribbons and medals, looking dashing and dangerous at once. He was devilishly handsome, but she tried not to be distracted by him. She knew the diamond was near and needed to keep her wits about her.

They'd left their chamber with plenty of time to spare since Quinn wanted her to go slowly. She was grateful for his thoughtfulness, but she felt much stronger.

She simply wouldn't remove the jet and silver jewelry for worlds. She even bathed with it on. A protective barrier had draped over her when she first clasped the jet to her chest. The shielding drove back the creeping darkness. She knew she violated several fashion dictums by going without gloves, but now that she wore all the silver and jet jewelry directly touching her skin, she felt almost normal.

Except for the low throb she heard from time to time on the other side of the invisible silver shield.

Baaghh kaa kkhuun was still there, still aware of her presence and still testing the strength of her defenses. The red diamond's nearness had no discernible effect on Quinn. She could only assume her gift made her more susceptible to its power and malevolence.

On the second story, they came to a gallery lined with oil paintings. Grand dukes, princes, and kings of Hanover from generations past all looked down their regal and prodigious noses at the mere mortals visiting their summer castle in Celle. As the subject of Her Royal Highness Queen Victoria, Viola wondered at the absence of any female dignitaries in the impressive hall.

She paused before a small glass-topped display case. "Finally. A woman."

A miniature of a rather plain young lady was embedded in midnight blue velvet. Even though her face could not be accounted pretty, her smile was infectious.

And the woman's bodice was cut so low, two pink nipples peeped above the lace.

Quinn laughed and leaned to whisper in her ear. "She has your sense of style."

Viola swatted him with her fan for reminding her of that exceedingly naughty fantasy. "I wouldn't actually go about with my breasts bared, you know."

"Pity."

She swatted him again.

"Imagine sitting for such a painting," she said, her own nipples tightening at the prospect.

Quinn's warm breath feathered by her ear. "I'm trying not to imagine you doing it for fear you'll hit me again."

She turned to him and he caught her in his arms. Even through the layers of her gown and petticoats, she felt his hard maleness pressed against her belly.

"Care to guess what I'm imagining instead?" he asked.

She smiled up at him. "Quinn, you're terrible."

"Ah, you're just saying that to make me feel good."

She rocked her hips into him slightly. "I think, sir, you're feeling quite good enough without any help from me."

"You're plenty of help." He grinned down at her. "Whether you're aware of it or not."

Someone cleared a throat at the far end of the hall and Viola sprang away from Quinn guiltily. Then she remembered that as far as the world knew he was her husband and she had no need to act as if they'd been caught in a compromising situation. She sidled close to him and looked down the hall. Neville was framed in the doorway.

"I see you've discovered the sad princess," he said as he started toward them.

"She doesn't seem sad to me." Quinn gazed back down at the risqué miniature with an appreciative smile. "She looks rather . . . rosy, actually."

Viola dug her elbow into his ribs and hissed, "Behave."

Neville's shiny Hessians clacked over the hardwood as he approached. "I assure you, Her Royal Highness Princess Caroline Matilda led a very tragic existence. It's always a pity when one born high is brought so low."

Neville tossed Viola a meaningful glance and she wondered if he slyly referred to her diminished status since her father had died. Her reduced state was the reason he'd tossed her aside, after all. Irritation raked her spine and she decided the next time Quinn wanted to throttle Neville, she might be disinclined to interfere.

"Caroline Matilda was a member of the British royal family and Queen of Denmark once she married His Royal Highness Christian VII," Neville went on. "She was exiled here at Celle for the last years of her life—till her unexpected death at twenty-four."

"Really?" Viola looked back down at the painting, which must have been done near the end of her short life. "She seems so lively one almost expects to hear her laugh. Why was she exiled?"

"She was an unfaithful wife. She had an affair with her husband's doctor," Neville said with a superior glow.

"Oh." Viola studied the small portrait again. Caroline Matilda seemed a bit wicked, with her little nipples exposed, but not entirely evil. It wasn't unheard of for a princess to have an affair, but it was always roundly condemned. Bloodlines were everything when it came to succession, after all. But if her husband was ill, that put an even dimmer light on the matter. "Was her husband's illness mortal?"

"No, he was just mad," Neville said. "Absolutely batty, they say."

Viola shrugged. The English were accustomed to mad kings. Flighty, immoral princesses were evidently another matter.

Still, Viola couldn't help feeling sorry for the vivacious young woman who was saddled with a doomed marriage. Any woman who posed for a portrait in that state of undress didn't seem the type to forego pleasure because the accident of her birth paired her with a lunatic.

"If the king was mad, I wonder that he even noticed his queen's affair," Quinn said.

"I'm sure someone brought it to his attention. One cannot pass over an insult to the crown, you know." Neville gave Viola a searching look. "But if a woman has no joy of her husband, I find it impossible to condemn her if she turns to another for solace. In fact, a man would be bound to welcome such a woman in need."

Viola felt Quinn's whole body tense beside her at the thinly veiled invitation.

"Husbands are a bit like kings in this respect, Beauchamp. They tend not to pass over insults either if someone troubles their wife," Quinn said pointedly.

"We'll be late for supper if we tarry further," Viola put in, tugging at Quinn's arm. "I find myself famished. Mr. Beauchamp, would you please show us the way to the dining hall?"

"This way, then." Neville strode ahead of them. "After supper, I've arranged for a troop of players to entertain in the castle theatre."

Neville stayed at Viola's side, introducing Lord and Lady Ashford to the other dignitaries in residence at Schloss Celle as they gathered in the parlor waiting for supper to be announced. Viola met an Austrian dowager duchess, a Hanoverian cousin to Prince Albert and an inebriated Frenchman who stumbled when he bowed over her hand and claimed to be the *Comte de Foix.*

For the first time in several hundred years, the English were uneasy allies with the French, but old animosities died hard. The count loudly told Neville he was "a silly fool of an Englishman" and if the British would only keep to their side of the Channel, the world would be a far better place.

"However, *cherie*," de Foix said as he made a second attempt at an elaborate obeisance over Viola's hand, "I have no aversion to the English sending us their women, provided they are as comely as you."

"The French had no aversion to our men fighting alongside them in Sebastopol either," Quinn said. He might have served in India, but he'd followed the battles in Crimea with intense interest.

"Ah! Lord Ashford, I perceive you are, like myself, a man of action. You, we will welcome." His words slurred slightly and he seemed to have forgotten he was in the kingdom of Hanover, not France, and was therefore in no position to welcome anyone. The French count sneered at Neville who had moved on to the next clump of dignitaries. "It is only your puling politicians we resist."

"In that, we find complete accord," Quinn said.

"Lady Ashford." Neville returned to them, leading a great bear of a man. "You will recall I mentioned a fellow who was recently returned from India. Lord and Lady Ashford, may I present Mr. Henry Chesterton, Esquire, lately of Peshawar, Delhi and Bombay?"

While Quinn made polite conversation with the newcomer about his time on the subcontinent, Viola's belly turned backflips. The Mr. Chesterton she'd seen in the ruby's vision had been slight and balding.

This man rejoiced in a full head of chestnut hair, a bit shaggy about the ears and definitely in need of a trim if he wished to affect a polished appearance. He was as tall as Quinn and easily outweighed him by two or possibly three stone.

Beneath the hum of multiple conversations and the clink of glasses, Viola heard the murmur of the diamond's low drone. It was closer. The genuine Blood of the Tiger was somewhere in Schloss Celle, probably secreted on the person of the man before her. She was sure of it.

But the gentleman before her was *not* the real Mr. Chesterton.

Of that, she was also sure.

CHAPTER 23

Schloss Celle had never been used as a military stronghold, despite the highly visible presence of guards patrolling the grounds. It served as a sort of summer palace for the House of Hanover and the many generations of dukes who'd claimed the place since the tenth century.

Since there was no true host in residence, Lord Cowley stepped into that role and seated himself at the head of the long table. Neville had arranged matters so he was seated opposite Viola. She gave her crockery her complete attention most of the time. Quinn languished at the foot of the table, between the aging mother of a baron, who according to his mother was "in want of a wife" and a flighty young contessa who giggled almost constantly and spoke only Spanish.

Dining beside Viola was the stolid baron from Sussex, whose mother had led him about as if he were a prize bull calf at a fair. He winced each time he heard her extolling his virtues at the far end of the table.

"You'll have to forgive Mother," he said to Viola, his voice mild as milk. "I've tried to explain to her that a wife and family would only detract from my study of ancient Persian, but she remains undeterred." The baron sighed. "She means incredibly well."

"Do I hear you right, monsieur? You have no use for *les femmes?*" the drunken French count at Viola's right leaned over her to ask the baron.

"No, it's simply that my life is ordered to my liking without a wife."

The Comte de Foix shrugged and spoke to Viola in a stage whisper that carried throughout the hall as well as the baron's mother's strident tones. "Vraiment, he has decided one woman telling him when to piss is enough, eh?"

Neville glared at the count. "My lord, there are ladies present. Kindly watch your tongue."

De Foix laughed uproariously.

"I fail to see what's so humorous," Neville said.

"The hell, it is over frozen," the count said. "An Englishman has presumed to tell a Frenchman what to do with his tongue when a lady is near. Believe me, the tongue is not for the watching. It has many other pleasurable uses which an Englishman obviously does not know."

Neville looked as if he'd just swallowed a bit of herring that had turned. Viola brought her napkin to her lips to cover her smile.

Tension eased when the butler and footmen brought in the dessert course and a comely serving girl distracted the men as she ladled on the clotted cream. Viola spooned up the last of her warm apple torte, wondering when she and Quinn would be at liberty to search through Schloss Celle for the diamond. Based on the low thrum, she knew it was near. She'd be able to follow the sound to its source if she had no distractions.

And wore her protective jet and silver. Somehow, she'd have to find a reason Quinn would accept for her to wear it even as she slept. So far, he'd been too concerned for her health to tax her with questions, but as she grew stronger, she knew that would change.

The Comte de Foix interrupted her musings when he disturbed the gathering with a drunken outburst again. "You

there, Monsieur Chesterton." The count waved a lacy handkerchief toward the fellow seated beside Lord Cowley. "You
have the stone for your English queen with you, non?"

All conversation stopped.

"*Quelle?* Do not make to give me the oh-so-shocked faces."
The count spread his hands before him in a classic Gallic gesture. "Come. We all know this man bears a fabulous gem
bound for the Royal Collection of the English queen, *n'est ce
pas?*"

"If we didn't, we do now," Neville said through clenched
teeth.

"*Alors*, we all are here to wait for your Prince's men to escort
it across the Channel, non?" the Comte de Foix said. "But I
am thinking, what would be the harm if Monsieur Chesterton
showed it to us here in the safety of Schloss Celle?"

It occurred to Viola that the count's speech was much less
slurred than previously. His dark eyes were bright and sharply
focused. He wasn't as drunk as he seemed.

"We will never see such a famous red diamond again," de
Foix said. "Do you refuse us a small peek only?"

Mr. Chesterton glared at the Frenchman, but Lord Cowley
put a hand on his forearm. "I think, sir, the burden you bear is
secure in this company," the ambassador said.

The man grumbled, but he drew a small silver snuffbox
from a pocket inside his waistcoat. Viola decided it was
deucedly clever of him to keep Baaghh kaa kkhuun in a snuffbox—a homely disguise for something so fabulously valuable.
When he opened the box, the low drone grew louder, but it
was still bearable. Viola was safe behind her silver and jet
armor.

Mr. Chesterton pulled a square of linen from his pocket and
used it to pick up the red diamond without touching it directly.

He knows, Viola thought. *He understands Baaghh kaa kkhuun's
power. And respects it.*

She also noticed Mr. Chesterton was wearing a pinky ring of tarnished silver set with a black stone.

He must also be sensitive to gems, she realized. She'd often wished she could speak to someone about her gift, but she'd never met another soul who shared her unusual ability. One glance at Mr. Chesterton's hard features told her he was not the one to whom she could unburden herself.

With extreme care, Mr. Chesterton slid the handkerchief with the diamond to the Austrian duchess at his left.

"Oh, my! It is so unusual," she said in heavily accented English as she touched the red stone. "This jewel gives me tingles right up my arm."

The men tended to pass the diamond along without touching it, not needing a case of the tingles evidently, but each woman felt compelled to run a fingertip over the rose-cut surface. When the count slid the handkerchief with the stone in front of her, Viola fully intended to pass it directly on to the Persian-obsessed baron.

Then the stone began speaking to her.

There were no words she could discern, but it was a definite summons. There was no pain or threat in it. Only a mesmerizing pattern in the low, undulating tone. Warmth. Light. Pleasure. When she lifted her hand toward the diamond, the sound intensified.

It began to stroke her, wrapping the rumbling timbre around her like a lover's caress. She felt the vibrations up her forearm before her fingertip reached the diamond's surface. It washed over her skin, slipping under her gown and tweaking her nipples to aching pertness. The waves rushed downward, flooding her groin with wicked sensations.

The room faded around her.

Someone moaned. It might have been her.

Quinn called her name, but she could no more have stopped her palm from covering the diamond than she could stop her heart from beating.

As it happened, that was something Baaghh kaa kkhuun intended to do for her.

"Viola! Viola!" Quinn would have leaped across the table if he'd thought it would get him to her side faster. He shoved the French count across the room. "Out of my way."

She was lying on the floor in a heap, having collapsed like a marionette whose strings had been cut. Her eyes were open, but unseeing, her face pale as parchment. Her body was limp except for one tightly clenched fist. Quinn dug the cursed diamond out of her curled fingers and slammed it back on the table, not caring where the damn thing went.

She sucked in a rasping breath and blinked three times.

Quinn clutched her to his chest.

She whimpered. "Away. Need to go. Away."

Quinn scooped her up. She trembled violently. "Somebody send for a physician to tend my wife."

He strode from the room and took the stairs two at a time up to their chamber. By the time he laid her on the bed, she'd stopped trembling but her breath still came in shuddering gasps. Quinn lit the candle on the nightstand and its light wavered uncertainly over her drawn features.

Neville rushed in, dragging behind him a man who claimed to be the ambassador's doctor. For once, Quinn was grateful to see Beauchamp.

The physician checked Viola's breathing with a mirror held beneath her nostrils. It fogged reassuringly. He put an ear to her chest.

"Is your wife increasing, my lord?" the doctor asked.

Quinn blinked in surprise. "I don't know. We haven't been together long."

"It doesn't take long," the doctor said with a wry grin.

"Could that cause her to . . ."

He had no words to describe the strange scene he'd just

witnessed. It was as if she were overpowered by the diamond, as if it *took* her, and she was powerless to resist.

"Women who're bearing do all sorts of odd things," the doctor said. "I've seen them keel right over and nothing to be done."

"You can't help her?"

"I didn't say that." The doctor reached for one of Viola's hands, but she pulled it away from him. "What's amiss here?"

Quinn took her hand and she allowed him to uncurl her fingers. The center of her palm was red and blistered around an angry mark roughly the size of the diamond.

"She's burned herself on something and it's set off some ill humors, no doubt." The physician rummaged in his bag and drew out a blood encrusted lancet set. "Bleeding always steadies a body."

"No," Viola said weakly, cradling her hand. "It doesn't even hurt. No bleeding. Quinn, please."

"You heard the lady," he said. One of his friends in India was an army surgeon who was fastidious about the cleanliness of his saws and lancets. It made sense to Quinn not to mingle Viola's blood with remnants of the doctor's previous ill patients. "What else can we do, doctor?"

"I suppose I could mix up a purge for her, if her ladyship will deign to listen to my advice," he said loftily. "After all, Lord Cowley trusts me implicitly."

"Then he must be fonder of chamber pots than I," Viola said, rolling on her side so she faced away from the doctor. "I need rest, that's all."

"Hmph! She evidently has no need for a physician since she's capable of self-diagnosis. Here's a salve for her hand if she'll let you use it on her." The man gave Quinn a small jar, replaced his instruments and closed his bag with an injured snap. "However, Lady Ashford will have to find rest on her own. I don't provide lullabies. Or laudanum, if that's what she's angling for. Too much resorting to opiates in my opinion."

Quinn agreed with the sentiment. He'd lost a couple friends to opium dens. He ushered the doctor and Neville out the door, then returned to hitch a hip on the edge of the bed. "Viola, what happened to you?"

"Go away." Her voice was strong and full of vinegar. Though she was pushing him away, her obstinacy eased his fears for her.

"Not until you tell me. Something made you ill. I want to know what happened. Do you think the doctor might be right?"

"Not likely."

"So you don't think you might be . . . with child?"

"No. You don't need to worry about that. My curse just ar—" She caught herself before she became indelicate. "Well, I'm certainly not bearing in any case."

Quinn was surprised to feel a stab of disappointment. If she was pregnant, it would give him an excuse to press her again on the subject of marrying him. "Does . . . do you often swoon when the custom of women comes upon you?"

"No. This is not something we'll discuss."

"Then what is it?" he asked, frustration creeping into his tone. "How can I help you if you won't tell me what's happening to you?"

She rolled over and looked up at him, her eyes clear, if a little bright. Her cheeks were pink with health. "You'll think I belong in Bedlam."

He smiled at her. "I already think that half the time, so you've nothing to lose."

She covered her mouth with her hand for a moment, her brows drawing together in distress. "But I've never told anyone."

"Have I given you reason to trust me?"

She nodded slowly.

He leaned over her and cupped her cheek. "Trust me with this."

She swallowed hard. "When I was a child, I loved seeing my mother's rings and necklaces and ear bobs, but I was never allowed to touch any of them. So my sister and I made daisy chains and fashioned love-knot pendants from locks of our own hair. On my eighth birthday, my father gave me my first piece of real jewelry. A moonstone ring. My birthstone."

Quinn was glad her father had taken note of her wants, but couldn't imagine how the story related to her collapse at dinner. He thought it was best to humor her so she would continue talking. "You must have been happy."

She shook her head. "I threw it down the well and told my parents I didn't know where I'd lost it."

"Why?"

"Because I couldn't sleep."

He raised a questioning brow.

"The moonstone wouldn't stop whispering to me."

CHAPTER 24

Viola covered her face with both hands. "There, you see. You think I'm a lunatic. I can see it in your eyes."

"No, I don't." He schooled his features into an impassive mask. She'd already told him her sister was dotty. Perhaps madness did run in her family and she was afflicted with a mild case, too. At least he hoped it was mild. "What"—he stopped, wanting to choose his words with care so she'd continue to confide in him—"what did the moonstone say?"

She arched a brow at him. "You don't think gemstones speak English, do you?"

"No, of course not. How . . . silly of me." He took the hand that had suffered the burn and stroked the back of it. "What language do they speak?"

"I don't know," she said with a sigh. "Not a human language. Just sounds, vibrations, screeches sometimes. Every stone is different."

Her mania had a sort of logic to it. If she was hearing voices, at least they weren't encouraging her to fly out a window or hack her family to pieces.

"That's how I can tell if a jewel is genuine. Paste gems are silent. Jet is the only stone I can bear for any length of time."

"Not very talkative?"

She rolled her eyes at him. "They merely hum. It's really rather pleasant."

Very logical. Her tale had the ring of truth, even if it was too outlandish to take seriously. "I take it the Blood of the Tiger spoke to you this evening?"

"Yes, but I could bear the sound because the jet and silver muted the power of the diamond's voice. When I became ill this afternoon, it was because I heard the stone arrive and wasn't wearing my shielding."

Her story was beginning to make sense. She did recover from that bizarre flash fever after donning her jet jewelry. "Score one for hokum," he said under his breath.

Fortunately she didn't seem to hear him. "Usually I have to touch a stone to hear it, but the Blood of the Tiger is very powerful."

There was a glaring flaw in her tale. "Several of the ladies at supper touched the diamond. No one else at the table was struck down."

"I'm beginning to think it's rather like hay fever. Some can work in a garden all day with no ill effects and others develop puffy eyes and runny noses at the first sight of a flowering plant. No one else at the table was susceptible to gems," Viola said. "Except perhaps the Comte de Foix. He's the one who insisted on seeing it after all. He must have sensed it was near. And of course, Mr. Chesterton. He took care not to handle the stone directly and he's wearing a jet and silver ring. Except . . . he's not really Mr. Chesterton."

"Who is he then?" Quinn's chest ached. She was making less sense by the moment.

"I don't know, but he's not the Mr. Chesterton the ruby in Paris showed me."

Quinn's gut roiled. She was more ill than he realized. "The ruby *showed* you?"

"If I maintain contact with a gem long enough, it sends me a vision." She sat up, as if to emphasize her point. "The ruby we almost pinched in the ambassador's office showed me the real diamond and its courier. I saw that the Blood of the Tiger would come through Hanover, even though I couldn't tell you at the time. I didn't think you'd believe me."

"Fancy that."

She evidently didn't hear the irony in his voice. "But I thought a short bald man would be carrying it. The jet and silver shield protected me from the diamond's voice this night, though I could still hear it." She shivered. "I shouldn't have touched it, but when the Blood of the Tiger sets itself to charm, you have no idea how compelling its song is."

Quinn hadn't heard a thing while the diamond was shuttled round the table.

"When I touched it, the diamond showed me the real Mr. Chesterton's murder." Her face crumpled. "It was horrible, Quinn. He begged and cried and—"

She covered her mouth with her hand and fresh tears streamed down her cheeks. "Oh, God, he wanted to live so badly," she said between gasping breaths. "Even after he . . . oh, Quinn, the man who killed him and took his place . . . he may look like a person, but he's really a beast."

She was sobbing inconsolably. Quinn put his arms around her and held her while she wept. An anvil settled on his heart. The woman he loved was mad and he feared her malady was beyond anyone's power to help.

"Hush, now," he said softly. He was a wealthy man. He'd find someone who understood the workings of an ill mind. They'd travel to the best sanitoriums in Europe looking for a cure. America, even, if need be. "It'll be all right."

"How? How can it be all right that a man was murdered and no one knows and—" She turned in his arms and slanted a look at him. "You don't believe me."

"If it's any consolation, Sanjay would believe every word."

"But you don't." She pulled away from him.

"Viola, I'm a simple man. A soldier. I trust what I can see.

What can be proven." He tried to smooth her tumbled hair, but she batted his hand away. "Try to look at it from my perspective. There's nothing to support what you say."

"You want proof?" She glared at him, her eyes brittle as glass. "Fine. I know what happened at the lake when you were a boy. I saw your brother drown."

"What did you say?" Quinn's face blanched and Viola's insides wilted. He was covered with guilt.

"You're not a simple man. Not just a soldier. You're a baron, in line for a viscountcy because your brother died. I've been trying to deny what I saw, but I can't any more. You're hiding a terrible secret. I saw you do it."

"Do what? What are you talking about?"

"Do you remember the day I fainted and had that headache in Paris?"

He nodded mutely.

"I had touched your signet ring while you were shaving. I thought it would tell me more about you, and I guess it did." The horrific images she'd tried to forget rushed back to her. "The stone showed me that day at the lake."

Quinn didn't move. He didn't speak. He seemed to be holding his breath.

"Your brother was floundering in the water. I saw you running along the dock, then you reached out a hand to him. He loved you so. He thought you were trying to help him." Her throat threatened to close over the words. "Then you held him under."

Quinn rose and walked to the window, leaving the circle of light thrown by the candle near her bed. He leaned against the sill. Backlit by the moonlight, he was a dark male shape outlined in silver.

"That's not what happened," he finally said. "It wasn't me."

"But I *saw* you." From her vantage point, through Reggie's eyes, she'd seen very little actually. Water weed and the underside of the rotting dock. But Quinn's young face in her vision was crystalline in its clarity. She'd remember Reggie's sense of terror and betrayal till she breathed her last. "I saw only you."

"Then your vision wasn't complete," he said wearily. "My father was there, too."

"Are you saying he's the one who did it?"

"Reggie was too soft, he always said," Quinn explained, with quiet bitterness. "Our father was never satisfied with either of us, but at least I showed some promise on a horse and could manage a cricket bat. Reggie was . . . a gentle soul. I loved my brother. I would never hurt him."

She desperately wanted it to be true. Viola scoured her memory. There'd been a look of panic on young Greydon's face as he pounded down the length of the dock. Then Reggie had disappeared beneath the surface again and she'd only seen the sickly green water. Their father might have been following at a distance and joined Quinn on the dock while Reggie was beneath the surface.

"I should have gone in after him, but . . . I was afraid. I'd heard a drowning person will take his rescuer with him often as not. I tried to reach Reggie from the dock, but my arm wouldn't stretch far enough."

Viola searched her vision. Yes, that much was true. Greydon had leaned out, his fingers splayed, his eyes wide.

"I was a damn coward," Quinn said. "And Father was so disgusted by Reggie's flailing attempts to swim, he held him down. 'To toughen him up,' he said."

Lord Wimbly had said Lord Kilmaine was hard on his boys. According to Wimbly, the viscount claimed to have been at the lake when Reggie tragically drowned. Now that she thought about it, Quinn's boyish fingers wouldn't have covered Reggie's entire crown the way the long, strong ones in her vision did. Quinn's version of the facts made sense. She hoped it was the truth.

"Oh, Quinn." Viola's chest ached for him. No wonder he

didn't want to be called Greydon because it was one of his father's names.

"I don't think he meant to, but he held him down too long. He was so angry when Reggie drowned. As if it was my brother's fault for dying. I thought he was going to throw me in next," Quinn said with a catch in his voice. He rubbed his forehead as if he could rub out the memory. " 'Sons are easy enough to get,' he said. He told me I'd better keep my own counsel if I knew what was good for me."

"You were only a child. It wasn't your fault."

"It's always felt as if it was." He slumped onto the bed by her feet. "The truth will never come to light. It would kill my mother. My father will never be called to account." He ground a fist into his thigh. "It's so damn unfair."

Viola realized that was why Quinn railed so against injustice wherever he saw it. Why returning the diamond to Sanjay's people was so important to him. If he righted other wrongs, somehow, he was making up for the wrong done to Reggie. The wrong that could never be undone.

"There is a Higher Court," she whispered. "Your father will face a reckoning someday."

"I hope you're right." Quinn looked at her searchingly. "Do you believe me?"

Viola nodded. She loved this man. She had to believe him. "Do you believe *me*?"

"It's hard, but I have to."

She moved to the end of the bed and wrapped her arms around his shoulders. "Let us agree to keep each other's secrets."

"Agreed." Quinn turned and tipped her face up to his, sealing their bargain with a deep kiss.

"I'm sorry I touched your ring," she said. "I shouldn't have done that. It was wrong of me, like reading your private journal."

Quinn gathered her in his arms. "I'm glad you did. I don't

want to have any secrets from you. I doubt I'd have believed yours any other way."

She smiled at him. "Careful. You're giving me permission to be nosy."

"Since your vision about Reggie wasn't completely accurate, I'm giving you permission to ask me anything instead." A frown pulled his brows together. "If the vision from the lake was incomplete, do you think you might be wrong about Mr. Chesterton, too?"

She explained that when she'd had the vision of Reggie's death, she'd experienced it all through his eyes. Her other Sendings had been viewed from a safe distance, which enabled her to see clearly what the stone wished her to see. In this case, there was no ambiguity. She was certain the man posing as Mr. Chesterton was a cold-blooded killer.

She shook her head. "We don't have to wonder what he intends. That diamond will never make it to the queen's collection. At some point, he'll switch it and try to fob a lesser stone off on the queen's men."

"Then we'll simply make the switch for him," Quinn said. "I have a ruby we can leave as a substitute."

"He'll know," Viola said. "He's like me. Jewels speak to him."

Quinn cocked a brow at her. "All right, I'll trust you on that. You'd know, if anyone would. What do you suggest?"

"We steal it outright."

"Fair enough. We'll have to be ready to fly afterward then, but I'm changing the rules. When we go for Baaghh kaa kkhuun, I'll be the one who actually lifts it. I don't want you to touch it. Not ever again," Quinn said. "Is that understood?"

"I'll try not to, but I can't promise I won't. The diamond is very compelling."

"Then I'll keep you from it." Quinn wrapped his arms around her and held her close. "I won't risk you. Not for anything."

It wasn't a declaration of love, but it felt like one. It wasn't about lust. It wasn't about thievery. It was about two souls who'd found their odd bits and pieces; their imperfections and private shames seemed to fit together to form a less broken whole. A warm glow shimmered over Viola. She relaxed in Quinn's embrace, perfectly content to remain there till morning.

An ungodly shriek pierced the night and lights winked on in every room of Schloss Celle.

CHAPTER 25

"Stay here," Quinn ordered.

"Not likely." Viola scrambled off the bed and toed on her slippers. Fortunately, she was still dressed, but even if she'd had to take to the drafty corridors of Schloss Celle in her nightshift and wrapper, after that scream nothing would keep her alone in the chamber without Quinn.

Viola couldn't say for sure whether it came from a man or a woman. It was bloodless. Disembodied. She gave a superstitious shudder.

Together, they bolted down the hall and took the stairs at a brisk place. Other guests joined them, all talking at once, all wondering what had happened.

"Quiet!" Quinn commanded and everyone fell silent.

Voices echoed from a lower level. The group followed the sound, keeping their own speech to a whispered hum. They slowed when they came to the foot of the stairs and found Neville Beauchamp and the ambassador with several other guests standing around a prone figure.

Viola peeked around Quinn. The French count was sprawled on the flagstones. His face was waxy and pale in the flickering light of the wall sconces. His unblinking eyes were bleached of all color, the irises mere shadows on the whites.

A serving girl sobbed into a corner of her apron and rattled on in German.

"What's she saying?" Quinn turned and asked.

"She doesn't know how it happened," Neville translated in a flat voice, clearly unnerved by the unnatural appearance of the count's body. "She found him like this."

Quinn squatted down and checked for a heartbeat at the French count's throat. He shook his head.

"Did he fall down the stairs?" Neville asked.

Quinn turned the count's head to one side. "No blood. No evidence of a blow. His neck's not broken."

"Where's that doctor?" Neville looked around, but the ambassador's physician wasn't among the group. "Check for a wound of any sort, Lieutenant."

Quinn moved the count's arm from across his chest. It was limp as a noodle. His fingers dangled as if his bones had dissolved inside his body. Quinn jerked his hand away and de Foix's arm flopped to his side, palm up.

"His hand," Viola said. "Look."

There was a burn in the center of the flesh between his lifeline and heartline. The angry hole was so deep it nearly went all the way through his hand. The burn on her own palm, which hadn't hurt at all before, flared in sympathy.

Viola had no doubt the Blood of the Tiger had killed de Foix.

Quinn glanced at her hand and a flash of understanding passed between them.

"Where's Chesterton?" Quinn asked, rising to his feet.

The ambassador cleared his throat noisily. "The prince's men arrived shortly after Lady Ashford was taken ill at supper with orders for Chesterton to depart with them immediately. The escort took time only to eat a quick meal in the kitchen while Chesterton packed. They should be leaving now for the port of Bremen to sail with the next available tide. The sooner the burden he bears reaches the Royal Collection, the safer it will be."

Viola realized Lord Cowley spoke the truth. The diamond's low drone was gone, but she couldn't say precisely when the sound had stopped. It had become such a habitual background noise, she'd ceased to note it since her silver and jet jewelry protected her from the diamond's power. She hadn't marked its absence until now.

Viola looked down at de Foix's body. She could imagine what had happened. Mr. Chesterton would have changed from his formal clothing into a traveling ensemble. The Frenchman must have realized the diamond was being taken away and moved quickly to snatch it while Chesterton packed.

But the comte wasn't cautious enough. Either he didn't know to protect himself from the stone or the diamond beguiled him into holding it in his bare hand while it sucked the life out of him.

If Chesterton was sensitive to the stone, he would have been aware in short order that it was no longer in his possession. He must have found the comte's body before the serving girl. Chesterton had pocketed the diamond and left de Foix as he lay, then strolled out to join the waiting escort without so much as a backward glance.

Quinn put his arm around her waist and led her back up the stairs, leaving the ambassador and Neville to see to the disposition of the body and any further investigation. "There's nothing more for us to do here."

She suspected he was talking about more than the poor comte. With the diamond gone, there was no reason for them to tarry in Schloss Celle. No reason to follow the diamond since it was unlikely they'd be able to slip past the prince's men.

No reason for them to continue the charade of being husband and wife. Their adventure together was over.

Her chest hurt. Her palm burned. She ached all over.

They continued in silence up to their room. The door thudded behind them with finality. She ducked behind the dressing screen to change into her night clothes.

"Viola, we won't follow Chesterton across the Channel," Quinn said.

"Naturally not. With the diamond under royal guard, we've little chance of pinching it now."

"No, it's not that. Whatever defenses a man can devise, another man can find a way around. But after what happened to de Foix, I don't want you near that thing."

His words sent hope dancing through her veins again. He did care about her. "Your reasons for wanting to steal the diamond are still the same, still strong."

"Yes, but now my reason for *not* stealing it is stronger."

She wished he'd say more, but she didn't want to press him.

He stepped behind the screen with her and undid the back of her gown without being asked, his movements easy and unhurried. It was a simple thing.

A husbandly thing.

He dropped a soft kiss on her shoulder, then left her to finish preparing for bed behind the screen alone. He undressed on the other side of the room, hanging up the pieces of his dress uniform so it wouldn't wrinkle. He made no effort to shield himself from her eyes, totally unconcerned by his own nakedness.

The soft light of the candle kissed the smooth skin of Quinn's broad back. Viola's gaze followed the line of his spine down to his bare buttocks and muscular thighs.

He was such a fine man. She wished he was truly hers. She wished her menstrual flow hadn't begun and she was bearing his child. She wished she could walk around the dressing screen and seduce him into loving her.

He pulled a silky banyan around his body and knotted the belt at his waist. When he turned, she averted her gaze.

"Do you need anything?" he asked.

Only you. "No," she lied.

"Then come to bed." He held out a hand to her.

She came around the dressing screen and took it with a little sigh. "Oh, Quinn, everything's gone wrong. Even if we did want to tail the diamond, we can't very well follow it to Bremen because Sanjay is still in Hanover. The fake Mr. Chesterton would recognize us and know why we followed him." She leaned her forehead against his chest, her crown fitting neatly under his chin. "What are we going to do?"

"We're going to bed." He cupped her chin, tilted her face up to his, and shot her a wicked grin. He kissed the tip of her nose. "There are plenty of delightful possibilities in that plan, but I think this time we should try to get some rest. I don't know about you, but I could sleep for a week."

She climbed into the bed and under the covers. He pinched off the candle flame and followed, pulling the bed curtains behind them to shut out the world.

But the world wouldn't stay out. Unresolved questions niggled at Viola's brain. "I wasn't asking what we'd do now. What will we do in the future?" She really wanted to ask what would become of *them*, but Baaghh kaa kkhuun seemed like a safer subject. "About the diamond, I mean."

"I know what you meant," he said, snuggling her close so her head was pillowed on his shoulder. "We're not going to think about it for the next twelve hours or so."

His breathing grew deep and rhythmic.

Viola raised her head and tried to make out his profile in the darkness. How did men do that? Could he really shove aside all the loose threads of their life and decide not to tug on any of them?

Apparently, he could.

But Viola's mind chased the endless possibilities around the bedpost for hours before exhaustion claimed her and she sank into oblivion.

* * *

The scent of musk and jasmine tickled his nostrils. Silk sheets caressed his skin. Quinn sat up abruptly. He was back in Padmaa's opulent bedchamber, but the Indian courtesan was nowhere to be seen.

What was he doing there? He'd left Padmaa and her athletic eroticism behind. Whether it made sense or not, he wanted only Viola.

She'd be devastated if she found him there.

Mother-naked, he rose from the thick bed of cushions, looking for his uniform. He must have discarded it somewhere. If he could find his clothes and slip out the open window, Viola never need know he—

He heard the soft pad of bare feet behind him.

He turned, expecting to find the courtesan. Instead of Padmaa's kohl-rimmed eyes, Viola's hazel ones greeted him above a gauzy veil. She unhooked the veil to remove all doubt of her identity.

She didn't seem surprised to see him there. Or hurt. The breath he'd been holding seeped out of him as he relaxed.

Viola was dressed as an odalisque, with only gossamer silk covering her form. Her pert nipples stood out clearly beneath the sheer fabric. The dark shadow of her pubic hair showed plainly.

Her gaze sizzled down his bare body and his cock responded with an aching stand. The corners of Viola's lips turned up, a slow sensual smile.

"What are you doing here?" he asked.

"Sh!" She lifted her fingers to his lips, then drew them down over his chest, around his nipples and on to his navel. Her fingertips marked him with wicked little charms. She wove lust spells into his skin. He ached for her to hitch her knee over his hip and press herself against him so he could rut her on the spot. Much more teasing and he'd bend her over and take her in a raging swive.

He moved to embrace her, but she straight-armed him. Evidently, she wanted to lead.

Very well. Quinn preferred to be in control, but there were times when a man was rewarded by letting his woman take the reins.

She walked a slow circle around him, trailing her hand at his waist and teasing his buttocks with maddening light touches. She *rubbed herself, catlike, against his back, her breasts unbearably soft, her nipples hard beneath the thin silk. His balls tightened.*

When she returned to stand in front of him, he plucked at a corner of the silk wrapper. She raised her lovely arms in surrender and did a slow turn as he unwound the fabric from her form.

Her skin glowed like alabaster lit from within by a hundred candles. He moved to stroke her, but she intercepted his hand, shook her head and returned it to his side. He swallowed hard and decided to let her continue to torment him.

She stepped closer so that her breasts nearly grazed his chest. His swollen cock found temporary relief rubbing against her soft belly. She cupped his scrotum and fondled his balls, running her nails lightly along the strip of darker skin that divided them.

He ground his teeth. He ached to touch her, to drive her to the same burning fury she whipped up in him. "Viola, I—"

"Choose, Quinn-sahib," she said.

The voice was not Viola Preston's. Padmaa's musical tones dropped from Viola's red lips.

He stepped back a pace. "Who are you?"

"Only a fool asks a question to which he already knows the answer," she said. "And you are not a fool."

"I choose Viola."

"Truly?" the spirit inhabiting Viola's body said. "You would choose one woman over all of Hind?"

Yes. The word sprang to his throat, but he couldn't force it out his mouth.

The woman opened her palm and he saw Baaghh kaa kkhuun pulsing in the center of it. The flesh around the scarlet diamond was blistered and reddened, but she gave no sign the burn pained her.

"If the Blood of the Tiger is not returned to the temple . . ." her voice faded and his vision swirled.

Angry men in turbans ran through the streets, shouting "Maro, maro!"

Kill, kill!

Flames engulfed the British cantonments. A terrified English-

*woman and her son were dragged from under the bushes behind their
bungalow.*

"No!" the young mother screamed. "He's only a child!"

The boy was hacked to death before her eyes.

*"One does not suffer an infant viper to live," the sepoy with the
machete said before he dispatched the wailing mother as well.*

*The horrific vision faded and Quinn was back in Padmaa's bed-
chamber.*

"Choose, Quinn."

*The woman before him was the dusky Padmaa, her palms tattooed
with henna, her plum-colored nipples standing pert.*

But Viola's voice came from her lips.

*The Blood of the Tiger growled its malevolence and burst into
flames.*

CHAPTER 26

Quinn's fork chased the eggs and sausage around his plate, but Viola didn't think much of the heavy breakfast made it into his mouth. Certainly none of the desultory conversation around the table made it into his brain.

When she'd woken that morning, Quinn was already dressed and standing at the window, watching dawn break over the castle walls. He hardly glanced her way while she rustled around behind the dressing screen.

He was quiet. Distracted. When she asked him to help with her laces, he rang for an abigail to come. He mumbled something about seeing her at breakfast and ducked out of the room before the maid arrived.

Most of the guests in residence were not up yet. Viola suspected the violent death of de Foix had left more than a few sleepless. Only Neville, the baron from Sussex and his loquacious mother, Viola and Quinn sat at the long table.

"Not hungry this morning, Lieutenant?" Neville asked, reverting to Quinn's rank instead of his title.

Probably thinks it will offend him, Viola guessed.

Neville would have given his right arm to inherit his uncle's title, but couldn't know Quinn didn't give two figs for his. She shot Neville a warning glare.

Don't poke the bear. She wished she possessed the ability to send her thoughts to others instead of the dubious gift of receiving visions from gem stones.

Neville wasn't disposed to take a hint. "Good Hanoverian fare not to your liking?"

"The food's fine." Quinn shoved his plate back and glowered at Beauchamp. "Must be the company."

Before they could start a real row, Sanjay strode into the room, having just arrived from Hanover. Viola was grateful for the interruption until she saw the Indian prince's expression. His hawkishly handsome face was drawn in misery.

"The *tar* has come from Delhi, sahib." He handed Quinn the telegram. "But it is not from your friend, Lieutenant Worthington. It is from Colonel Tibbets, his commanding officer."

Quinn opened the envelope and ran his gaze over the page. As he read, a muscle in his cheek ticked and a vein bulged on his forehead.

"Quinn, what is it?" Viola asked.

"It's happened. And it's still happening," he said woodenly. "The sepoys have mutinied."

Neville was on his feet demanding to know more.

"The uprising started in Meerut." Quinn continued to stare at the telegram, but Viola suspected he saw little of it. "And spread to Delhi. They have no estimate of the dead yet, but women and children were not spared. By either side."

"You say the news doesn't come from Lieutenant Worthington," Viola asked, her chest aching for Quinn. His warnings to his commander of an impending rebellion were the reason he'd been demoted to lieutenant and shipped Home. She was sure he wished he'd been wrong. "What does the telegram say of your friend?"

"There's a British magazine at Delhi, an arsenal of arms and ammunition," Quinn said. "If the mutineers got control of that, they'd have been able to take the subcontinent. So Worthington and a few others blew it up." Quinn's jaw went rigid. "From inside."

"After all we've done for those people," Neville said, "this is how they repay us."

"What precisely is it you think we've done for them?" Quinn asked in a deceptively mild tone. Viola feared he'd go off like the magazine at any moment.

"Schools and roads and clean water, for God's sake," Neville said. "We've even built them a railroad."

"Without asking if they wanted one." Quinn chuckled mirthlessly. "Did you know the ranks of the Indian military are filled with princes and noblemen? They volunteered to fight for us purely for *izzat*, for the honor of it."

"So much for their honor." Neville sneered.

From the corner of her eye, Viola saw Sanjay's posture stiffen, but he maintained his deferential façade.

"What set the heathens off?" Neville demanded.

"We did," Quinn said. "We gave them the new Enfields and somehow the rumor started that the paper cartridges were greased with either pig or cow fat. I heard the rumor myself." Quinn's eyes took on a faraway light and Viola suspected the sumptuous dining hall had faded around him. "I didn't think anyone would believe it. But if a lie is repeated often enough, it becomes the truth. It was the perfect spark to light the tinder."

Neville frowned at him. "What possible difference should grease make?"

"To load the Enfield rifle, you must bite open the cartridge first." Quinn shook his head. "Pork is pollution to a Muslim. Eating beef destroys a Hindu's caste. Maybe we didn't mean to, but by insisting they use the Enfield we attacked their *religions*, Beauchamp. Is there any uglier reason for war on earth?"

Quinn stood and stalked out with Sanjay in his wake.

"Apparently, we must go," Viola said to Neville. Considering the news he'd just received, she'd forgive Quinn's abominable manners. "Please convey our thanks to the ambassador for his hospitality."

"Viola, you don't have to leave," Neville said.

"Oh, yes I do. Good-bye, Neville." Wherever Quinn went, she must go too. It was as simple—and as complicated—as that.

Once Quinn reached their room, he began throwing his few possessions into a valise. Sanjay stood by, watching him.

"We need to move quickly. Aren't you going to help me?" Quinn demanded.

"That depends on what you intend to do, sahib."

The chamber door opened and Viola entered. Quinn tossed her a glance. He didn't dare look at her for longer than a blink or his resolve might weaken.

"I intend on returning Lady Viola safely to her family"— Quinn ignored the rustle of her skirt as she strode toward him—"and then we'll take ship for Bombay on the next available berth."

"You will go without orders?" Sanjay asked.

"Given the gravity of the situation, do you really think they'll quibble over having another officer, with or without orders?" Quinn said, studiously not looking at the female form bristling at the corner of his vision. "It'll take us a couple months if we leave for India today. If I wait to be recalled, I may arrive too late to do any good."

"And what of the good you might do on this side of the world?" his friend said.

Quinn shook his head. "I speak the language of your people. I understand them, as much as any Englishman can at any rate. If I'm there, I can try to find cooler heads on both sides and get them together." He checked the safety on his Beaumont-Adams and stowed the revolver in his luggage. "There's nothing I can do from here."

"Then you have abandoned Baaghh kaa kkhuun."

"Yes. I can't muck about after a single jewel when the sub-continent is ablaze. I'm done with it."

"Well, I'm not," Viola piped up. "I'll still help you get the diamond, Sanjay."

The Indian inclined his head to her in a gesture of respect. "My people and I will thank you, Lady Viola."

"Wait just a minute." Quinn rounded on her. "Weren't you paying attention last night? The damn thing attacked you when you touched it and we both know it killed that Frenchman. You're not going anywhere near it."

Viola glanced up from folding her belongings and stowing them in her trunk. She smiled sweetly at him. "You haven't a thing to say about it."

"The hell I don't."

She shot him a purse-lipped look. "There is no need for such language."

"There is when you're talking suicide. Stay away from that diamond. I mean it. I won't have it."

"Contrary to what you've been telling people, you're not really my husband," Viola said evenly. "I don't answer to you, so it doesn't matter a fig what you'll have or not have."

"You don't have to do this, Viola." Anger simmered in Quinn's belly. "I'll still split the jewels with you as I promised, if that's what you're worried about."

She narrowed her eyes at him. "That's not why I'm doing it."

"You little fool!" He grasped her upper arms and made her face him, giving her a small shake. "You know the power of that stone. You know what it can do."

"Yes, I do," she said, her eyes wide, her lips pale. "Can you imagine what the Blood of the Tiger will do to our queen if it comes into her possession? To our country?"

"The red diamond seeks only to destroy," Sanjay added. "Only in the temple can its evil be balanced with its power and turned for good."

"That's why I have to steal it back." She grasped Quinn's

hand between both of hers. "You want to help our people and Sanjay's find peace. What better way to start than by returning something they treasure?"

Quinn's gut knotted and he palmed her cheek. "But I don't want to risk what *I* treasure."

She blinked in surprise at him. "Are you saying you treasure me?"

It wasn't the time to speak his heart, not with this thorny problem dividing them and with Sanjay looking on, grinning from ear to ear at his discomfort. "Viola, I can't let you do this alone."

"Then do it with me. I won't have to touch the diamond if you're there, too. You've never shown the least sensitivity to gems, but you should have a jet and silver ring, just in case and—"

He covered her mouth with his to quiet her, kissing her into silence and delicious oblivion. The door latch clicked and Quinn realized Sanjay had slipped out to give them privacy.

He'd tried to choose India. He'd tried with all his might to do the honorable thing. The just thing.

But his heart was too bound up with the woman in his arms.

He knew Sanjay would say Quinn had managed to choose both, since he would be protecting Viola during the theft of Baaghh kaa kkhuun. And the theft would benefit Sanjay and the people of Amjerat.

"You have bound two worlds with one knot," his friend would say.

But Quinn knew better. He didn't give a damn about the red diamond. Or what it might do to England. Or for Amjerat.

All that mattered was Viola.

Mr. Chesterton had already sailed by the time Viola, Quinn, and Sanjay reached Bremen. They had to wait till the next day to find a ship bound for Dover.

Viola chafed at the delay. If the red diamond was presented to the queen and disappeared into the Royal Collection, she didn't know how they'd manage to pinch it. Willie's contacts in the underbelly of London, who provided her with intelligence about where the ton's personal wealth was stashed, would be of no help in planning a foray into the Tower.

The ruffians might be useful for breaking *out* of a prison fortress, but never *in*.

When they finally reached London, Quinn insisted on taking Viola straight home. Her mother greeted them at the door, so Viola could only surmise their doddering servant was once again down with an ailment.

"Oh, my dear," the Dowager Countess of Meade exclaimed. "What are you doing home so soon? You should be off to Italy or some such romantic place. Why didn't you tell me? Come in, come in, you sly boots!"

Viola's mother cast an assessing eye at Quinn and then swatted him with her fan. "Couldn't have waited to have the banns read, eh? Well, no matter. So long as you make my daughter happy, I'm pleased to have you as a son-in-law, Lord Ashford. Welcome to the family."

"Mother, where did you hear—"

"Lady Wimbly sent word back from Paris to Lady Hepplewhite and then of course, your secret was out," Viola's mother prattled on. "Quite scandalous to elope like that, but everyone so approves the match. Except perhaps your father, Ashford. By all accounts, he's frightfully put out that you didn't consult him before you spirited my daughter off to Gretna Green."

Viola's chest constricted. "Mother, I have to tell you. We're not—"

"Not set up to receive visitors yet," Quinn interrupted, "but as soon as Viola redecorates my town house, we'll have a reception to celebrate. I fear it's a bit of a boar's nest now. Needs a woman's touch."

"Oh, lovely. Viola does have a flair for such things," Lady Meade said. "Perhaps your father will come round to the match by then. I believe the poor man has taken to his bed over it. After all, even if she doesn't come with a handsome dowry, my Viola is the daughter of an earl."

Lady Meade continued with minimal input from Quinn or Viola. She admired the serpent wedding ring, declaring it quite the "done thing," though she deplored the choice of silver and jet jewelry.

"A bride ought not wear black!"

Viola's belly jittered too much for her to contribute to the conversation. With each passing moment, the web of deceit around her and Quinn grew thicker and more difficult to untangle.

"Oh! And you won't have heard since you've been out of country, but there's to be a ceremony at Buckingham this afternoon. The presentation of some fabulous jewel from India to our queen. Came right from one of their temples, they do say. Quite an honor, evidently, for such a treasure to be allowed to leave India according to those who ought to know. Makes one quite proud of our empire's distant possession."

Evidently, news of the sepoy rebellion hadn't leaked to the press yet or Viola's mother wouldn't have been so lavish in her praise of their "distant possession."

"Everyone who's anyone will be there." Lady Meade clasped her hands together. "Say you'll go with me."

"Of course we will," Quinn said, taking Viola's hand in his. "It'll be our first outing in London society as husband and wife."

She wished she were strong enough to squeeze his fingers off. He kept making it more and more difficult to make a clean breast of things.

"Well, then we'll—oh gracious, look at the time!" Viola's mother consulted her brooch watch, the last of her remaining jewelry from her days as a countess. "If we wish to have a proper place for viewing the queen, we'll need to go now. Let me fetch my parasol and we'll be off."

Viola's mother scurried out of the room before she could see her daughter give her new husband a smack on the back of the head.

CHAPTER 27

"Ow!" Quinn rubbed the back of his head. "That was rather less cordial than a man expects of his bride."

"That's because I'm not your bride," she hissed. "Why are you making things more difficult?"

"More difficult? I should think you'd have been pleased." Did she *want* him to destroy her reputation? He'd intended to tell her when her mother left the room that he meant to make the rumors true, wanted her to reconsider his offer of marriage. But if she was set on being so prickly, he'd let her stew a bit longer. "Isn't it better to be thought impetuous than ruined?"

She glared at him. "It's better to be honest, and much easier to remember the truth than a whole pack of lies."

Quinn snorted. "I'd forgotten thieves were such sticklers for the truth."

"I didn't think you were so adept with lies." She fidgeted with her gloves, unbuttoning them as if she intended to remove them and then refastening the closures.

"Viola, what's wrong with you? You're nervous as a cat."

She stood and paced before the cold fireplace, her elegant ensemble casting the room in a shabbier light. Though the parlor was furnished with an eye to correctness, it was obvious all the items of value had been sold off long ago.

"We're too late," she fumed. "There'll be no catching Mr. Chesterton with the jewel ahead of time now."

"Viola, let it go," Quinn said.

"How can you say that? Didn't you drag me across the continent for the diamond?" She stopped pacing and glared at him. "You know what the Blood of the Tiger is capable of, what might happen once it reaches the Royal Collection. How can you be so indifferent?"

"I'm not indifferent." That was an understatement. He loathed the red diamond for several reasons, but highest on the list was the hold it seemed to have on Viola. "But I think we need to regroup and consider our next move. In war, one often doesn't know where the battle will be joined until the enemy commits himself. I'm not without other resources. Be patient. Let's see what the day brings."

Lady Meade returned, her wrinkled face flushed and gay as a girl's. "I trust you have appropriate transportation for us, Ashford."

"Of course, ma'am. It is my honor to escort two such lovely women to this momentous occasion." He offered his arm to Lady Meade. *May as well milk the cow to get the calf.* "And please, call me Quinn."

They arrived at the stands erected near the royal dais in time to secure a premium space for viewing the ceremony before the rest of the ton filled in the available seating. The regal box was festooned with red and blue bunting and appropriately gilded in preparation for Her Majesty's arrival. The green space before Buckingham Palace filled with commoners and laborers who hoped to get a glimpse of their queen and the fabulous jewel she was supposed to receive as tribute from a distant point in the empire.

Viola's mother preened for her acquaintances and introduced Quinn as her new son-in-law to all who spoke to them.

Lady Meade was making the most of her freshly elevated status, clearly anticipating that her daughter's wealthy husband would care for their needs as her own nephew had not. With Viola in line to become a viscountess, the Dowager Countess of Meade and her family might find their way back into the mainstream of the ton.

With each offer of felicitations from those who'd recently ignored her mother, Viola wondered how she'd extricate herself from the increasingly sticky tangle. She resisted reminding Quinn that he'd offered to marry her in Paris. If he were serious about it, surely he'd broach the subject himself.

Yet if he was only resigned to marrying her to avoid a scandal, she wasn't sure she'd accept. She didn't want to be someone's burden, someone's inevitable responsibility.

The only other respectable way out was to announce that their "marriage" had been annulled. But that would compound one lie with another.

What a perfectly vicious little circle.

A brass ensemble blasted out a fanfare by Handel, interrupting Viola's thoughts. Her Majesty processed past the viewing stands so burdened with regalia she was like a frigate under full sail. The queen mounted the dais and settled onto her throne. An impressive entourage of courtiers bobbed in her wake.

No ceremony was complete without speechifying. Several dignitaries found it necessary to drone on about the sun never setting on the British Empire due, no doubt, to the beauties and superiority of the English culture.

As if everyone present didn't already believe that implicitly.

Almost everyone.

Quinn was restive during the speeches. When one scholar who'd made an "extensive three week tour of India" started pontificating about the blessings England had bestowed on a backward nation, Viola felt the muscles in Quinn's thigh tense where it touched hers.

"Only three bloody weeks of gallivanting and he thinks he's an expert." Quinn snorted.

Viola shushed him. If they were ever to get close to the diamond again, alienating the queen's people was not the way to go about it.

Finally, Mr. Chesterton, who was introduced as one of the Crown's premier gemologists, appeared with an honor guard of Beefeaters flanking his steps. He bore a vermillion pillow with a small jewel box nestled on it instead of the snuffbox. Even though the musicians were still playing, Viola strained to hear the low voice of the diamond.

"Something's not right," Viola whispered to Quinn.

"Make that 'everything' and I'll agree," he answered back.

"No, it's not here. I can't feel the diamond."

Quinn sat up straighter as Chesterton passed directly before them. "Maybe it's the box. It looks like it's made of silver, inlaid with dark stones."

"Maybe." Viola frowned, unclasped her jet and silver wristlets and stuffed them into her reticule.

Still nothing.

She removed her earbobs. Only the delicate necklace remained but since it was hidden under her high-collared day dress, she couldn't remove it without a tussle. Though the diamond couldn't harm her from a distance while she wore her silver shield, its voice was strong enough she ought to be able to hear Baaghh kaa kkhuun.

She leaned and cupped her hand around Quinn's ear to whisper. "Even with the shielding, I should sense the stone's presence. Without the wristlets, I should be nauseous. I tell you, whatever is in that box, it's not genuine."

"Wait till it's opened," Quinn said.

Viola scrunched the extra fabric of her skirt between her fingers. After all that had happened, he still didn't believe her.

Mr. Chesterton dropped to one knee before the queen,

holding the pillowed jewel box aloft. Viola hoped to heaven she was right. If not and if the queen was sensitive to gems, the red diamond might claim yet another victim as it had the Comte de Foix.

The queen leaned forward with interest as one of her advisors stepped up to open the box. The stick-thin man lifted the silver case from the pillow and presented it to the queen with an elaborate bow. She smiled at the stone and nodded. Her advisor returned to her side, holding the silver box before him. The deep red stone winked in the sun, making it seem larger than its five or six carats.

"Who's that holding the jewel box?" Viola asked.

"Hubert Fenimore, another spare son like me, but he's not likely to inherit. He has three older brothers," Quinn said. Another dignitary had launched into a pedantic speech about the rarity and splendor of the red diamond from Amjerat's temple. "Fenimore was a couple years ahead of me at Eaton. Is he in danger?"

"Not unless there's a stiff wind," she said. She'd never seen a more sepulchral figure. Fit the man with a cape and a breeze would send him aloft like a kite. "That's not Baaghh kaa kkhuun he's holding. Chesterton must have provided a convincing fake."

"Good," Quinn said. "Then we still have a card or two to play."

"What do you intend?"

"Someone needs to inform Her Majesty that the jewel she accepted isn't genuine."

"I don't see how that will get us the stone."

"The authorities have the power to arrest Chesterton and demand the real item. Then I'll have to convince them it's in our country's best interest to return the diamond to Amjerat." Quinn studied his former schoolmate. "Since it seems I have a friend in high places, it just means a word in the right ear."

"Shh! Really, children, I can't concentrate with your constant whispering," Lady Meade scolded. "Save your sweet nothings for when you return to your own home."

Viola didn't feel like whispering sweet nothings to Quinn. She was much more likely to box his ears. If his commander in India wouldn't listen, why did he think London bureaucrats would be any more receptive to his arguments?

As long as the authorities thought they had the real stone, they wouldn't notice when the genuine Baaghh kaa kkhuun went missing. If she and Quinn successfully relieved Mr. Chesterton of the red diamond, he couldn't very well report the theft since he'd have to admit he'd switched gems on Her Majesty.

"But Quinn, that—"

"That's how it'll be," he interrupted in a whisper so as not to antagonize her mother. "I don't want you anywhere near that diamond. Let me handle this."

The ceremony was winding down. A brass ensemble launched into a spritely Purcell tune as Her Majesty rose and retired from the fray. Hubert Fenimore clapped the jewel box shut and followed her through the deep velvet curtains that provided the backdrop for the dais.

Quinn rose. "My apologies, ladies. Some business requires my immediate attention, so I'll be unable to accompany you for any additional excursions this afternoon. However, I'll leave the brougham for your use. Perhaps you'd enjoy a little shopping together. My credit's good wherever you choose to go. I daresay Harrods has a few nice things your mother might like."

Lady Meade made a giggly, cooing noise of delight. Viola sent him a glare that should have rendered him a smoldering pile of cinders. He was determined to go forward with his own plans without even giving hers the dignity of a full hearing.

Quinn lifted Lady Meade's hand and pressed a very correct kiss on her bony knuckles. Then he bent and brushed his lips over Viola's cheek.

Smart man. If he'd put her hand anywhere near his mouth, she'd have curled her fingers into a fist and clouted him a good one.

"I'll see you at home later, dearest."

"You know how we women are when we're shopping." She smiled venomously at him. "Don't wait up."

Quinn lifted a brow at that, but kept a smile firmly in place for her mother's sake. "Yes, well, try not to spend all my money in one place."

"Of course not," she said sweetly. "I know lots of places to spend all your money."

His smile was less convincing as he turned and walked away from them.

Viola's mother was so excited about the idea of shopping, she kept up a lively conversation, complete with several changes of topic, with very little input whatsoever from her daughter.

All the way to Harrod's.

Viola merely nodded and made approving noises from time to time as Lady Meade led their retail expedition. As soon as her mother's acquisition lust was slaked and she was returned to her town house, Viola had some business of her own to attend.

Quinn might have a friend in high places, but Viola had, if not a friend, at least an associate, in the lowest. Willie used to boast that a mouse didn't fart in Cheapside without him smelling it. A crude boast, but a true one. He'd be aware which collectors were brazen enough to purchase an item stolen from the queen herself. If anyone in London knew where Mr. Chesterton made his domicile, where he might have stashed the red diamond, and what he planned to do with the stone, it was Willie.

Viola was going to make him tell her everything he knew.

CHAPTER 28

"Ashford, what a surprise!" Hubert Fenimore said from behind his burled walnut desk. "Last I heard you were still mucking about in India with all them savages, what? Always one for adventure, weren't you? Come in, come in. Make yourself comfortable."

Quinn removed his hat and took the seat Hubert indicated. Undersecretary to one of the queen's advisors, Fenimore's office wasn't ostentatiously appointed, but Quinn recognized the gleam of ambition in Hubert's eyes. He'd make use of the information Quinn was about to share if for no other reason than the hope of advancement.

"What could have dragged you away from the Gorgeous East? Ah, I know why you've returned Home. You've come back to take up the reins of the Kilmaine estate from your father. He's been poorly I've heard. An apoplectic fit from all accounts." Fenimore's thin lips twitched in a suppressed smile. "How trying for you."

If Fenimore had been in line for his father's title, Quinn had no doubt he'd be circling the family seat like a carrion bird every time his old pater came down with a case of the sniffles.

"I'd heard Lord Kilmaine was ill, but this is the first I've heard of apoplexy," Quinn said. "We're not on speaking terms, he and I."

"Perhaps you'll bestir yourself to visit for your mother's sake then," Fenimore said, with a sly smile. "And perchance look over the estate ledgers while you're there."

"Perhaps," Quinn said. Apoplexy. His father might not ever recover, depending on how bad the fit was. Some lost the power of speech or the use of their limbs on one side after a bout with this illness. His mother would be beside herself. "But for now, I have an urgent matter to bring to your attention. First of all, congratulations on your part in this afternoon's ceremony. It was singularly impressive."

"Thank you." Hubert smoothed down his mustache with the backs of both hands. "Contrary to popular opinion, most of the real work of governance is done by those of us without the fancy offices or positions. The ceremony this day was quite gratifying, however, in that it showed I do enjoy a certain amount of royal favor. Advancement to a more senior post is only a matter of time."

"Indeed. But a queen's favor can be a fickle thing. The smallest thing can turn it. For example, are you aware that the jewel you presented to our queen is not, in fact, the Blood of the Tiger?"

"The devil you say."

"Have the stone examined by a qualified gemologist. You'll find I'm telling you the truth. Chesterton still has the real diamond, or knows where it is. But time is of the essence. If he hasn't already sold the jewel, he's undoubtedly planning to. The damn thing is worth the earth."

Fenimore sat perfectly still for the space of a minute. Quinn could practically see the cogs of his brain turning in his shifting eye movements.

"How did you come by this astounding intelligence?"

Quinn waved away the question. "That's not important."

"It is if you expect me to take you seriously." Fenimore

leaned back in his chair. "Can you imagine the loss of prestige our sovereign might suffer if it became known she'd participated in a public ceremony at which she accepted a fake diamond?"

How typical of a political appointee to focus on perception rather than reality. "Not if the real one is recovered in a timely manner. It would only highlight the efficiency and strength of our queen's rule." Quinn stood as if he intended to leave. "But perhaps you lack the authority to send runners to arrest Chesterton. I shall take my case elsewhere."

"No, no," Fenimore said. "Don't be hasty, Ashford. These things require a certain delicacy. I will certainly act, but I need assurances that your information is correct. Again, how do you know the diamond in the queen's vault is not the Blood of the Tiger?"

Quinn didn't want to admit it, but saw no other way to convince Fenimore. He settled back into the chair. "The Mayfair Jewel Thief told me."

Fenimore's pale eyes narrowed. "You know the identity of the thief who's been plaguing London?"

Again, Hubert focused on the wrong thing. "That's not the point. The main issue is this. Will you be the man who delivers the true jewel to his sovereign or will you not?"

Hubert templed his fingers on the desk before him. "Sending runners to arrest Chesterton would create a sensation and spread the story wide enough that the press might catch wind of it."

"The reward is worth the risk. The British press seems rather oblivious at present."

"Why do you say that?"

"Because no mention of the sepoy rebellion has reached our shores yet," Quinn said.

Fenimore blinked in surprise. "No one is supposed to know about that."

"You see, I do have my sources." Quinn frowned at his old

schoolmate, who obviously already knew about the disaster in Delhi. "Is the government quashing mention of the uprising in the papers?"

"Nothing so Machiavellian. A delay only. Once we've dealt with the brigands, it will be appropriate to release the information. Not before."

"It could take months, maybe years, to quell this rebellion. Our military cannot complete the pacification on its own. We must make political overtures to the people of India as well."

When Hubert's eyes glinted with interest at the mention of politics, Quinn decided to press Sanjay's claim to the throne of Amjerat. Diplomacy would appeal to Fenimore more than tales of an inherently evil diamond.

Hubert listened and nodded occasionally as Quinn detailed the inequity of the Doctrine of Lapse and how the reinstatement of Prince Sanjay's rule would improve the natives' opinion of the British Raj.

"If you could convince the queen to return the real diamond to the temple from which it was stolen," Quinn said, "it would purchase so much good will, cooler heads would surely prevail in the current crisis."

Hubert studied his desk top in silence for a few moments, digesting the new information. Finally he nodded. "I will take this to my superior. I believe I can convince him to issue a decree in Her Majesty's name reinstating your Prince Sanjay to his throne. It's just the sort of benevolent action that would appeal to our gracious sovereign."

Hubert leaned forward and lowered his voice. "But the disposition of the diamond is another matter and I can make no promises in that regard. I will, however, see what may be done. In return for these considerations, you must do something for me."

"Anything." Quinn could hardly believe he'd convinced someone in authority to take action on Sanjay's behalf.

"You say you know the Mayfair Jewel Thief. Very well. I'd

rather not have a scandal erupt over accepting a fake jewel into the Royal Collection, so using official means to retrieve the real diamond won't do. Let us make use of this scallywag who's been the bane of the ton instead. If he can steal the Blood of the Tiger back for the Crown, I'll see what I can do about a pardon for him."

Quinn frowned. After the French count's death, he didn't want Viola anywhere near that diamond. "The thief may not wish to do it. I believe . . . he's had an attack of conscience and means to retire from thievery."

"Then you must convince him to make one last burglary or all deals are off." Hubert spread his hands before him.

"You mean unless I convince the thief to steal back the Blood of the Tiger, you won't see Amjerat restored to its rightful prince?"

Hubert shrugged. "One must be prepared for quid pro quo in this world. Political bargains are ever made in such ways. I trust you'll be as convincing with him as you have been with me."

"I'll see what I can do." Dissatisfied, Quinn rose and took his leave.

Hubert crossed to his small window and watched Lord Ashford exit the building below and hail a hansom. Then Fenimore rang for his assistant.

"Send for a Bow Street Runner to tail Lord Ashford. I want reports on his whereabouts at all times."

Hubert reached into his bottom drawer and pulled out a shot glass and flask of whisky. It was time for a celebratory drink. Not every day was a man handed a fortune on a plate. He'd collect the sizable reward for the Mayfair Jewel Thief and put a fabulous diamond in his own pocket before this business was done.

He'd arrange matters so Lord Ashford would take the blame for the theft of the Blood of the Tiger. It would do his old school chum no lasting harm. Everyone knew a man with

Lord before his name could get away with anything short of murder.

But court deliberations ground slowly. By the time Ashford was acquitted, Hubert would be long gone. He'd be visiting South America or deciding which villa to purchase in Tuscany. Possessing unlimited means was such a delicious prospect, he gave himself the rest of the day off to contemplate it.

And lay out plans for making his rapacious dreams a reality.

Viola's mother wallowed in a full afternoon of acquisitive frenzy the likes of which Harrods had rarely seen. But Lady Meade would have had a conniption fit over the next stop if she hadn't already been dropped off at her town house with a full dozen parcels, three hatboxes, and a firm promise that Viola would call again soon.

Quinn wouldn't be too keen on this shop either, Viola thought. *But what Quinn doesn't know won't hurt me.*

The brougham rattled down the narrow lanes of Cheapside and came to a stop before Willie's disreputable establishment.

"I do not think this place is fitting for such a one as you," Sanjay said from his perch on the driver's seat. "Are you sure you wish to do this, memsahib?"

"Not really, but I'm sure I *have* to do it. I won't be an instant longer than I must be."

After the thrashing Quinn had given Willie in Paris, she doubted she'd receive a warm welcome. But if anyone had the information she'd need to find Chesterton and the diamond, it was her old fence. She hoped the information's price wouldn't be too dear.

Viola straightened her spine, screwed up her courage, and pushed open the door to Willie's shop.

When Quinn returned home, no one was waiting for him at his town house. He supposed he ought to be thankful Viola was still out spending his money. The only thing in danger was his net worth and he was sufficiently flush not to be overly concerned by the price of a few gewgaws and gizzwickies.

He sank into one of the wing chairs by his back parlor fireplace where the furniture was unfashionable, but comfortable, and wished he knew what to do. At every turn, it seemed fate conspired to make him choose between Viola and his adopted country. As if the powers that be weren't listening the first time he chose the woman he loved.

There was also the news that his father was ill. Quinn had thought he'd greet that information with a loud huzzah, till he remembered his mother's devotion to the old devil. She'd be devastated if Kilmaine died.

It was a puzzlement to Quinn how a woman could live with a man for so many years and not know him for the coldhearted bastard he was.

Perhaps Lady Kilmaine didn't want to know.

Quinn decided he had no stones to throw. After all, he loved a thief, someone who set his carefully constructed sense of *ought-ness* on its ear. He knew Viola. Knew her faults and weaknesses and it didn't change his feelings for her one bit.

Love really is blind.

A smile tugged at his lips. She probably felt the same way about him. He hoped.

But he wasn't sure.

She made love with abandon, but it occurred to him that she'd never expressed her feelings for him as openly as she'd shown her desire for his body.

She *had* turned down his proposal. Perhaps she didn't love him at all.

Though the thought made his chest ache, it didn't change how he felt about her one jot.

The front door scraped over the threshold and he heard voices. Quinn rose and peered down the hall of the town house toward the entrance.

"Thank you, Your Highness," Viola was saying to Sanjay,

who carried in a pair of hatboxes with a brown paper parcel tucked under his arm.

"Please, milady, do not use my title," Sanjay said. "I was once a prince in Amjerat, but no more. And I may never be again."

The injustice boiled in Quinn's veins. The unfairness didn't have to continue. He'd been too afraid, too weak to stand up to his father and help his brother, but he could help his friend. He could right the wrong, but only if he was willing to put the woman he loved in danger.

If it was simply his own neck in jeopardy, there'd be no hesitation.

Resolve stiffened his spine. He'd drape Viola in silver and jet. He'd stand between her and the evil in the stone. Somehow, he'd make sure he was the one taking all the risks.

"Yes, you will, my friend," he said softly. "Never doubt it. You will be a prince of Hind once again. And Viola will be my wife in truth."

CHAPTER 29

Quinn listened with growing consternation as Viola told him about her visit to her former fence's shop.

Willie had greeted her with a surly glower, rebuffing her initial queries for news of the Blood of the Tiger, but once Sanjay joined her in the shop, he'd turned surprisingly accommodating. Yes, Willie had admitted, the word slithering around Cheapside was that an illicit purchase of legendary proportions was about to take place.

Quinn frowned. "You shouldn't have gone there."

"Nonsense," Viola said. "I was perfectly safe. Though I had no idea how threatening Sanjay can appear when he wishes."

"It was not me, Lady Viola," the prince said with a self-deprecating shrug. "A Beaumont-Adams in one's sash always makes a suitable impression."

"I suspect your snapping black eyes and fierce scowl helped immeasurably. Thank you, Sanjay."

The Indian prince bowed and left the room, claiming he needed to prepare the brougham for the evening's plans.

"What plans?" Quinn asked.

"Willie gave us all we need to intercept the diamond before it changes hands."

"Out of the goodness of his boot-black heart?" Quinn folded his arms across his chest.

"No, I had to promise him a goodly sized ruby, but I believe you have one you can spare." Viola untied her bonnet and laid it on the side table, then tore open one of her parcels to reveal its contents. She handed Quinn a black domino and shook out a folded garment that turned out to be a matching silken cape. "You'll need this."

"Why? Are we going to a masquerade?"

"After a fashion. The buyer of Baaghh kaa kkhuun wants to maintain his anonymity." She held a purple half mask before her face. "Mr. Chesterton is meeting him this evening at Vauxhall on the Druid Walk sometime between eleven and midnight."

"How is this good news?" Quinn demanded. "Didn't your fence know where Chesterton was staying? We might provide a diversion to draw him away from his domicile and then you and I could break in and snatch the diamond."

"That's no good. According to Willie, the diamond never leaves Chesterton's person. Apparently he learned his lesson when he almost lost it to the Comte de Foix." Viola crossed over to Quinn, put her arms around him and kissed his cheek. "Don't look so glum. Trust me. This will work to our advantage."

He buried his nose in the juncture of her neck and shoulder and inhaled her sweet scent. How could he put her in jeopardy, even for the sake of his adopted country?

He certainly couldn't reveal her identity to that blasted Fenimore. He might have promised a pardon, but Quinn wouldn't bet a farthing on it. Even if a pardon was forthcoming, Viola would be devastated if her adventures as the Mayfair Jewel Thief became grist for the gossip mill, as they would if the authorities were involved. Nothing in government was ever a secret for long. Perhaps the best course would be simply to give the damn diamond to Sanjay and let him return it quietly to the temple of Shiva. Yes, that would settle matters after a fashion.

His mind made up, he kissed her neck.

But if he gave the diamond to Sanjay on the sly, the bureaucrats would sort out the sepoy rebellion in their usual ham-handed way without even the hint of an olive branch to offer the Indians once they were "pacified." Of course, the whole argument was moot since there was still no sure way to steal The Blood of the Tiger back.

"I don't see how the fact that Chesterton has taken to keeping the diamond on him will help us," Quinn admitted.

"Really?" She pulled away from him and held out her palm. One of his pearl wrist studs shimmered up at him. He hadn't felt her take it. "Do you see now?"

"How did you do that?"

"Before I mastered the tumbler lock, I realized most people forget they are wearing jewelry and if properly distracted, won't notice it's missing until much later." Viola shrugged and bit her bottom lip. "You have no idea the number of hours I practiced lifting items from a dressmaker's dummy in the attic before I tried it on a living person. I thought my heart would leap from my chest the first time, but I must confess"—her hazel eyes sparkled with hidden fire—"it's really rather exciting."

Lady Light-fingers. She certainly lived up to the name he'd first given her. He didn't doubt she could do it, but Baaghh kaa kkhuun was one jewel that might very well steal her in return. "No, Viola. I don't want you to touch that bloody diamond."

"But that's the beauty of this plan. I won't have to." She smiled, her face as flushed and excited as a debutante at her coming-out. "We already know Mr. Chesterton keeps the diamond in a silver snuffbox in his waistcoat pocket. So long as I wear my shielding jewelry and keep the box closed, I'll sense its presence, but the diamond won't be able to harm me."

"But what about him?" Quinn asked. "Do you think Chesterton can sense the diamond's presence as well? He might notice it was gone sooner than we'd like."

"He wore a silver and jet pinky ring at Schloss Celle, but that's all. Fairly light shielding." She frowned, considering the matter. "That shows he understands some of the diamond's power—enough to take precautions against it—but I don't think he's that sensitive or he wouldn't have been able to withstand the stone this long." She sighed. "It does call to one."

Like a siren on the rocks, if her longing expression was any indication.

"Come, Quinn. It's the only chance we have of retrieving the diamond." Viola put her arms around his neck again and pressed her body against his, drawing her palms down his arms. "It'll be fun. I promise. Please."

He grasped her wrists and held them immobile. "Am I about to lose something else?"

She laughed musically. "No, silly. In fact, I just put your stud back."

He snapped his wrist up between them. Sure enough, the pearl stud was back in place. He shook his head and smiled. "You're good at being bad."

She pulled his head down for a bruising kiss.

"No, I'm a good thief," she said breathlessly when their lips finally parted. "You're the one who taught me to love being bad."

The woman crowded his senses, pushing aside everything else. His body roused to her with a granite-hard cockstand.

"If we're quick about it"—he thumbed open the buttons in a line down the front of her bodice—"there's time for another lesson in debauchery."

"Lead on." To his delight, she swung one leg around him and hooked her heel at the base of his spine. There were layers of petticoats and lace between them, but he could feel her heartbeat throbbing between her legs. Her head lolled back as he kissed the exposed skin above her chemise and corset.

"Oh, yes, Quinn," she slurred. "Tell me we'll find the diamond tonight."

His head snapped up at that and he looked down at her. The last thing he wanted to hear from her before he swived her silly was more about the damned diamond.

Her lips were parted and her eyes closed. A fine sheen of perspiration bloomed on her skin. She trembled. If someone had told him she was an opium fiend in need of a fresh dose, he'd have believed it.

The red diamond's power was a drug to her, he realized with a jolt. It had touched her once and made her long for it again, even though it had tried to kill her.

Her eyes fluttered open. "Quinn, what's wrong?"

He unhitched her leg from around him and forced a little distance between them. "If we go for the diamond, you must promise me something."

"What?"

"If I think it's too risky, if I don't like the situation we find, we'll stop then and there. And if I call it off, there will be no argument. Understand?"

She sighed. "I understand, but it'll be fine. You'll see."

"As soon as you have the snuffbox with the diamond, you must give it to me immediately. Agreed?"

She didn't answer.

"This is nonnegotiable, Viola. I don't want you to hold the box a second longer than absolutely necessary."

"Quinn, you're being a tyrant."

"No, just a man who doesn't want to see you hurt. I mean it. I'll have your word on it or we're not going anywhere this night, even if I have to tie you up to keep you here."

For a moment, Quinn imagined her strapped spread eagle to his four-poster, breasts bound with silk, her secrets bared and vulnerable. He could keep her teetering on the edge of release for hours. How prettily she'd beg before he'd relent and let her come.

"In fact, that's the best idea I've had in ages." He put his mouth to her ear and whispered a few of the lewd and loving things he'd like to do to her.

Her eyes flared with scandalized surprise. "As much fun as letting you tie me up sounds, I'll pass on it for now. You have my word." She stood on tiptoe to kiss him. "I'll give you the diamond as soon as I have it."

She kissed him again. Her mouth under his pushed all thoughts of the diamond out of his mind. She gave herself over to him, helping him free her breasts from their whalebone prison.

He captured a nipple and suckled hard till she moaned his name. Then he turned his attention to her other nipple. Her nimble fingers teased their way down the front of his trousers. She unfastened the horn buttons at his hipbones and shoved his smallclothes aside, plunging her hands in to fondle and stroke him.

He yanked up her skirt. She guided him through the slit in her drawers and he swived her against the wall, mindless as a ram in rut.

"Harder," she urged.

Her words released him and he stopped holding back. She welcomed his feral thrusts with little cries of pleasure. Her body stiffened and her release pounded around him. He joined her, spilling into her in hot pulses, the precaution of a French letter the last thing on his mind.

He gasped for air, not realizing he'd held his breath while they throbbed as one. When the insanity of lust faded and he started to help refasten her bodice, he realized something. He needed Viola like he needed food and water and his next breath.

She was his opium, his own private poppy field. Each time he loved her, he wanted more of her. She enslaved him with each sigh, each kiss, each bone-jarring swive. Though he ought to have been fully spent, his cock rose again, ready to claim her as his.

She was his light, bright enough to blind him, but he couldn't look away. She was salt, preserving and abrading at once, but without her, his life was tasteless and flat. She was the lifeblood coursing through his veins. She might be addicted to the red diamond, but he was addicted to her. He'd never be free of his obsession with Viola Preston until he was dust.

Please God.

For almost two hundred years, Vauxhall Gardens had lured Londoners out to revel in its groves. At one time, Handel's music debuted in its pavilions and the upper crust dined on Vauxhall's famous paper-thin ham. Families with children rode across the Thames in little coracles to see the spectacle of the gas lamps winking on throughout the expanse of green.

Of course, since the pleasure gardens were open to the public, the seedier side of the city had always enjoyed its own brand of revelry there as well. Young bucks and girls of questionable virtue could be seen cavorting about pagan, vaguely phallic Maypoles. Bonfires blazed and instead of Handel, gypsy tunes filled the air in the less lighted sections of the garden. All manner of sexual congress was available for a price behind the thick shrubbery of the Druid Walks.

The gardens had fallen on exceedingly hard times. The ton had all but abandoned Vauxhall, except for those looking for a randy adventure with the added spice of anonymity. Almost everyone of consequence wore masks or dominoes to conceal their identity.

Viola and Quinn strolled the length of the Druid Walk, looking for Mr. Chesterton, no mean feat since that part of the park was not lit by gas lamps and the moon was on the wane.

Every time a man of the correct height and girth appeared, Quinn asked Viola if it were he.

"No," she said, cocking her head to strain for the low sound. "The diamond isn't here."

She might not recognize the man, but there would be no mistaking Baaghh kaa kkhuun. When she'd first heard the stone at Schloss Celle, its voice had been excruciating to her, nearly knocking her flat. But after she'd actually touched the stone, the sound changed.

She ached to hear its deep, rhythmic song again. There was something primal about the diamond's voice, elemental as the rush of the tide, a good hard swive, or the beating of her own heart.

Sanjay claimed Baaghh kaa kkhuun was evil and he was probably right. But that didn't stop her from wanting to be near it again. She couldn't help it. The diamond had claimed part of her and she wouldn't feel whole until she heard its music, inexorable and demanding, pounding inside her head.

She hoped it wouldn't be too terrible or too beautiful to bear.

The nearly-healed burn on her palm tingled. Her lust for the diamond made her shiver as they walked along, though she wasn't the least cold.

She wondered if she'd recognize the diamond's buyer based solely on his desire to possess the stone. Her own wanting was so keen-edged, she suspected if she were naked she'd find her nipples perked and her crotch damp. She moaned in frustration.

Quinn pulled her close. "Are you all right?"

"Yes." She leaned into his warmth. Solid. Male. Comforting. Quinn would protect her. Even from herself.

Then, as if from a great distance, she heard it—a *basso continuo* melody so low, it was on the farthest edge of sound. Perhaps she didn't even hear it with her ears. Perhaps the vibrations in her chest shuddered up her spine to roll slowly around her brain and then out her ears instead of in. She stumbled.

"No. I'm not all right," she admitted.

Only Quinn's arms kept her from collapsing.

The diamond's seductive tones wove a spell around her, setting her palm stinging. Her breathing hitched. Pleasure shot through her, arcing from her breasts to her womb and pooling between her legs, as if Quinn had touched her special spot with his tongue.

She grasped Quinn's lapels with both hands and clung to them like a drowning victim going down for the last time. He was her only anchor to reality in the face of the diamond's potent and sensual power.

"Baaghh kaa kkhuun," she whispered. "It's coming closer."

CHAPTER 30

"All right, that's it. We're done." Quinn gathered Viola in his arms. "I'm getting you out of here. You're in no condition to do this."

She leaned on him and sucked in a deep breath. She almost agreed with him. She hadn't located Chesterton yet and was already in danger of losing herself to the diamond's seductive summons.

Then she realized if she focused on the solid thump of Quinn's heart, it drowned out Baaghh kaa kkhuun's voice. She stopped trembling and wrapped her arms around his waist. Viola pressed her ear against his chest and drew from his strength. One thought formed in her mind with clarity and brilliance that outshined the finest jewel.

She loved this man.

Come ruin. Come scandal. Come desertion or disaster she couldn't yet imagine.

She loved Greydon Quinn.

He needed her to do one small thing for him, to pluck the jewel from a man who had murdered, and would do so again to possess it. Then she must hand it over to Greydon. Such a simple thing, really, when weighed against the love she bore him. She could do it with her eyes closed, if need be.

She tipped her face up to him and he kissed her. Their breaths and souls mingled, tangled together, inseparable. When their lips parted, she smiled up at him, her vision clear, her mind unfettered by the diamond's drone.

"I'm ready, Quinn. I can do it." She glanced down the walk at the shadowy figure moving in their direction. "That's him. I need to you do something for me, though."

"What?"

"Whistle something."

"Excuse me?"

"Anything. Whistle. I need to hear you."

Quinn broke into a jaunty version of "Rule Britania."

The diamond's low buzz began to drown out Quinn's tune.

"No, not that." Viola steeled herself against the Blood of the Tiger's voice. "Hum something. A love song."

Quinn switched to the haunting "The Water Is Wide." The deep hum of unsatisfied love and longing rumbled in her chest and the diamond's sound faded.

"Much better," Viola said, hooking her hand through his arm and walking toward Mr. Chesterton. As far as he would be able to tell, she and Quinn were two lovers strolling the dark walks in search of the perfect trysting spot.

Mr. Chesterton came closer, almost meeting them on the narrow path.

Another few steps, and Viola pretended to catch her toe on an exposed root and stumbled forward, clutching at Mr. Chesterton in what she hoped was a convincing approximation of someone who didn't want to end up facedown in the dirt. As his beefy hands caught her shoulders, her hand snaked into his waistcoat and she palmed the silver snuffbox.

"Darling, are you all right?" Quinn grabbed her and pulled her back to him, taking the box from her and secreting it in his pocket in a smooth motion. "Thank you, sir, for your assistance."

He hustled Viola away. "You really ought not have so much sherry after supper. Come, dear, let's get you home."

Her feet barely touched the ground as Quinn propelled her along, but they hadn't gone ten paces before Mr. Chesterton bellowed at them to stop.

"Yes, you two," he growled. "Turn around."

Viola's heart sank to her toes as she and Quinn faced Mr. Chesterton. Starlight glinted on the muzzle of a pistol. She hadn't considered that Chesterton might be armed.

Quinn stepped in front of her to shield her. "What seems to be the trouble, my good man?"

"You know." Chesterton's voice dripped malice. "Tell your doxy to fork it over."

"Now see here—"

"No, you see. Thought you'd take advantage of a man in the dark, did you, you and your light-fingered wench? Almost worked, too. Give it back now." When Quinn didn't move, Chesterton raised his gun. "The dead are easy to search."

"Our mistake, sir," Quinn said quickly, fishing in his pocket and coming up with the silver snuffbox. "Here you are and no harm done."

He flipped the box toward the large lilac bush next to Chesterton, the silver flashing as it turned end over end.

"Run!" Quinn turned and gave Viola a shove down the path.

She lifted her skirts and ran, knees and elbows pumping. Quinn was right behind her, his footfalls in time with hers. Brush rattled behind them, the fragrance of crushed lilac sweetening the air. Mr. Chesterton rooted in the bush for the snuffbox, swearing a blue streak as he sought it frantically.

A shot rang out. The slug ripped through the clump of birch Viola ran past, setting the stand of spindly trunks shivering. Her feet sprouted wings and she poured on more speed as the path took a sharp turn. Quinn, behind her, urged her on.

Viola's side began to ache. She couldn't draw a deep enough

breath to continue. When she faltered, Quinn scooped her up and flung her over his shoulder.

Though there were no sounds of pursuit, Quinn didn't stop till they reached the brougham where Sanjay waited in the driver's seat. Quinn yanked open the coach's door and tossed Viola in.

"Drive!" he bellowed at Sanjay from the coach's step, not bothering to wait till he was in and the door closed.

Sanjay snapped the reins over the geldings' backs and the brougham lurched forward, clattering over the cobbled streets into the night.

Quinn closed the door after himself and settled into the tufted velvet beside her. Yellow light from the street lamps cast him in stark relief followed by deep shadows as the brougham raced from one post to the next.

Still dragging in shallow breaths, Viola was overwhelmed by despair. Her chest ached. All the trouble. All the expense. All the chasing around the capitals of Europe and, in the end, they'd still lost the diamond.

"I'm so sorry," she murmured.

"What for?"

She rolled her eyes at him. "In case it's escaped your notice, we lost the diamond."

Quinn shoved a hand deep into his pocket and came up with a silver snuffbox. "You mean this diamond."

He opened the box and she heard Baaghh kaa kkhuun's low drone. She recognized its voice, but it was fainter than before. She didn't have to fight against its pull. Her love for Quinn had driven the lust for the stone from her heart. It no longer beguiled her with mesmerizing seduction.

"How did you—"

He snapped the box closed and the diamond's song faded to such a soft buzz, Viola wondered if she only remembered what it sounded like.

"I simply flipped Mr. Chesterton my Uncle Bertram's old snuffbox instead. Silver containers all look alike in the dark." Viola wrapped her arms around Quinn's neck. "You're brilliant. Now Sanjay can return it to the temple and it won't trouble anyone anymore."

"You're content to let it go?" he asked as he pulled her into an embrace.

"More than content." She was so relieved and happy, she had no thought for anything but the man whose strong arms surrounded her.

As they barreled through the night toward Quinn's town house, neither of them noticed their progress was being shadowed by another coach a couple blocks behind them.

Viola and Quinn left Sanjay to unhitch the horses in the stable behind the town house. Quinn had tried to help, but the prince insisted that so long as he bided on English soil, he must maintain the carefully constructed ruse that he was merely a servant.

"Besides, I owe you a great debt, sahib. You have returned a great treasure to my people," Sanjay said, his heart shining in his dark eyes.

Viola noticed Quinn didn't acknowledge Sanjay's mention of the Blood of the Tiger going back where it belonged. They walked in silence through the back door of the town house and through the kitchen.

"You are planning on returning the diamond to Amjerat, aren't you?" Viola asked, once they headed down the corridor toward the front parlor. She hoped the stone hadn't gripped his heart with the same lust she'd felt for it.

"I was planning on it," Quinn said softly as he helped Viola off with her cloak. "But as Robert Burns says, 'The best-laid schemes o' mice an' men gang aft a-gley.' "

"What do you mean?"

" 'e means, Peach, that even a fancy-arsed bloke like 'im

can't see all the twists and turns ahead." Willie rose from the shadow of one of the wing chairs with a blunderbuss tucked in the crook of his arm. "Aw, now, milady, don't pull such a face at ol' Willie. Surely ye knew I'd be 'round to collect what's due me. Did ye not promise me payment for the information ye wrung from me this afternoon?"

"Yes, but you shouldn't have come here, Willie," Viola said, peeping around from behind Quinn. Every fiber of his body rippled with tense watchfulness as he'd put himself between her and Willie. Viola knew he was regretting that, for the second time that night he'd insisted Sanjay keep his revolver. "You won't get the red diamond."

" 'ell, no, and I wouldn't want it. What would a simple feller like me do with such a thing? I've been waitin' 'ere since ye left this evenin' cause there's somewhat else I've a mind to have." Willie's smarmy smile turned hard. "Ye didn't think ye'd get rid of me with just one little ruby, did ye? I want that fistful of uncut stones the lieutenant's been talkin' so free about. Be a love and nip off to get 'em for me, yer ladyship, while I keep me old blunderbuss pointed at your lover's most important parts."

"This is outrageous!" Viola said, hoping to awe him with aristocratic indignation as she had on a few other occasions.

"Stow it, milady. Lest me finger slips and I accidentally hit something the lieutenant holds more dear than jewels." Willie laughed raucously at his own wit.

"Go on, Viola," Quinn said quietly. Willie must not have heard the cool menace in his tone, but Viola did. "You know where I keep them."

Reluctantly, she left the men in the front parlor and padded up the stairs to Quinn's bedchamber. She knew better than to try the safe. True to form, he'd left the fortune in jewels in his stocking drawer.

She dumped the contents of the stocking on the damask counterpane folded over the foot of his bed. Willie didn't know how many gems there actually were, so she quickly culled out the least precious ones to return to the stocking, careful to salt in a small ruby, two emeralds and one of the diamonds so as not to rouse his suspicion.

She returned the best of the jewels to another stocking in Quinn's chest of drawers, then headed toward the door.

She jumped when a loud bang sounded below her and she was showered with tiny splinters of wood. The blast of the blunderbuss blew a fist-sized hole in the floor a couple feet from where she stood.

CHAPTER 31

"Quinn!" Viola ran for the stairs and pounded down to the first landing. She had a clear view into the parlor, where Quinn and Willie fought for control of the weapon. Though it was only good for one shot, the blunderbuss made a formidable club. Willie laid about him, smashing a blue and white porcelain vase and reducing a small Louis XIV table to kindling.

"Viola, stay back!" Quinn shouted.

She sank down on the steps, peering through the banister rails, unable to tear her eyes from the fight boiling in a tight circle. She wanted to help Quinn, but she realized she might be a distraction. She bunched her skirt between her fingers and hoped Willie's next blow didn't connect with Quinn's head.

Quinn feinted right, then delivered a crushing left to Willie's jaw. The man's eyes rolled back in his head and he crumpled to the floor.

Viola breathed a sigh of relief and started to rise, when a loud crash froze her in place. The front door flew wide and swung drunkenly from its ruined hinges. A stream of peelers in dark blue uniforms pushed through the opening and surrounded Quinn and the downed Willie in the parlor.

Hubert Fenimore, the man Viola had seen accepting the fake diamond on the queen's behalf, stepped through the front door and strode into the parlor with a self-important flip of his long cloak.

"Excellent work, Lord Ashford," he said, giving Quinn the slightest of bows. "You have handed us the Mayfair Jewel Thief on a silver platter." Fenimore pointed at Willie's unconscious form. "Gentlemen, arrest that man."

The peelers picked up Willie and carted him out the front door, knocking his noggin on the jamb a couple times as they went.

Viola watched in shock, her thoughts scrambling wildly.

Quinn must have told Fenimore he was working with the Mayfair Jewel Thief. There was no other way Quinn's old schoolmate could've known about his involvement with the notorious criminal.

He meant to turn me over to the authorities. She doubled over as if she'd been gut-punched.

She'd loved him. She'd trusted him.

And he'd betrayed her.

That was far worse than Neville's feckless inconstancy. Neville's rejection was only a by-product of the way her cousin had stolen her family's position and means.

This time her heart was robbed.

It was only dumb luck that the official had mistaken Willie for the notorious thief. And only a matter of time before Quinn corrected the erroneous assumption.

Sick at heart, Viola pulled off her serpent ring and left it on the landing. She crept back up the stairs and then down the servant's back staircase. She slipped into the alley behind the row of town houses skirting the stables to avoid Sanjay as she moved through the shadows to the main street, hoping to hail a hansom.

She clutched the stocking to her chest, wishing she'd been more generous with Willie's share of the jewels because they were now hers. There wasn't time to waste on a more equitable division of the treasure she'd earned.

The real Mayfair Jewel Thief had to disappear.

Quinn and Hubert watched the peelers carry Willie off. Once they were out of earshot, Hubert cleared his throat noisily.

"Of course you realize, Ashford, I cannot publicly acknowledge your part in the thief's apprehension."

"Naturally," Quinn said. "I would prefer you didn't."

So Hubert intended on claiming the reward for the capture of the Mayfair Jewel Thief for himself. He was welcome to it. Especially since Willie would screech his innocence once he regained consciousness. No one would believe such an uncouth bungler could be responsible for the string of thefts that could only be described as elegant crimes.

Quinn hoped fervently that Viola would remain safely upstairs till he was able to shuffle Fenimore out the door, lest the man reconsider his assumption.

Hubert's pale eyes fixed him with a stare. "We understand each other then. There is another matter."

"Yes. I trust you were able to secure a decree reinstating Prince Sanjay's rule," Quinn said.

"Oh, that. Here it is." Fenimore pulled a document from his waistcoat pocket bearing the royal seal. "It is in our best interest to show our benevolence as we settle the troubles in India now. I assume your prince will aid us in quelling the unrest."

"He will lead his people well," Quinn said, knowing Sanjay might not lead them in the direction Fenimore wished.

Fenimore held the document out, but when Quinn reached for it, he drew it back.

"Chesterton is dead," Fenimore said flatly.

"What?"

"His body was found in Vauxhall shortly after your brougham left the pleasure garden. A single wound. Likely a saber of some sort. A military weapon." Hubert arched a brow at Quinn. "Any idea who might have killed him?"

Obviously Chesterton's buyer for the red diamond wasn't amused by Uncle Bertram's empty snuffbox.

"No?" Hubert said. "I have a theory that includes you, my friend. I assume you are in possession of the real red diamond. No stone was found on the body."

He continued to wave the decree that would reinstate Sanjay back and forth, as if Quinn were a cobra to be charmed. "A swap then. The red diamond for your friend's kingdom."

Honesty, Viola always claimed, was the best policy. For a thief, she was quite a stickler for truth. Quinn hoped it would serve him well as he pulled the snuffbox from his pocket.

"Here it is." He held it out to Hubert, careful not to hand it over since he was not yet in possession of the document. "Whether you believe it or not, Chesterton was alive when I last saw him this evening. I have no trouble turning the diamond over to agents of the Crown, but be warned. Baaghh kaa kkhuun has some strange properties."

The men made the swap, the box for the paper, in a swift simultaneous move.

"Nothing good will come from that diamond being in England," Quinn said. "I urge you to encourage your superiors to return it to the temple of Shiva from whence it came."

Hubert laughed. "You think my superiors will ever know the stone now in the queen's vault isn't the real thing? No, old chap, I'll keep your secret about Chesterton's killing and you'll keep mine. This diamond will never see the inside of the Royal Collection and it damn sure won't be returned to some heathen temple." He opened the snuffbox and stared down at the stone. "It's mine."

Hubert picked up the diamond with his bare hand.

"No, Fenimore, don't!"

The man closed his fist over the jewel, his eyes blazing.

"You realize what this means, don't you? I'll be able to leave that grubby little government office and do anything I damn well please. Why, I could buy and sell you, Ashford! Along with most of the ton, come to that."

Fenimore's whole frame shuddered but he didn't loosen his grip on the diamond. He cocked his head as if listening intently. "Do you hear that?"

Quinn didn't hear anything, but he recognized the distracted, enthralled expression on his old schoolmate's features. He'd seen the same look on Viola's face when the stone called to her. The diamond had unleashed its seductive power.

"Let it go or it'll take you, man." Quinn leaped forward and tried to force Fenimore's hand open.

"No! It's mine." Unnaturally strengthened by the Blood of the Tiger, the smaller man shoved him away with such force, Quinn sailed through the air and smacked against the mahogany paneling.

He slid down the wall and landed with a thud on the hardwood floor. When he fingered the back of his head, a tender lump was forming. Quinn gave himself a shake, wondering if he'd lost consciousness for a moment.

He scarcely recognized Hubert. The whites of Fenimore's eyes glowed with an unnatural light and his irises paled to the color of three-day-old suet. The hand in which he clutched the diamond began to tremble violently.

"I can't let it go," he slurred. Fenimore stared at his own fist, then began shrieking and trying to pry open his fingers with his other hand. Blisters bubbled along his skin.

He collapsed to the floor, writhing in agony.

Quinn started to go to him to try to wrest the diamond from him, but a pair of strong arms grasped him from behind. Sanjay had slipped into the room as silently as a python slides over a rock.

"No, sahib," Sanjay struggled to hold Quinn back. "It is too late. When the diamond feeds on a soul, it is too strong to resist. If you touch him, Baaghh kaa kkhuun will only consume you as well."

Fenimore's spine arched and his jaw clenched. The convulsions stopped suddenly and a long stream of air hissed from his lips. Then his entire body relaxed, save for the fist that clutched the diamond.

"He is gone," Sanjay said. "It is safe to remove the stone now, but do not touch it with unprotected skin."

Quinn knelt beside Fenimore and pried open his fingers. He pulled a handkerchief from his pocket, using it to lift the diamond from the hole it had burned in its victim's palm. He dropped the stone back into the silver snuffbox and closed the lid.

"Take the damned thing," he told Sanjay. He stooped to retrieve the document that reinstated his friend's rule in Amjerat. He must have dropped it when Fenimore and the diamond's malevolent force flung him across the room. "And take this as well."

Sanjay's dark gaze flicked over the document. "You have done it, my friend. The cost has been great, but you have restored my kingdom and my people's treasure. I owe you more than I can repay. How may I serve you?"

"For now I'll settle for you running to fetch a doctor. A singularly stupid one, for choice. Someone needs to certify that Hubert died of heart failure or some virulent case of the pox." He ran a hand over his face, feeling suddenly tired enough to sleep for a week. "Viola, it's safe. You can come down now."

There was no answer.

He headed up the stairs calling her name, but stopped on the landing when he felt something crunch under his boot heel. It was misshapen from his weight, but he recognized the mangled silver and gold as her serpent ring.

Her wedding ring.

Panic seizing him, he ran the rest of the way up the stairs.

CHAPTER 32

"Oh, Ashford, I'm ever so glad to see you, dear boy," the Dowager Countess of Meade said, walking across her parlor toward him with her hand outstretched. She was so obviously confused by his middle of the night arrival, she hadn't bothered to dress, coming to meet him in her nightshift and robe de chambre. Her iron-gray hair streamed in a long plait down her back. "This has been a most peculiar night, most peculiar indeed."

"Is Viola here?" He took her hand between both of his instead of making the requisite obeisance over it.

"There you see. No pleasantries, no inquiries after my health. You're not being the least polite and I find that peculiar, too." She patted his shoulder and settled onto the threadbare settee. She waved absently, indicating he should sit. "No, Viola's not here, but she was. Shall I ring for tea?"

"No, thank you. Where is she now?"

"Oh, I haven't the foggiest," Lady Meade said. "That girl vexes me sore. She came home in the middle of the night. She left me a stocking full of gemstones, with no explanation of how she came by them, and then she went. Uncut gemstones! Now I ask you, what am I to think? What am I to *do* with them?"

The dowager countess was really quite helpless in practical matters. The older woman's plaintive tone made Quinn realize what a heavy burden Viola had shouldered since her father's death. "She got the gems from me."

"Oh. Well. That's fine then, isn't it?" She sighed with relief. "One doesn't want to think badly of anyone, but honestly, what would you think in my position?"

"I believe you should think your daughter loves you and was trying to provide for your welfare, madam," Quinn said testily. "Now please, I need you to remember. What exactly did Viola say when she left?"

"Well, I was so flustered by all those jewels, I'm not sure I was attending properly. And why are you asking me? She's your wife." Lady Meade turned her head and scrutinized him with one eye half closed. "Did the two of you have a lover's spat? What did she say before she left your home?"

Quinn leaned his elbows on his knees and buried his face in his hands. "I suppose I wasn't attending either."

He had no idea what had sent her scurrying off. The evening's events scrolled past his mind's eye. The last time he'd heard anything from her, he was fighting with Willie and he'd ordered her to stay back. Then Fenimore and the peelers had burst in and arrested her fence, thinking he was the Mayfair Jewel Thief.

Could that have been it? Was she afraid Willie would regain consciousness and expose her for a thief?

"Did she take anything with her?" Quinn asked.

"I should say so! She took all my pin money," Lady Meade said indignantly. "But I suppose the jewels are worth a bit more than that."

"A good deal more, I should think."

"Oh! And she took one of yesterday's loaves of bread."

"I need something on my stomach if I'm to be a pleasant sailing companion, bread for choice." Viola's words when she'd boarded

the *Minstrel's Lady* rose up to taunt him. She was preparing to take ship.

"Oh, Lord, she could be headed anywhere." Quinn bolted for the door without so much as a fare-thee-well to Lady Meade. He'd apologize later if he must. If he missed Viola on the London wharves, he'd never find her unless she wished to be found.

Dawn was breaking when Viola reached the docks at Wapping, but men were already at work, loading and unloading the vessels riding at anchor. The fragrant aromas of tobacco leaves and coffee beans mingled with tar and the stench of hides and pungent rum fumes. Chains attached to the unloading cranes rattled and workers grunted a boisterous and off-color sea shanty as they hauled on heavy ropes. A forest of masts dipped and swayed with the swells of the Thames and a steamer preparing to depart belched black clouds of smoke.

Viola couldn't afford passage on the steamer, not even if she was willing to travel steerage. She pressed on toward the smaller sailing vessels, looking for something like the *Minstrel's Lady*, that might offer passenger accommodations for less. Her meager cash would have to stretch into the foreseeable future, at least until she lighted somewhere and figured out what to do with herself.

She could continue with thievery, she supposed, but it made her stomach lurch to think of it. Having a near brush with arrest was a sobering experience. For the first time, she felt the full weight of the consequences of her actions and couldn't bear the thought of her mother and sister, not to mention little Portia, being tainted with her shame.

She'd find work. Honest work. She might serve as a governess or a tutor or even a shop girl with a clear conscience. But she had to quit England before the peelers discovered they'd arrested the wrong person and came looking for her.

And she had to put as much distance between her and Quinn as possible.

Her chest ached at the thought of him. A lump of caring rose in her throat. He'd betrayed her, but she still loved him. Why didn't her heart have a tap she could shut off?

She switched her single valise to her other hand as she threaded her way through the crowd of milling people. "At least Quinn can't say I'm not traveling light this time," she murmured.

"What if he's not happy about you traveling at all?" came a masculine rumble behind her.

She turned around to find Quinn dogging her steps. He smiled at her.

Damn the man, he had the audacity to smile.

"What's it to be, Quinn? A Judas kiss?" Her gaze darted about, looking for the authorities he must be dragging in his wake. "Oh, no. How silly of me. You prefer to shag those you mean to betray."

His brows shot up at her casual obscenity. "Betray? What are you talking about?"

"You told Mr. Fenimore you were working with the Mayfair Jewel Thief. Fortunately for me, he assumed Willie was your accomplice." She turned back around and started walking away with a determined stride. He fell into step beside her. "However, Willie will promptly denounce me, so Fenimore probably knows and is on his way to take me into custody."

"No one is after you, Viola. Who'd believe anything Willie says? I'm the only one daft enough to want custody of you," Quinn said, "and I'd never turn you over to the authorities. Besides, Fenimore is dead."

She stopped and looked askance at him.

"I didn't kill him if that's what you're thinking. It was the diamond. Just like de Foix." Quinn shrugged. "But Sanjay has his kingdom back and the Blood of the Tiger will be returning to the temple of Shiva."

"Oh." She started walking again. "Congratulations. You accomplished your goal."

"I did a good deal more than that." He reached over and took her valise from her, still keeping step with her.

"Oh?"

He stopped her with a hand to her forearm. "I fell in love."

"Oh!"

He caught her hand and brought it to his lips, pressing a soft kiss on her palm. "I love you, Viola. If you're still intent on running away, I'll run with you, but I hope you'll stay here with me."

Her heart leaped at that, but she knew he'd never intended on staying in England. "You're not going back to India?" It had been his first thought when he received news of the uprising.

His brows drew together slightly. "No. My father's ill. From what I've heard, it's probably mortal. And that means I'm needed at home."

Viola glanced up at him, sensing tension in the set of his shoulders. "But you want to go back to India, don't you?"

"I'll always love that land, but once I take my seat in the House of Lords, I'll be in a position to do more good for England and Sanjay's country here than I would as a line officer there." He pressed her hand to his chest. "I'm heir to a title I wasn't born to, that shouldn't be mine. I'm drawn to a land halfway around the world, but I've been exiled from it. I've never quite known where I belong." He palmed her cheek. "Until now."

He bent and kissed her, right on Wapping Dock, in front of God and everybody. A trio of sailors walking by broke into loud huzzahs.

"You are my home, Viola. I belong with you. Marry me."

"Oh, Quinn." She wanted to believe him. Wanted to trust, but she'd had to fend for herself for so long, it was hard to put so much hope in another soul.

"Don't you love me?"

"Of course, I do." If she loved him any more, her living heart would leap out of her chest.

"Don't you believe I love you?"

She didn't answer right away.

"You can hear what a jewel has to say, but you can't sense the love I bear for you?"

He pressed his forehead to hers and suddenly she felt it, a Sending more intense than from any gem she'd ever touched. Quinn's love washed over her, a warm sea, buoying her up on its waves, fierce, then gentle. She could trust her heart, her life to this man.

"I feel it," she admitted. "And I love you too."

"Then say yes." One corner of his mouth curved up. "You've already stolen my heart. You may as well take the rest of me."

"When you put it like that"—she stood on tiptoe to nip his bottom lip—"what self-respecting thief could resist?"

AUTHOR'S NOTE

Touch of a Thief is a work of fiction, but there are a number of historical facts embedded in it.

My story begins with a scene featuring the *Kama Sutra*, a third-century Hindu text written by a holy man, Mallanaga Vatsyayana. It is considered far more than a manual of sexual positions: like the Kabala and the Song of Solomon, it has spiritual implications as well.

The kingdom of Amjerat in my story is my own invention, but many real principalities were stripped from their hereditary rulers under British India's Doctrine of Lapse. Lord Dalhousie added in excess of three million pounds sterling to the coffers of the East India Company with this policy—per annum. In the case of one princely state, when the rana died without a son to succeed him, his queen, Lakshmi Bai, adopted an heir. Since royal adoption was foreign to Britain, this was not accepted by the British and the state devolved to the Crown. Not to be set aside lightly, Lakshmi Bai donned warrior's gear and led her people in armed rebellion. The uprising was put down, but she died fighting at the head of her force and has become an icon of feminine courage in India.

The Sepoy Mutiny is a sad fact of history. The reason given for it in *Touch of a Thief*, the greased cartridges for the new infantry rifles, is actually said to have been the spark that ignited the growing Indian resentment of the British.

The specific red diamond named Baaghh kaa kkhuun is another invention of mine. Red diamonds do exist, but they are so rare that few jewelers have ever seen one—fewer than twenty exist. The largest pure red diamond ever recorded is the Moussaieff Red. Only 5.11 carats, it sold for nearly $8 million in 2001.

Lastly, we come to my heroine's unique gift—the ability to receive information from gemstones. This is known as *psychometry*, and there are those who claim to be able to discern things about people through touching their possessions. Some believe that part of an individual's energy is imprinted on the objects around them. Personally, I've never met anyone for whom "the rocks cry out," but I won't discount it either.

I hope you enjoyed *Touch of a Thief*. Please stop by my website, www.miamarlowe.com, for news of my upcoming releases, contests, and more. I love to hear from you!

I wish you romance unending.

If you liked this book, you've got to try
DEMON HUNTING IN DIXIE,
the debut from Lexi George, out this month!

Addy shot off the couch like she'd been bitten. The sword-carrying, creature-of-darkness-fighting dude from the park gazed down at her without expression. In the semi-darkness he'd been handsome. In the bright light of her living room he was devastating, a god, a wet dream on steroids. Tall and powerfully built, with wide shoulders and a broad chest that tapered down to a lean waist and hips, he was the most handsome man Addy had ever seen. His long, muscular legs were encased in tight-fitting black breeches, and he carried a sword in a sheath across his back. He was also a stranger, a very big stranger, and he stood in her living room.

"Who the hell are you?"

"I am Brand." He spoke without inflection. "I am a Dalvahni warrior. I hunt the djegrali."

"Of course you do." Hoo boy, the guy was obviously a nut case. Real movie star material, with his shoulder-length black hair and disturbing green eyes, but a whack job nonetheless. Addy grabbed the back of the couch for support as a wave of dizziness assailed her. "That would explain the flaming sword and the medieval get-up you're wearing. Nice meeting you, Mr. . . . uh . . . Brand." She flapped her hand in the general direction of the door. "If you don't mind, I'm a little freaked out. I'd like you to leave."

"I cannot leave. The djegrali that attacked you will return."

Addy clung to the couch for dear life as the room began to spin. "Look, I appreciate the thought, but I'll be fine. Really." She closed her eyes briefly and opened them again. "Dooley will protect me."

He crossed his arms on his chest, his expression impassive. "Dooley? You refer, I presume, to the animal that led me to this dwelling?"

This guy was unbelievable. His superior attitude was starting to tick her off.

"The 'animal' is a dog and, yeah, I mean her."

"This I cannot allow." He spoke with the same irritating calm. Dooley, the traitor, ambled across the room and sat at the man's feet, gazing up at him in adoration. "She would not be able to defend you against the djegrali."

"Cannot allow—" Addy stopped and took a deep breath. She was dealing with a lunatic. He wouldn't leave and she couldn't run. She was too woozy to make it to the door. Best to remain calm and not set the guy off. Besides, the spike in her blood pressure made the dizziness worse. "Okay, I'll bite. What exactly is this juh-whats-a-doodle thing you keep talking about?"

"The djegrali are demons." He raised his brows when she gave him a blank stare. "Evil spirits. Creatures of dark—"

"I know what a demon is." The guy thought he was a demon chaser, for Pete's sake. "Okay, just for grins, let's say this demon business is for real. What's it got to do with me?"

"The demon has marked you. He will return. He will be unable to resist."

"Oh, great, so now I'm irresistible. Just my luck he's the wrong kind of guy. Don't worry, I've got a .38, and like a good Southern girl I know how to use it, so you can leave." She waved her hand toward the door again. "I'll be fine. If this demon fellow shows up, I'll blow his raggedy butt to kingdom come."

The corner of his lips twitched, and for a moment she thought he might smile.

"You cannot kill a djegrali with a mortal weapon."

"I'll rush out first thing tomorrow morning and get me one of those flamey sword things, I promise."

Again with the lip twitch. "That will not be necessary. I will protect you."

"Oh, no, you won't!" Addy straightened with an effort. Her chest still hurt like a son-of-a-bitch. "I'd never be able to explain you to my mama."

"This mama you speak of, she is the female vessel who bore you?"

"Yeah, but I wouldn't call her a vessel to her face, if I were you."

"You fear her?"

Addy rolled her eyes. "Are you kidding? The woman scares the crap out of me. *Thirty-two hours of labor, and don't you ever forget it,*" she mimicked. "*You owe me. Big time.*"

The eye-rolling thing was a mistake, because the room started to spin again.

"The mama will not be a problem," he said.

"You're darn tootin' the mama won't be a problem, 'cause you're not going to be here!"

She stepped way from the couch and her knees buckled.

One moment he was across the room, his shoulder against the wall, the picture of aloof boredom, and the next she was in his arms. She closed her eyes and swallowed a sigh as she was lifted against his hard chest. The man sure had muscles, she'd give him that.

"You will recline, at once." His tone was stern.

Okay, muscles and a few control issues.

She opened her eyes as he lowered her to the couch, and saw a grimace of pain flash across his features. It was the first expression of any kind she'd seen on his face, unless you counted the lip twitch thing. The man could give a marble statue lessons in being stoic.

She caught his arm as he started to rise. "That thing hurt you!"

He stilled, his gaze on her fingers wrapped around his wrist. "You are mistaken. The djegrali did not injure me. It is your touch that disturbs me."

Addy stiffened and drew back. "Well, excuse the hell out of me."

He caught her by the hand. "You misunderstand. You do not repulse me."

He knelt down beside her. He put his fingers under her chin and tilted her face with gentle fingers. Addy stifled a gasp. Who was this guy? The merest touch from him and her breasts tingled and she felt all hot and wobbly inside. What was the matter with her?

"Look at me," he commanded.

Sweet Sister Ruth, he had a voice was like whiskey and smoke. She shivered and raised her eyes to his. He stroked her cheek with his thumb, a rapt expression on his face. His thumb drifted lower to brush her bottom lip. "You must be patient with me, Adara Jean Corwin. The Dalvahni do not experience emotion. It would be superfluous. We exist for one purpose and one purpose alone: to hunt the djegrali. For ten thousand years, this has been my objective, until now."

"Ten thousand years, huh?" With an effort, she squelched the sudden urge to scrape the pad of his thumb with her teeth. No doubt about it, she was in hormonal meltdown. "Sounds boring. You need to get a new hobby, expand your horizons."

"Earth is but one of the realms where the Dalvahni hunt the djegrali."

Oh, brother, too bad. He was paying a visit to schizoid-land again. Then the impact of his words percolated through the fog of lust that set her brain and her body on fire.

"Hey, wait a minute, I didn't tell you my name!"

"The animal you call Dooley informed me of many things, including how to find this dwelling."

"You don't say? Funny, she's never said a thing to me in four years."

He put his hand on her shoulder as she tried to sit up. "You will not rise," he said with annoying calm.

"Oh, yeah? That's what you think, bub."

She pushed at his arm, an exercise in futility. The man was built like a proverbial brick outhouse.

His hand slid over her abdomen and down her running shorts to her legs. She froze. His hand felt hot against her bare skin.

"Dooley, come here," he said.

The dog rose and trotted over to the couch.

Brand traced an intricate pattern with his fingers along the skins of her inner thigh. Addy began to shake. What was happening to her? This was so unlike her. All her life she'd struggled to rein in her reckless nature, the wild streak that made her mama wring her hands in despair. Self-control was her hard-earned mantra. Think first and feel later. But this guy . . . this guy really got her going, made her want to throw caution to the wind. She wanted to arch her hips against his hand, a *stranger's* hand.

"Speak, Dooley," Brand said with is gaze on Addy's face.

"DOOLEY LOVE ADDY. LOVE, LOVE, LOVE," the Lab said in the growly voice of a three-pack-a-day smoker. Flinging up a back paw, she scratched her ear. "CAN DOOLEY HAVE CHICKEN LEG IN COLD BOX? CAN DOOLEY?" Her head snapped around. "OH, LOOK, A BUG!"

There was a long moment of silence as Addy gaped at her dog in shock. Slowly, she raised her eyes to Brand's.

"Who *are* you?"

A slight crease appeared between Brand's brow. The expression in his eyes grew puzzled. "Until tonight, I though I knew."

Lowering his dark head, he kissed her.

There's nothing sexier than a BIG BAD BEAST.
Keep an eye out for Shelly Laurenston's latest,
out now!

Ulrich Van Holtz turned over and snuggled closer to the denim-clad thigh resting by his head. Then he remembered that he'd gone to bed alone last night.

Forcing one eye open, he gazed at the face grinning down at him.

"Mornin', supermodel."

He hated when she called him that. The dismissive tone of it grated on his nerves. Especially his sensitive *morning* nerves. She might as well say, "Mornin', you who serve no purpose."

"Dee-Ann." He glanced around, trying to figure out what was going on. "What time is it?"

"Dawn-ish."

"Dawn-*ish?*"

"Not quite dawn, no longer night."

"And is there a reason you're in my bed at dawn-ish . . . fully clothed? Because I'm pretty sure you'd be much more comfortable naked."

Her lips curved slightly. "Look at you, Van Holtz. Trying to sweet talk me."

"If it'll get you naked . . ."

"You're my boss."

"I'm your supervisor."

"If you can fire me, you're my boss. Didn't they teach you that in your fancy college?"

"My fancy college was a culinary school and I spent most of my classes trying to understand my French instructors. So if they mentioned that boss-supervisor distinction, I probably missed it."

"You're still holding my thigh, hoss."

"You're still in my bed. And you're still not naked."

"Me naked is like me dressed. Still covered in scars and willing to kill."

"Now you're just trying to turn me on." Ric yawned, reluctantly unwrapping his arms from Dee's scrumptious thigh and using the move to get a good look at her.

She'd let her dark brown hair grow out a bit in recent months so that the heavy, wavy strands rested below her ears, framing a square jaw that sported a five-inch scar from her military days and a more recent bruise he was guessing had happened last night. She had a typical Smith nose—a bit long and rather wide at the tip—and the proud, high forehead. But it was those eyes that disturbed most of the populace because they were the one part of her that never shifted. They stayed the same color and shape no matter what form she was in. Many people called the color "dog yellow," but Ric thought of it as a canine gold. And Ric didn't find those eyes off-putting. No, he found them entrancing. Just like the woman.

Ric had only known the She-wolf about seven months, but since the first time he'd laid eyes on her, he'd been madly, deeply in lust. Then, over time, he'd gotten to know her, and he'd come to fall madly, deeply in love. There was just one problem with their becoming mates and living happily ever after—and that problem's name was Dee-Ann Smith.

"So is there a reason you're here, in my bed, not naked, around dawn-*ish* that doesn't involve us forgetting the idiotic limits of business protocol so that you can ravish my more-than-willing body?"

"Yep."

When she said nothing else, Ric sat up and offered, "Let me guess. The tellin' will be easier if it's around some waffles and bacon."

"Those words are true, but faking that accent ain't endearing you to my Confederate heart."

"I bet adding blueberries to those waffles will."

"Canned or fresh?"

Mouth open, Ric glared at her over his shoulder.

"It's a fair question."

"Out." He pointed at his bedroom door. "If you're going to question whether I'd use *canned* anything in my food while sitting on my bed *not* naked, then you can just get the hell out of my bedroom . . . and sit in my kitchen, quietly, until I arrive."

"Will you be in a better mood?"

"Will you be naked?"

"Like a wolf with a bone," she muttered, and then told him, "Not likely."

"Then I guess you have your answer."

"Oh, come on. Can I at least sit here and watch you strut into the bathroom bare-ass naked?"

"No, you may not." He threw his legs over the side of the bed. "However, you may look over your shoulder longingly while I, in a very manly way, walk purposely into the bathroom bare-ass naked. Because I'm not here for your entertainment, Ms. Smith."

"It's Miss. Nice Southern girls use Miss."

"Then I guess that still makes you a Ms."

Dee-Ann Smith sat at Van Holtz's kitchen table, her fingers tracing the lines in the marble. His kitchen table was real marble, too, the legs made of the finest wood. Not like her parents' Formica table that still had the crack in it from when Rory Reed's big head drunkenly slammed into it after too many beers the night of their junior-year homecoming game.

Then again, everything about Van Holtz's apartment spoke of money and the finest of everything. Yet his place somehow managed to be comfortable, not like some spots in this city where everything was so fancy Dee didn't know who'd want to visit or sit on a damn thing. Of course, Van Holtz didn't come off like some spoiled rich kid that she'd want to slap around when he got mouthy. She'd thought he'd be that way, but since meeting him a few months back, he'd proven that he wasn't like that at all.

Shame she couldn't say that for several of his family members. She'd met his daddy only a few times, and each time was a little worse than the last. And his older brother wasn't much better. To be honest, she didn't know why Van Holtz didn't challenge them both and take the Alpha position from the mean old bastard. That's how they did it among the Smiths, and it was a way of life that had worked for them for at least three centuries.

Hair dripping wet from the shower, Van Holtz walked into his kitchen. He wore black sweatpants and was pulling a black T-shirt over his head, giving Dee an oh-too-brief glimpse at an absolutely superb set of abs and narrow hips. No, he wasn't as big a wolf as Dee was used to—in fact, they were the same six-two height and nearly the same width—but good Lord, the man had an amazing body. It must be all the things he did during the day. Executive chef at the Fifth Avenue Van Holtz restaurant; a goalie for the shifter-only pro team he owned, The Carnivores; and one of the supervisors for the Group. A position that, although he didn't spend as much time in the field as Dee-Ann and her team, did force him to keep in excellent shape.

Giving another yawn, Van Holtz pushed his wet, dark blond hair off his face, brown eyes trying to focus while he scanned his kitchen.

"Coffee's in the pot," she said.

Some men, they simply couldn't function without their morning coffee, and that was Van Holtz.

"Thank you," he sighed, grabbing the mug she'd taken out for him and filling it up. If he minded that she'd become quite familiar with his kitchen and his apartment in general, after months of coming and going as she pleased, he never showed it.

Dee waited until he'd had a few sips and finally turned to her with a smile.

"Good morning."

She returned that smile, something she normally didn't bother with most, and replied, "Morning."

"I promised you waffles with *fresh* blueberries." He sniffed in disgust. "Canned. As if I'd ever."

"I know. I know. Sacrilege."

"Exactly!"

Dee-Ann sat patiently at the kitchen table while Van Holtz whipped up a full breakfast for her the way most people whipped up a couple of pieces of toast.

"So, Dee"—Van Holtz placed perfectly made waffles and bacon in front of her with warmed syrup in a bowl and a small dish of butter right behind it—"what brings you here?"

He sat down on the chair across from her with his own plate of food.

"Cats irritate me."

Van Holtz nodded, chewing on a bite of food. "And yet you work so well with them on a day-to-day basis."

"Not when they get in my way."

"Is there a possibility you can be more specific on what your complaint is?"

"But it's fun to watch you look so confused."

"Only one cup of coffee, Dee-Ann. Only one cup."

She laughed a little, always amused when Van Holtz got a bit cranky.

"We went to raid a hybrid fight last night—not only was there no fight, but there were felines already there."

"Which felines?"

"KZS."

"Oh." He took another bite of bacon. "*Those* felines. Well, maybe they're trying to—"

"Those felines ain't gonna help mutts, Van Holtz, you know that."

"Can't you just call me Ric? You know, like everyone else." And since the man had more cousins than should legally be allowed, all with the last name Van Holtz, perhaps that would be a bit easier for all concerned.

"Fine. They're not going to help, *Ric*."

"And yet it seems as if they are—or at least trying."

"They're doing something—and I don't like it. I don't like when anyone gets in my way." Especially particular felines who had wicked right crosses that Dee's jaw was still feeling several hours later.

"All right," he said. "I'll deal with it."

"Just like that?"

"Yep. Just like that. Orange juice?" She nodded and he poured freshly squeezed orange juice into her glass.

"You don't want to talk to the team first?"

"I talked to you. What's the team going to tell me that you haven't? Except they'll probably use more syllables and keep the anti-feline sentiment out of it."

She nodded and watched him eat. Pretty. The man was just . . . pretty. Not girly—although she was sure her daddy and uncles would think so—but pretty. Handsome and gorgeous might be the more acceptable terms when talking about men, but those words did not fit him.

Don't miss BODYGUARDS IN BED, the anthology from
Lucy Monroe, Jamie Denton, and Elisabeth Naughton,
coming next month! Turn the page
for a preview of Lucy's story . . .

Danusia wiggled the key in the lock on her brother's apartment door. Darn thing always stuck, but he wouldn't make her another one. Said she didn't come to stay often enough for it to matter.

Yeah, and he wasn't particularly keen for that to change either, obviously. He'd probably gotten the wonky key on purpose. Just like the rest of her older siblings, Roman Chernichenko kept Danusia at a distance.

She knew why he did it at least, though she was pretty sure the others didn't.

Knowing didn't make her feel any better. Even in her family of braniacs, she was definitely the odd one out. They loved her, just like she loved them, but they were separated by more than the gap of their ages. She was seven years younger than her next youngest sibling. An unexpected baby, though never unwanted—at least according to her mom.

Still, her sister and brothers might love her, but they didn't get her and didn't particularly want her to get them.

Which was why she was coming to stay in Roman's empty apartment rather than go visit one of the others, or Heaven forbid, her parents. She did not need another round of lectures on her single status by her *baba* and mom.

The lock finally gave and Danusia pressed the door open, dragging her rolling suitcase full of books and papers behind her. The fact the alarm wasn't armed registered at the same time as a cold cylinder pressed to her temple.

"Roman, I swear on Opa's grave that if you don't get that gun away from me, I'm going to drop it in a vat of sulfuric acid and then pour the whole mess all over the new sofa Mom insisted you get the last time she visited. If it's loaded, I'm going to do it anyway."

The gun moved away from her temple and she spun around, ready to lecture her brother into an early grave, and help him along the way. *"It is so not okay to pull a gun on your sister . . ."* her tirade petered off to a choked breath. *"You!"*

The man standing in front of her was a whole lot sexier than her brother and scarier, which was saying something. Not that she was afraid of him, but she wouldn't want him for an enemy.

The rest of the family believed that Roman was a scientist for the military. She knew better. She was a nosy baby sister after all, but this man? Definitely worked with Roman and carried an aura of barely leashed violence. Maxwell Baker was a true warrior.

She shouldn't, absolutely *should not*, find that arousing, but she so did.

"You're not my brother," she said stupidly.

Which was so not her usual mode, but the six-foot-five black man, who would make Jesse Jackson Jr. look like the ugly stepbrother if they were related, turned Danusia's brain to serious mush.

His brows rose in mocking acknowledgment of her obvious words.

"Um . . ."

"What are you doing here, Danusia?" Like a really good aged whiskey, even his voice made her panties wet.

How embarrassing was that? "You know my name?"

Put another mark on the chalkboard for idiocy.

"The wedding wasn't so long ago, I would have forgotten already." He almost cracked a smile.

She almost swooned.

Max and several of Roman's *associates* had done the security on her sister, Elle's, wedding, which might have been overkill. Or not. Danusia suspected stuff had been going on that neither she, nor her parents had known about.

It hadn't helped that she'd been focused on her final project for her Masters and that Elle's wedding had been planned faster that Danusia could solve a quadratic equation. She'd figured out that something was going on, but that was about it. This time her siblings had managed to keep their baby sister almost completely in the dark.

A place she really hated being.

Not that her irritation had stopped her from noticing the most freaking gorgeous man she'd ever met. Maxwell Baker. A tall, dark, dish of absolute yum.

Once she had seen Max with his strong jaw, defined cheekbones, big and muscular body, not much else at the wedding had even registered. Which might help explain why she hadn't figured out why all the security.

"It's nice to see you again." There, that sounded somewhat adult and full points for polite conversation, right?

"What are you doing here?" he asked again, apparently not caring if he got any points for being polite.

She shrugged, shifting her backpack. "My super is doing some repairs on the apartment."

"What kind of repairs?"

"Man, you're as bad as my brother." They hadn't even made it out of the entry and she was getting the third-degree.

Really as bad as her brother and maybe taken it up a notch. Roman might have let her get her stuff put out of the way before he started asking the probing questions. Then again, maybe not.

"I'll take that as a compliment." Then Max just waited, like he had all the time in the world to wait for her answer.

Like it never even occurred to him she might refuse to do so.

Knowing there was no use in attempted prevarication, she sighed. "They're replacing the front door."

"Why?"

"Does it matter?" Sheesh.

He leaned back against the wall, crossing his arms, muscles bulging everywhere. "I won't know until you tell me."

"Someone broke it." She was proud of herself for getting the words out considering how difficult she was finding the simple process of breathing right now.

This man? Was lethal.

"Who?" he demanded, frown firmly in place.

Oh, crud, even his not-so-happy face was sexy, yummy, heart palpitatingly delicious. "I don't know."